# Silent Whispers

M. KATHERINE CLARK

This is a work of fiction. Names, characters, places and incidents are the product of the author's imagination or are used fictitiously, and any resemblance to any actual persons, living or dead, events, or locals is entirely coincidental.

ISBN-13: 978-0-9909915-7-1

# Other Works by M. Katherine Clark

The Greene and Shields Files:
- Blood is Thicker Than Water
- Once Upon a Midnight Dreary
- Old Sins Cast Long Shadows
- Tales from the Heart

Soundless Silence a Sherlock Holmes Novel

Love Among the Shamrocks Collection:
- Under the Irish Sky
- Across the Irish Sea – Coming Soon
- In Dublin Fair City – Coming Soon

The Wolf's Bane Saga:
- Wolf's Bane
- Lonely Moon
- Midnight Sky
- Star Crossed
- Moon Rise – Coming 2018

*For my ancestors, kin and all the Scots who died at Culloden.*
*And for James David Hardy, Jr. Though I never met you,*
*Grandfather, your love of Scotland lives on in my mother and*
*now in me. I promise I'll write the MacHardy Saga soon!*
*Alba Go Bragh*

# Chapter One

Alistair needed me. He was wounded already. Running as fast as I could, I saw another damned English Redcoat race to my friend. Blood, from the pistol shot he had nae ducked away from fast enough, dripped off his fingertips. A front kick straight to Alistair's gut had him falling onto his back but I was there before the Red could do anything more than sneer.

Thrusting my sword home through the English before him, the bloody bastard fell with a womanly scream.

"I had it handled, MacPherson," Alistair stated from his place on the ground.

"Aye, thought I'd take a wee bit of yer glory, Sutherland. Too much'll go to yer head," I offered my hand and helped him up. "How bad?" I asked seeing the blood continue to drip from his right arm.

"I'll live," he grunted squeezing his hand around the hilt of his basket sword as if getting the feel of it in a hand he did not usually favor. "How does the battle fare?"

"Charlie's a fool. Angus was right," I said. "A fool and a coward. He fled."

"Nay!" Alistair shouted.

"Murray's and Drummond's divisions have been decimated," I went on. "The Farquharson's have lost heavily."

"What?" He demanded. "Nay! Me wife's brother is one of them!" After a moment, he shouted. "I will kill every last one of these damned whoresons!"

"The battle's lost, Alistair," I said.

"No' until I draw my last breath!" He yelled. Crying his clan's battle cry he raced back toward the fray.

"*Eejit*," I muttered but followed him. Cutting through some English who were nae older than me, I made my way toward Alistair but I could nae longer see him. We were too far separated.

Five minutes passed but to me it felt like hours. I did nae feel human while I was fighting. I was a warrior. I felt nothing as I killed a boy nae older than fourteen who attacked me. I felt nothing when I killed an old man, old enough to be my father. I put all thoughts aside. I was fighting for the future. The future of Scotland. The future of my clan.

Just as that thought entered my mind, I felt it... I was a dead man. Two pistol shots blew through my back.

Jerking awake at my alarm clock's shrill beep, I sat straight up in bed and looked around my room, calming my raging heartbeat. Reaching beside me, Daren wasn't there but my paperback was.

"Okay," I breathed. "No more Scottish romance novels before bed." Silencing my alarm clock, I checked my phone for a message from my boyfr... my *ex*-boyfriend.

Nothing.

Couldn't say I was surprised. Three months had gone by since he'd broken up with me and every morning my phone looked the same; emails, new twitter followers and a possible upgrade to my laptop, but nothing from my ex. I was somewhere between the anger and acceptance stages of my grief but unlike so many days where I rolled over and hit the snooze button, I smiled, jumped out of bed, ran down the stairs of my townhouse apartment and turned on the coffee. Waiting for the nectar of the gods to brew, I flipped through the pamphlet of Castle MacCulloch. I still couldn't believe I had been accepted to the League of Extraordinary Writers. It was a dream come true. The coffee done, I poured a cup and hurried upstairs again.

Too hot to drink, I set the cup on my bathroom counter and ran the hot water for a shower. As I stood under the water, my dream came back to me. It was unlike any I had had before. Who were the two men? Where was I? Going off their accent and clothing, it was Scotland. Their kilts were well ingrained in my memory.

Determined to write everything down before I forgot it, I shut the water off and reached for my towel. Before I had a chance to grab a pen, my phone rang.

"I'm here, honey," Dad's voice came over the speaker. "Want me to help you with your luggage?"

"Come on in, Dad. Coffee's made," I told him and hit the button to buzz him in.

He needed to get to the tenth floor, so I had some time. Scribbling what I could remember of my dream, I just finished when I heard the front door open and close. Dad gave one of his signature whistles and headed into the kitchen.

"Ready for Scotland?" He asked when I walked down the stairs to the kitchen, my coffee mug pressed between my hands. It was a surprisingly cool August morning in Chicago.

"Don't I look it?" I teased, looking down at my red, white and blue shirt, jeans and flats. "I have a change of clothes for when I land so I don't look quite like an American Tourist." Dad chuckled but looked deep in my eyes.

"You all right, sweetheart?" he finally asked. "You look a little pale."

"I'm okay," I answered taking a drink of the black caffeinated goodness. "I just had this weird dream."

"Wanna talk about it?" He asked.

"It's not important. I just think I shouldn't read anymore just before bed," I teased.

"Your mother has said the same thing," he answered. "She used to have the weirdest dreams."

"Have you heard from her recently?" I asked.

He shook his head as he took a sip of his coffee.

"Only when she calls to see how you are doing," he replied.

"I'm sorry," I said. "I know it was tough for you after the divorce."

"Oh Nikki, we stopped talking long before that," he answered. "But how are you? Really?"

"I'm hanging in there, Dad," I sighed.

"Have you talked to him?" he asked.

Shaking my head, I turned back to the sink, hiding my tears.

"He won't answer my calls," I admitted.

Dad reached around me to set his coffee mug down near the sink and turned me into him. "You're much too good for him," he cooed as he pressed my head to his chest.

"I love him, dad," I said softly.

"I know. I know you do, sweetheart," he sighed. "Go to the writer's retreat and clear your head. It'll all look better after you get away from it. And who knows, something wonderful could happen."

Taking a deep breath in, I held on to his familiar and comforting cologne.

"Now are you ready?" He asked resting his hands on my shoulders and pushing me slightly away from him. "Scotland awaits."

"Ready," I answered. Eight weeks in a Scottish castle, sexy men in kilts with accents that make you a blithering idiot before you even have a chance to say hello? That sounded like my kind of place. And the fact I would be surrounded by kings and queens of their genre might just break the writer's block I had since the breakup.

Safely landed in Heathrow, I pulled out my phone and texted my dad to let him know I was all right and that I'd call him when I had a moment. After I cleared customs, I was able to find my gate for my connection to Edinburgh and a seat near the Starbucks kiosk.

During the seven-and-a-half-hour flight, I contemplated

my dream from the night before. The two men intrigued me but as I stared at the cursor on my laptop, my writer's block won out. Desperate to at least write something, I groaned in frustration when my sentences looked like an elementary school student writing about a purple unicorn.

I hadn't opened my laptop while I waited for the connecting flight. I couldn't bring myself to read how terrible it actually was. Closing my eyes for a moment, I leaned my head back. After what seemed like only a couple minutes, I opened my eyes and looked around. *Stupid,* I thought. Falling asleep in the middle of a busy airport and alone. Thankfully my laptop was there with my whole life and career still intact.

As I fished my phone out of my pocket, I could smell fresh coffee from the kiosk behind me. A good strong cup would help my jetlag, I got in line and checked my phone, about to call my dad seeing two missed calls from him and three texts asking if I had gotten on the flight. Confused, I looked up at the time and froze, my stomach flipped and landed somewhere near my feet. Three o'clock glared at me. After a moment of disbelief, I raced to the ticket counter.

"The two-oh-five to Edinburgh, has it left yet?" I asked anxiously as the terminal attendant looked at me like I was crazy.

"It left about fifty minutes ago, ma'am. Is something the matter?" she asked.

"Yes, I was supposed to be on that flight. Is there another flight to Edinburgh?"

"That was the last one today, ma'am," she answered.

"No, surely not," I stated. "Please check again."

"I'm sorry, ma'am, but there is no other flight today," she explained.

"I need to get to Edinburgh by tonight. Is there anything you can do?" I pleaded.

The writer's retreat had sent a car to pick me up, there would be welcome cocktails at the castle's bar and Elliot Ross was speaking. There was no damn way I was missing him; President of the League of Extraordinary Writers and bestselling author of *Highlander's Heaven* series, *Rosewood, Pindrop Silence*, and *Rival Brothers*... Oh yeah, I was getting to

Edinburgh if I had to walk.

"The best we can do, ma'am is to get you on a flight to Glasgow at eight-fifteen tonight," she answered. "Then a connecting flight in to the capitol at ten."

"How far is it to drive? Is there a train?" I asked.

"There is ma'am, a train leaves Heathrow for Paddington every fifteen minutes," she explained.

"And you are sure there is no other earlier flight?" I asked.

"Positive ma'am," she answered. "I'm sorry."

"No no, it's my fault. Is there by chance a train set to go up to Edinburgh?"

"I'm not sure, ma'am, we don't have the railway information, but I can get you the website," she explained.

"No, that's all right, thank you, though. Could you by chance see if there's room on that flight to Glasgow."

Once it was settled I would be on the flights and land around ten-thirty, I desperately needing a glass of wine and some food. Asking where the closest restaurant was, I slid into a seat at the bar, and ordered a large glass of white wine and a chicken spinach wrap.

"Great, Nik really great," I berated as I took a gulp of wine. "Your first vacation by yourself and you manage to screw it up. How difficult is it to get to Edinburgh? You had one task, get on that damn plane but no, you manage to fall asleep and miss your flight."

"'Scuse me," a voice beside me startled me. White wine dribbled on my hand and down my chin as I pulled the glass away startled. Grabbing a cocktail napkin beside me, I set the wine down and patted the drops. "Sorry, dinnae mean to startle you."

"No, it's okay," I answered and, for the first time, looked at the intruder of my personal brow beating.

*Oh. My. God.* My eyes trailed up to blue eyes set in a pale face with short dark hair and a grin that made my mind go blank.

"Uh…" I so eloquently said.

"Sorry, I could nae help but overhear ye," he started and of course he had a Scottish accent. My subconscious rolled her eyes. "But I heard you needed to get to Edinburgh today?"

I nodded, thankful to have some semblance of intelligence return to me in the face of this beautiful man.

"Well, me and the lads are flying out in a couple minutes. We have an extra seat if you wanna join," he indicated three others at a table. One man was in his mid-fifties, the other two were about the same age as my handsome stranger.

"Oh… well, thanks, I appreciate it," I said as the bartender came out with my lunch. "But I have a flight out at eight to Glasgow."

"Right, I just thought you might need it. It sounded like you needed to get there soon," he explained.

"It's my first time on vacation without my boyfriend and I fell asleep, missed my flight," I stated. His face contorted for a moment into a frown. "Ex-boyfriend, really. Sorry, it's been a while but I just can't bring myself to say it."

A slow grin spread across his face as he slid onto the bar stool beside me and waved the bartender over.

"I understand," he stated. "Jamie," he addressed the bartender. "Another for the lady and my usual."

"Very good, Mr. Sutherland," the bartender replied turning away to fill the order.

"Ross Sutherland," he introduced himself reaching over for a handshake.

"Sutherland," I said remembering my dream as I accepted his hand.

"Aye," he answered then looked at me questioningly. "Is it an all right name?"

"Sorry, yes, it's a great name," I replied. "I'm Nikki Thompson."

"Pleasure to meet you. What brings you to our bonnie shores?"

"I'm a writer," I answered.

"Oh, grand, anything I would have read?" he asked.

"I doubt it," I answered taking the white wine the bartender placed in front of me. The wrap stared at me and my stomach growled softly.

"*Sláinte mhath*," he cheered and clinked his glass against mine. "So, Miss Writer, are you working on anything else?"

"Not yet, but hopefully soon," I answered. "I haven't

been very inspired recently."

"Oh?" He asked taking a sip of his whisky. "Ah, the ex?"

"Yeah, it's been a couple months but he's still here," I tapped my temple indicating my mind.

"Oh, I understand," he replied. "Some people linger with us. But you're headed to Scotland, the home of romance novels. I'm sure you'll find something to write about."

"Oh, I'm not a romance writer," I replied. "Though I do read it, I prefer mystery or suspense."

"Ah, my favorite genre to read," he smiled. "Listen, I'm gonna head back to my lads so you can eat but I'm serious, if ya need a lift to Edinburgh, I'd be happy to provide it. We'll be in terminal B gate forty-two. And um... I'm no' a sexual sadist or kidnapper if you're wondering. I just hate to see a beautiful woman upset," he nodded to me as he slipped off the stool and downed the rest of his whisky. "Jamie, put the lovely lady's drinks and food on my tab."

"Very good, Mr. Sutherland," he answered.

"Oh no really, that's not necessary," I replied.

Ross didn't say anything, only winked and headed back to his friends. The men smiled and greeted him with a pat on the back. I turned my attention to my lunch. As much as I wanted to stare at them, even his friends were handsome, I needed to eat.

Not wanting to make them feel awkward, I focused on eating half of the wrap before I looked back. Their table was empty and Jamie, the bartender was cleaning up. When he found a note, he looked over at me and smiled.

"I think this is for you," he said handing it to me.

Thanking him, I opened the folded napkin and read.

*Miss Writer,*

*Thank you for the conversation. I find you very intriguing. My friends and I are heading to catch our plane. If you would like to get to Edinburgh today, my offer still stands. The plane leaves from B42 in twenty minutes. Take the escalator down and around to the right, you'll pass the caviar stand and the purfumeria. Please come.*

*My very best regards,*
*Ross Sutherland*

I didn't have time to think about the fact chivalry is dead and no man would offer what Ross Sutherland was offering without expecting something in return, namely us joining the Mile-High Club. All I could think about was getting a chance to go to the welcome event tonight and meeting Elliot Ross.

Grabbing my laptop case, I turned to Jamie, about to ask for my bill and for the food to be packaged up, when he handed me the to-go box.

"Mr. Sutherland is well known, miss, you'll be fine. I promise," he assured.

"Thank you," I answered. "What do I owe you?"

"Nothing, Mr. Sutherland's tab took care of it," Jamie said. Taking out some cash, I thanked him and gave him a tip.

"Oh, can I ask you something?" I turned back to him.

"Of course," he replied.

"What kind of whisky does he drink?"

Jamie grinned and handed me his glass. "Smell for yourself."

The peated scent hit my nose and I took a deep breath in. It smelled like a bonfire mixed with wet earth and pine.

"That smells divine," I groaned.

"Laphroaig," he replied. "Ultra peated."

"Thank you," I smiled. "Can I buy a bottle from you for him?"

He looked around the room and winked. "Since you're the only one here, aye, but don't be telling anyone," he said.

"I promise, how much?"

After I purchased the bottle of whisky, he gave me a bag for my leftovers and the bottle. He wished me luck and I hurried to catch the plane, hoping I didn't miss it while talking with Jamie.

Making my way to the escalators, I passed the caviar stand and raced down the hall. I passed another pair of escalators with flashing cameras, squealing girls and big guys in sunglasses. I had no time to see which celebrity had just arrived but with my luck, it would have been Prince Harry or Benedict Cumberbatch. Still, I couldn't stop. I had to make that flight.

Passing the purfumeria, I turned to Terminal B.

"Oh, you've got to be kidding me," I stated seeing a wall

of huge men in black suits with sunglasses and earwigs blocking my path. One of them deigned to look down at me and demanded to know my name. "Nikki Thompson? I'm supposed to meet Ross Sutherland." I stated.

My blocker looked at another one who nodded once.

"Welcome to terminal B, Ms. Thompson," he said stepping aside and allowing me in.

"Thank you." Passing him, I stepped onto the escalator and once at the top, looked around and gasped. The terminal had two bars, a coffee and pastry shop, one souvenir shop and plush chairs. Famous actors and even some American and English Millionaires spoke together or sat at the bars and coffee shop. Walking forward, surprised by some of the faces, I looked for gate forty-two.

"Nikki," that sexy Scottish brogue made me smile and nearly had me in a puddle. Turning, I locked eyes with Ross. "Glad you decided to join us."

"Mr. Sutherland," I said with a nod. "Thank you for your kind offer. I hope I haven't kept you waiting."

"Ross, please," he commented. "And it's my pleasure. We're boarding." He turned and guided me toward the gate. I fell into step beside him. "Did you find your way here all right?"

"Yeah," I answered. "Quite a crowd."

"Oh yeah," he shrugged.

"Can I ask why you were at the restaurant and not here?"

"Jamie and I went to university together, I visit him whenever I'm in Heathrow," he explained.

"Oh, I nearly forgot," I took out the bottle of Laphroaig. "I wanted to thank you."

"Ah, grand," he accepted it with a slanted grin. "Thank you. You did nae have to."

"I wanted to. And Jamie told me it was your favorite," I said.

"He knows me well," he replied. "Thank you. Come on, I'll introduce you to the lads."

We walked down some stairs and out a door. The sun hitting me directly in the eyes, I barely had a chance to see the personal jet Ross was heading toward. He took the steps two at a time and offered his hand to me as I climbed the last step.

Entering, a man and woman waited just inside, a pleasant smile lit their faces.

"Melanie, John," Ross began. "This is Nikki Thompson. She'll be flying with us today."

"Welcome aboard, Miss," John said with a slight English accent. "I'll be your pilot and my beautiful wife will be your flight attendant."

"Welcome, Miss Thompson," Melanie replied. "May I take your bags?"

"My bags? Ah hell," I sighed in frustration.

"What is it?" Ross asked.

"My luggage was on my previous flight," I said pulling out my phone trying to figure out who to call.

"Oh, John'll take care of that, don't you worry," Melanie smiled placing a hand on her husband's arm.

"Absolutely," he replied. "You go ahead and get settled. Leave it to me, Miss."

"Oh, thank you," I was grateful and too tired to think any more.

"Allow me show you to your seat," Melanie offered.

"I got it, Mels," Ross replied and guided me into the cabin. "Nikki, allow me to introduce to you to three of the randiest lads in all of Scotland and my best mates; Graeme and Gerard Fergus and my... *chaperone* MacDonald."

The three men stood to greet me.

"Hell, Sutherland," one of his best friends said. "Take pity on your oldest friend and teach me some of your tricks. How do I get a beautiful lass to follow me after only a five-minute conversation?"

Laughing, the other man stepped forward, identical twin to the other, and extended his hand to me. "Och, forgive my brother, Miss Thompson. He forgets himself. Gerard Fergus," he introduced.

"Nikki," I answered taking his hand.

"We're taking off in a moment, lads, let's sit down and strap in," Ross said and indicated an empty seat for me. He took my laptop case and placed it in a stowaway compartment just as John's voice came over the intercom.

"Ladies and gentlemen, we'll soon be taking off. We are

third in line. The weather is fair and we should make good time. Our ETA is three hours forty minutes. Oh, and Miss Thompson, I was able to contact the Edinburgh airport, as soon as your original flight lands they will find your luggage and hold it in the main office."

"Thank you," I called.

"Now, just sit back, relax," he began. "And enjoy the flight."

# Chapter Two

If I had any concern about Ross Sutherland, all those fears were put to rest after about thirty minutes into the flight. I had never laughed as much as I did in those few minutes. Graeme and Gerard were identical twins and the three of them had been best friends since they were babies, their parents knowing each other for years. All in their early thirties and very much single as Graeme made sure to tell me.

Gerard owned a farm near Ullapool his grandfather had willed to him several years ago. Graeme was older, albeit by only a couple minutes but as such he stood to inherit the family's whisky distillery which sold all over the world. I was certain I had seen a bottle or two in Dad's collection back home.

Ross was a little more tight-lipped about what he did for a living. All I could get out of him was, he was self-employed and did rather well for himself. *No shit, Sherlock,* I thought looking around the jet. Then their attention turned to me.

"So, tell us, lass," Graeme exaggerated his Scottish accent. "What brings you to Bonnie Ole Scotland? All Ross said was, you're a writer."

"I am," I answered. He grinned and glanced over at Ross

who was fixing his famous, according to both men, Whisky Sour.

"What have you written? Are you published?" Graeme went on.

"I am. I write mostly suspense. Though it seems nothing sells anymore unless it has a hot sex scene in it," I said.

"That's all I read," Graeme teased. "Skip through the book until that bit."

"It's terrible though," I laughed. "My dad reads my books."

"Oh god," the twins winced.

Ross came around with a tray of drinks and winked. "As bad as that would be, there's nothin' wrong with a few scenes."

"No, it's just not my style," I replied. "Not that I'm a prude," I clarified.

"More of a fade to black or fireplace close up?" Graeme asked.

"Exactly," I answered.

"Who is your favorite author?" Gerard asked.

"Elliot Ross," I answered without hesitation. The twins beamed and Graeme's eyes drifted to Ross's back as he replaced the tray.

"Hear that, Sutherland?" he called.

"Aye, I heard it," Ross replied. "Why would you like *that* old timer?"

"Old timer?" I sat up. "You've seen a picture of him?"

"Has anyone? Ever?" Ross asked sitting in his seat across from me, crossing his ankle over his knee.

"Well, no," I answered. "But I've read his work and I can't imagine him being old." The three men chuckled at some unknown joke and I continued, "I'll meet him tonight, thanks to you all. Maybe I'll let you know."

"What's the one you have out now?" Ross asked.

How he knew I had only one book out, I wasn't sure. But I ignored it, *sláinte mhath*'ed with them and drank my Whisky Sour.

"Damn well done, man," Gerard complimented Ross's drink. Ross raised his glass to him in thanks.

"So, lass, donnae leave us in suspense here. What have you written?" Graeme asked.

"Oh, it's called *Secret Revenge*," I said. "It's about a CIA agent who uses her training to disappear after her partner-lover is killed. She has to survive on her own and hide because she's pretty sure she was the intended target. She disappears for five years until the man she had found out was responsible for her lover's death, is running for president. She gets a job in his campaign and slowly, secretly, she puts her plan of revenge in motion," the men were staring at me. I couldn't help but smirk, hiding it behind my drink. "It did fairly well," I said as I took a sip.

"I'm hooked," Graeme said.

"Me too," Gerard replied. They both pulled out their tablets.

"Just bought it," Graeme said triumphantly.

"Beat me to it, ya bugger," Gerard said. "There, done. Got two more fans and I just liked your Facebook page." I chuckled and thanked them. "I'll finish it first," Gerard went on.

"Oh right, when do you have time to read?" Graeme asked.

"I'll make time," Gerard replied.

As I watched them, I felt Ross' eyes on me. Turning, his heated gaze lit me on fire.

"Any plans for a sequel?" Ross asked, his voice thick.

"I've tried a few ideas but nothing has really stuck."

"Donnae worry, Nikki," Gerard said. "Scotland is filled with stories, I'm sure you'll find your inspiration again."

"Oh, I do have an interesting idea. Came to me in a dream," I admitted. "Oddly," I looked at Ross. "Your last name was in it."

"Invading women's dreams again, Sutherland?" Graeme teased. "How many times do I have to tell ye it's no' gonna win you any dates."

Ross laughed and downed the rest of his Whisky Sour. Standing, he took Gerard's empty glass and headed back to the bar area. The brothers were laughing and teasing each other and it gave me a moment to look at all of them individually without being caught.

Gerard's dark blonde hair was short, military cut on the sides and in the back but flopped in his face in front. I caught the faintest glimpse of a sleeve tattoo on his arm. Graeme's longer, curly and shaggy blonde hair hung past his ears and his light eyes gave him a playful look. Daren's two younger sisters would be hanging on their every word.

I liked Ross' quiet demeanor. Looking up at him, our eyes locked and he gave me a lazy smirk. Knowing I had been caught red-handed observing his two friends, I decided to see if my flirting skills were as rusty as I thought. Raising the Whisky Sour, I kept my eyes on him the whole time. Walking back to me, he resumed his seat and crossed his ankle over his knee showing off his dark wash jeans and slip on dress shoes.

"So, you don't have any time to read, Ross?" I asked in a sultry tone.

"I prefer my thrillers with a little more… thrill," he replied. Loving the way his words heated my dormant blood, I set the glass aside and leaned forward grateful for the low-cut t-shirt as his eyes dropped to my chest. Not as rusty as I thought.

"Oh? And who says I won't give you a thrill?" I asked.

"Fade to black?" he looked up. "Fireplace close up? As much as I am a fan of prudish behavior anywhere *but* the bedroom, books are where fantasies come true," Ross explained. "And I am sure you have some fantasies, don't you, Ms. Thompson?"

"Several, Mr. Sutherland," I answered taking my drink again. Before he could respond, Graeme called to me.

"You know, Nikki, if you need a tour guide while in Edinburgh, you only need to ask me. I went to Edinburgh University and lived in the city for a while. Know it like I do the back of me own hand."

"Oh aye, he'd show you around all right. To all the pubs and clubs and his bedroom. That's all he did in Uni. Now me on the other hand, I know how to show a lady a good time," Gerard said.

"I offered first," Graeme winked at me.

"Thank you, Graeme that's very sweet of you. But I'm not going to be in Edinburgh for more than a couple minutes. I'm expected north."

"Och, aye?" Graeme asked. "Where would that be?"

"MacCulloch Castle about fifty miles north of

Edinburgh," I explained.

Both sets of eyes flashed to Ross. "Really?" Ross asked unfazed. "And what will you be doing there?"

"I'm here for a writer's retreat," I explained.

"So you're gonna hole up in some musty old castle and write?" Graeme was skeptical.

"Hopefully," I said. "I haven't been doing much of it lately but I am hoping to write my next bestseller. Who knows, you all might be in it."

"Be sure to get my prince's good looks and my charming demeanor right," Graeme teased.

"Oh trust me, Graeme," I replied. "I will be sure to write all of you correctly."

After an interesting exchange with the large breasted woman at the main office of Edinburgh airport, Ross and I left with my luggage and joined the rest of the party near the taxi lane.

"Wynda?" Gerard asked Ross. Ross blew out a breath and nodded.

"Who's Wynda?" I asked looking from one to the other of them.

"The daughter of Ross's mother's friend," Graeme answered.

"They went to the pub once," Gerard explained.

"That's no' all they did once," Graeme replied.

"Wow, real classy, Sutherland," I said. "And you never called?"

"We men donnae always remember to," Ross answered.

"No wonder she looked about ready to kill me," I stated.

MacDonald walked up behind us and nodded once to Ross before taking my bags.

"Thank you, MacDonald," turning back to me, Ross continued. "He called you a cab."

"Oh, I appreciate it," I said looking over at MacDonald standing stoically by Gerard. He bowed stiffly but said nothing. "Really I don't know what I would have done if I hadn't met you guys. You saved me a lot of stress. I will have to tell Elliot Ross about you, my knights in shining armor."

"It was our pleasure," Ross replied. "That old codger does nae need any more ideas, trust me. But I'm sure he'll get a kick out of it."

"So you do know him," I bit my lower lip.

"Aye, all right, I know the old fox. Known him me whole life in fact."

*Dad? Uncle? Brother?* I wondered.

"But enough of that, thank you for the whisky. I'll think of you when I drink it," he winked.

"You better," I answered. Ross's slanted grin appeared again just as the twins spoke up.

Graeme took my hand and made a show of bowing and kissing it. "Parting is such sweet sorrow, me wee lass," he said. "But I look forward with immense pleasure to reading your novel."

"It was a pleasure, Mr. Fergus," I said. "And um..." leaning in, I lowered my voice. "There's a pretty steamy scene in the first chapter."

"Excuse me, I have a book to get to," Graeme said loudly.

"See you around, I hope, Nikki," Gerard replied.

"Absolutely," I answered. "You guys know where I'm staying. Consider this a standing invite to come and see me. I'm sure I'll need some inspiration." Turning back to Ross, I said. "I can't thank you enough. I will be sure to dedicate my next best seller to you."

"I'll hold you to that," he said.

As it turned out, MacDonald had told the cabby where I was going and, at the order of Ross Sutherland, paid for my fare.

Looking out the window seeing the Scottish countryside roll passed, only one face reflected in the beauty and threat of rain.

Ross Sutherland.

Handsome.

Sophisticated.

Sexy.

Wealthy.

Scottish.

Secretive… I practically knew Graeme's and Gerard's life history but I hardly knew anything about Ross Sutherland. Grabbing my phone to send a thank you text, I realized I didn't have any of their phone numbers.

*Shit,* but they did like my author page. I pulled out my iPad to check my Facebook page and found their names. Immediately sending personal friend requests, I searched their friends for Ross, but he did not have a profile. Huffing a sigh, I noticed my notes app was open in the background. Clicking on it, a message popped up on my screen.

*Miss Writer,* and I grinned.

*Grabbed this while you used the facilities on the plane, hope you don't mind. I wanted to tell you, I am very glad you decided to join my friends and me. I do hope you are having as much fun as I am… Something I wanted to tell you about MacCulloch Castle might whet your suspense writer's appetite. Like all Scottish Castles of at least a hundred years old, it is reputedly haunted. The ghost of Fearsome MacPherson roams the halls. I have included a link to his biography and some sightings. I do hope you find this as interesting as I find you.*

*Trust me, if I could, this flight would be a lot longer than four hours. It hardly seems fair.*

*I can hear you moving about in the cabin. I'll return this to your bag but before I do, I have to tell you… you look so damn sexy in those skinny jeans and your American Pride t-shirt. It was for selfish reasons I invited you along. I couldn't stop looking at you and trust me, I really don't want to. I have a feeling we're going to be seeing each other again very soon.*

*Graeme and Gerard send their love and wanted me to take their picture. Check your photos, lass.*

*Yours Respectfully, (But not too respectfully)*
*Ross Sutherland*

The cab suddenly grew very warm. Leaning back into the seat, I grinned. I was very much looking forward to seeing him again.

Skype rang on my iPad and I cursed the little jolt of hope I had that it could be him. Clicking connect, I squealed with joy to see my dad on the other end. But joy quickly turned to guilt. He was frantic. I had forgotten to call him during the whole fiasco. Trying to calm him down, I launched into the story of what happened in Heathrow.

I skyped with Dad until the cabbie pulled into the drive of Castle MacCulloch. Telling him for the ninetieth time I was fine, not to worry and everything worked out, I promised to call him later and show him the grounds. After I hung up with my dad, I got out and thanked the cabbie. He helped me with my luggage and tipped his hat to me. He was heading back to the driver's side door, when I called him back and offered a twenty pound note.

"No need, ma'am," he said shaking his hand at the money. "Mr. Sutherland already took care of everything."

"Oh," I replied. "Great, thank you for driving me all this way."

"No problem at all," he grinned. "I hope you have a wonderful stay."

A clap of thunder made me jump and as soon as I felt large drops on my arm, I thanked him and raced to get under the awning. A little disappointed I didn't get a chance to see the old place, I looked around in the dying light trying to see as much as I could. Grey stone faded with age, battlements and guard towers wrapped the main part of the hotel and the Scottish flag fluttered in the rainy wind.

I grabbed my two bags and headed up the steps to the main doors. Immediately my stomach twisted in knots. This is my last chance to break through the writer's block Daren had caused. The people inside were going to be famous and hopefully available for me to talk to. I needed a new agent and a new marketing strategy. The market was saturated with suspense and mystery novels, it was difficult to set your work apart.

*Deep breaths.*

"Hello," I heard a breathy voice say behind me.

"Hi," I forced a grin and turned but no one was there. "Hello?" I called out again. "Anyone there?"

The only answer was the rain beating the pavement and a cold chill snaked its way up my spine. Shivering, I tugged my leather coat tighter around me and took a step toward the open door. Just as I reached for it, it slammed shut. I screeched and stumbled back.

"Okay not funny! Whoever's playing around, just stop," I yelled.

"You all right, lass?" A man's voice startled me. I whirled around. "Sorry about the door, it does that when there's a storm and someone opened the door to the back. Causes a wind tunnel."

"Oh, sorry, it's just been an interesting day," I answered walking passed the older man and going into the lobby. "Nikki Thompson, I'm here for the writer's retreat."

# Chapter Three

Once I received my room key, I was told the cocktail party was in half an hour and was semiformal. Elliot Ross had arrived and was in his room looking forward to meeting everyone. The receptionist asked me to confirm my signature and understanding of the League's social media policies as well as understanding no large parties were permitted inside the guest rooms. After signing a waiver and a promise I wouldn't burn the castle down or wreck the room, I thanked the older lady behind the counter and followed the signs to the elevator, pulling out the welcome packet pamphlet as I waited for the car to arrive at my floor.

Spa.

Pool.

Bars.

Movie Theater.

All those words stuck out to me but mostly the word: libraries, as in more than one, caught my attention. Call me a geek but that got my blood going more than *spa* or *bar*.

Reaching my room, I unlocked the door and gasped. It opened to a sitting room decorated in Louis XV style. Two gold and ivory embroidered canapé sofas faced each other with a cherry stained center table, standing on delicately thin legs inlaid with gold ormolus of cherubs and roses, between them. A bay window with the most beautifully ornate desk in front of it, overlooked the gardens and fountain. A gigantic fireplace, with a roaring fire already lit, had two wingback chairs and a tapestry-like-rug laying between them.

Walking through, I went to the door connecting the sitting room to the bedroom.

"Oh come on," I muttered as I took in the king-sized bed, a chest of drawers, highboy and two nightstands. A floor to ceiling mirror reflected my awed image as I turned to a second fireplace and a painting of a man and woman in eighteenth century dress hanging above it.

Walking toward the bed, I rolled my suitcases to the corner and took the card resting in front of the gift basket on the bed.

*For literary success and those sleepless nights only a writer would understand. Sláinte mhath, Elliot Ross, President of the League of Extraordinary Writers, Castle MacCulloch, 2014*

There would be plenty of those sleepless writing nights if I had anything to say about it. Glancing through the basket, there was my favorite bottle of champagne, cheese, salami, nuts, dried fruit, crackers, tea bags, a mug emblazoned with the league's logo, chocolates and Scottish shortbread. Before I could look through it any further, the phone on the bedside table rang.

"Nikki Thompson speaking," I answered.

"Good evening, Ms. Thompson, this is Lorna, Mr. Ross's assistant. He has asked we call all the rooms to give everyone a twenty-minute warning. He wishes to start promptly at seven," the disembodied voice said.

"Of course, thank you," I answered.

"Cocktails are already being poured in the library bar if you are ready please feel free to come down now. Also, please remember, it is semi-formal," she went on.

"I understand, thanks," I said. "I'll be down in a couple minutes."

"Grand, and welcome to the League of Extraordinary Writers and MacCulloch Castle," she replied.

"Thank you. I am looking forward to my stay."

She hung up and I rolled off the bed hurrying to my bags. Unhooking my garment bag, I hung up my little black cocktail dress and found my Prada pumps. Rushing to the bathroom, I turned on the shower and stripped out of my clothes. There was no way I was going to greet Elliot Ross looking like something the cat dragged in.

The hot water felt amazing on my aching shoulders. Once dry, I applied some light makeup and smoky eyes then slipped into the dress and high heels.

Using the time frame as my excuse, I grabbed my hairspray, bent over and sprayed my hair upside down. Shaking it out, what greeted me was a distinctly *come hither* look but I was newly single and on vacation. Not to mention I was meeting my favorite author. Ross's face flashed before my eyes and I almost wished he could see me. I'd give him a little more thrill...

Shrugging, I did a final inventory check in the mirror and grinned. Grabbing my clutch as I headed out the door, I happened to glance at the time. Seven minutes till. *Perfect.*

"Hey, gorgeous," I heard behind me as I locked the door. Turning, a vaguely familiar face greeted me. "Going my way?" I laughed at the wiggling eyebrows in his mocha chocolate face. "Chad Neugan," he introduced.

"Of course," I smiled remembering his interview on national television. He had revolutionized LGBTQ literature and lived with his partner in Maine.

"Nikki Thompson," I replied.

"Oh right," he grinned. "My boyfriend loves spy thrillers. He'll be so jealous to know I met you. You heading to cocktails?" He asked falling into step beside me.

"Yes," I answered seeing his tailored suit jacket with a black superhero t-shirt under it and designer shoes. "Can't wait to meet Elliot Ross."

"Me too," he replied. "I heard he is gorgeous."

"You've never seen a picture of him either?" I asked as we reached the elevator.

"Honey," he laughed. "No one has. He has that deal with

his publisher not to show his face. Why, I don't know. Maybe he's a beast or disfigured or something," he teased. "But I was so intrigued when I got that NDA with the packet, I Googled him and I seriously couldn't find a single photo! In today's day and age! I mean, seriously?"

I laughed having done the exact same thing when I signed the Non-Disclosure Agreement that strictly said pictures of the authors were forbidden and if violated, could cause you to be kicked out of the league and everything up to being sued. They couldn't stop us from using our phones of course but basically photos of any person would need to be screened by staff.

"To think we may have passed him on the street and would never know he was Elliot Ross," I said. "I seriously can't wait to meet him."

Chad checked his watch as we both stepped off the elevator and followed the signs to the library bar where several other authors had already gathered.

"He should be starting in a couple minutes," Chad said. "Get you anything?" He indicated the bar.

"Oh thanks," I answered. "Champagne, brut?"

"Done, I tell you, so glad it's an open bar, but I could get in trouble," he teased.

As he retreated to order our drinks, I took in the room around me. Several other authors filled the small space. In America, it would be considered cramped; in Scotland, it was cozy.

And it truly was a library. Books lined the walls in shelves and cases, chairs flanked the lit fireplace and a large chandelier hung from the ceiling.

Chad returned with two glasses of bubbling champagne in crystal flutes.

"Cheers," he clinked his glass with mine.

"To writer's retreats with open bars," I grinned.

"I'll drink to that," he replied taking a hefty sip. "They told me they would be passing glasses out all evening so if we want something different we could go to the bar but our champagne is covered."

"Don't tell me that," I laughed. "Champagne is my bane."

"Good to know," he laughed.

The hall clock chimed the top of the hour and a hush descended over the group. The lady I had spoken with earlier on the phone stood and addressed the crowd.

"Ladies and gentlemen," she announced in a crisp but subtle Scottish accent. "On behalf of the League of Extraordinary Writers, I am pleased to welcome you all to Castle MacCulloch. We are very excited to announce this is our largest event to date. Thirteen authors from six different countries are here today. I hope you all have come prepared for the adventure ahead. Two months together and with luck, hard work and determination, let's get a couple bestsellers done, shall we?" Whoops of cheers went up around me. The excitement in the air was palpable. As I looked around, I saw kings and queens of their genre all gathered together. Realization I was now a Fellow of the League of Extraordinary Authors made me giddy.

"So without any further ado," the woman went on. Chad grabbed my arm and squealed his delight. "The man of the hour. It is my pleasure to welcome, our Founder and President, Mr. Elliot Ross!"

A side door opened. My pulse pounded in my ears as I waited to see him. The authors applauded and gathered together blocking my view. All I saw was a flash of plaid, a white shirt and brown hair. I moved this way and that trying to get a good look at him. Chad stretched to his full height a good half a foot taller than me and gripped my arm.

"Oh my god!" he mouthed, then fanned himself indicating Elliot Ross was hot. I grinned but I still couldn't see. Eventually, the crowd quieted down.

"Thank you all for that warm welcome," Elliot Ross began. His voice was silky smooth and Scottish accented. But what surprised me was I had heard that voice before. "It certainly is a pleasure to be here and host this tenth annual writer's retreat. It is my honor to have you here and I very much look forward to getting to know you all. Many people have asked me why it is I write but long ago when my first novel, *Rosewood* was published, I was being interviewed and the journalist asked me the same question. He didn't really care, he was just asking a set of canned questions to fill space in an interview column. I didn't answer at first because it got me thinking. Did I really want fame and money? Women throwing themselves at me simply to get their one minute of fame? But come now men, we all know that was in the back of my mind," the men around me chuckled and a couple of them raised their glass to toast him. "Or did I want to write just for the hell of it? That's when I realized I wanted people to read my words simply because they wanted to. They want to be transported to another realm. For three hundred and fifty pages, they want to forget the hassles of the day, the busy job, the kids yelling and screaming, the mess the dog just made. They want to be so absorbed in another world that the problems and pain and heartbreak of this world," he snapped his fingers. "Vanish. They donnae want to know it is fiction, they want to revel in the idea the characters they love are real.

"So that was when I decided to make a deal with my publisher to never have my face printed on a book or in an article, interview, or newspaper. And you know what? I am very happy with my decision. I've never looked back... I do have a point to this by the way," the authors chuckled. "What I'm trying to say is I was free of distractions and because of that, I am able to do what it is I love. I hope we have created a little place here where you all can share in that peace. It is definitely a little slice of heaven here at the castle and in Scotland... But I may be a wee bit biased. Now, I am sure you are all as eager as I am to take advantage of the open bar, delicious foods, and excellent conversation so, I would like to propose a toast. In my country, we have a saying; *Sláinte mhòr agus a h-uile beannachd duibh.* Great health and every good blessing to you! *Sláinte mhath*!"

We all repeated the last phrase with our glasses held high and drank. The crowd began milling about as the general buzz of conversation began. Chad turned to me, a brilliant smile on his lips.

"Oh my god, talk about one man there needs to be more pictures of," he let the idea trail off. "You okay, honey? You look a little... flushed."

I answered his suggestive grin with one of my own.

"Hang on a sec, I need to check something out," I said. "You good?"

His grin widened. "Some*thing* or some*one*?"

"Go flirt," I smacked his arm playfully. He winked and walked in the general direction of a group of two other American authors.

Winding my way through the crowd, I searched for the owner of that voice. I couldn't believe he was there. I couldn't believe it was *him*. That little... Walking out of the library bar, a whisky glass was on a table beside an open glass door leading outside. Taking the tumbler, I smelled the contents. Bonfire mixed with wet earth and pine; definitely his whisky. Peeking out, the grounds glowed in the soft lights lining the pathway. The rain had stopped earlier but the sudden change of temperature made me shiver. Wrapping my arms around myself, I stepped through the small door and onto the terrace. I took a moment to enjoy the fresh air and the view before me. The grounds were absolutely lovely. The wide green space was divided by a mass of thick trees matured at least a hundred years. In the dim light, they looked like silent sentries. Walking over to them, I ran my fingers over the rough bark and smiled.

"If only you could talk, what stories you would tell," I breathed. Walking through the line of trees the stillness of the air left me breathless as the forbidden feeling growing in the pit of my belly mixed with the absolute freedom I felt being in my maternal grandfather's homeland.

As the sounds of night crept in, the insects, the wind rustling the leaves, the wild life coming alive all around me, I could tell why Grandpa Brodie loved this place. Taking a deep breath in, I closed my eyes humming the tune he always used to sing to me. Loch Lomond, slow and soft.

After the first verse, I felt something brush against my leg. Looking down, I couldn't see anything in the dim light, but I movement to my right caught my eye. A man stood a few feet away from me, his kilt of crème and black stripes shone in the moonlight, his knee-high soft leather boots, covered his legs and a black doublet with an extra bit of plaid flung over his shoulder was fastened with a silver brooch at the lapel. He stood in a ray of moonlight and his brown hair flopped in his face while his penetrating light blue eyes stared at me as if I was the most intriguing thing he had ever seen. Roughly forty years old, he was broadly built with athletic looking muscles and oddly something drew me to him. Quite a handsome man, mystery surrounded him and I could not stop my feet from taking a closer step toward him.

"Looking for me?" a familiar voice called. As soon as I turned to see who was walking up, I knew my strange visitor in the kilt would be gone. Glancing back, the only thing I saw in the moonlight was an old rusted water pump surrounded by white heather. The man had reached me by then and called my name. "You all right? You look pale. Are you cold?" He shrugged out of his jacket and draped it across my shoulders. His heat surrounded me and I moaned as goosebumps rose on my arms. I met his eyes and that lazy smirk raised one side of his mouth.

"So is it Mr. Ross or Mr. Sutherland?" I asked.

"Ross will do," he replied.

"You could have told me you were Elliot Ross," I said playfully slapping his arm.

"Where would the fun be in that?" he answered.

"So what is your real name?" I asked.

"Ross Sutherland like I said," he answered. "I go by a pen name when I write."

"Known him all your life, huh?"

"Not a lie," he replied. "I have known me my whole life."

"Did you know who I was?"

"No' at first," he answered. "When I approached you, I saw a beautiful woman in need. Then, when you introduced yourself, I knew. I make it a point to read the books of everyone who comes here."

"You read my book?" I asked surprised.

"Cover to cover, Ms. Thompson," he replied in a low voice. "In twenty-four hours, by the way. You owe me eight hours of sleep for that... And I think you're wrong. There's plenty of material there for a second one. So why have you really stopped writing?"

"I don't have to tell you anything," I snipped. Ross said nothing only raised a single eyebrow. "I'm sorry," I replied. "It's a sore subject with me at the moment."

"I do understand how a bad breakup can affect writer's block, you know," he said. "When you are ready or would like to talk, I'm here," he took a step closer to me. "Would you like to go back inside? I hear Elliot Ross goes all out for this thing. The food is supposed to be fantastic."

"Yeah, okay," I replied. We turned to head back into the house when I stopped again. "Ross," he looked down at me. "Why didn't you tell me?" My voice soft.

"Because I was intrigued by you, Ms. Thompson," Ross said. "And I wanted to give you a reason to be intrigued by me."

We dropped the subject and soon slipped back through the door. His whisky glass was gone from the table. Making our way through the crowd, I met Chad at the bar, ordering a glass of scotch. He turned to us, a wide grin on his face as he took in my flushed face and Ross's coat draped over my shoulders. Quickly shrugging out of it, I handed it back to Ross and picked up a glass of champagne from the passing waiter.

# Chapter Four

Throwing open the heavy drapes covering my windows, I reveled in the shining sun streaming through the glass. *What a glorious day!* I wrapped my arms around myself and squealed with delight. It was early morning and my jet lag was surprisingly nonexistent. As I gazed out to the garden below, I saw two of the more famous writers in the group together with pens and notebooks in hand. I watched as they walked toward another section of the maze garden. Ross greeted them as he came out of the hedgerow entrance and into my line of sight.

It wasn't right for a man to be that good looking. Ross oozed sexual awareness. I remembered too well how his gaze lowered to my open shirt in the airplane, his sexy lazy smirk, teasing about liking more thrill, and how his gaze pierced my resistance. I realized, too late, I was biting my lip as I watched him. If I put half the energy I spent fawning over him into writing, I would have ten books written by the end of the retreat. Resolved, I turned back to the room and went to my suitcases.

Half an hour later, I heard a knock at my door. Putting down the last sweater from my suitcase, I went to answer it.

Peering through the peep hole, I recognized dark violet, slightly bloodshot, eyes in the handsome chocolate face of Chad Neugan. Grinning, I opened the door.

"Drink much?" I teased.

"Morning to you too," he moaned rubbing his temples.

Laughing, I opened my door wider for him, grabbed two Alka Seltzer tablets and dropped them in a glass of water. Chad had fallen into one of the chairs beside the sitting room fireplace.

"How are you so perky?" he asked grumbling. "You had like ten glasses of champagne."

"Five and water after each one," I winked. "Did you mix your alcohol?"

He looked up at me accepting the glass with the medicine. "Possibly."

"Well don't worry, I think I got all the incriminating pictures of you dancing topless on the bar," I teased.

"Oh good, send them to me, would ya? I'll get them to my boyfriend."

"Trying to make him jealous?" I asked.

"No, just showing I miss him."

"Awe," I pouted. "Poor baby. It's a beautiful morning though, isn't it?"

"Mm, the sun is too bright when I'm this hungover," he replied.

"Oh, but it's so nice," I answered and went to the side table to pour myself a mug of coffee from the pot I had made earlier. "Want one?" At his nod, I poured another and sat across from him in the other wingback chair. "I want to explore more. I was out in the grounds last night. There is something mystical about this place."

"This excitement wouldn't have anything to do with a certain drop dead gorgeous, kilt wearing, dreamy eyed, bestselling author, would it?" He asked with a knowing stare.

"He is dreamy, isn't he?" I teased sitting back down.

"Are you going to tell me how you met him?" he asked.

"Outside, last night," I covered.

"You are a terrible liar," he chuckled.

"A girl's gotta have some secrets," I winked. "But now I'm

starving. Did I read there was a buffet breakfast?"

"Every morning," he answered.

"Feeling better?"

"Good enough to be able to eat," he stated standing.

"Good," I replied. "Let me change out of these yoga pants and into some jeans."

"Want me to head on down?" he offered.

"I'll be two seconds," I said. "You can stay here if you want."

"Thanks," he sat back down. I went to the bedroom and left the door cracked. "You know this room is pretty nice," he called. "Louis XV is a beautiful style."

"Yeah, I didn't know when I filled out that questionnaire they would take it this far," I called back, remembering the ten page get-to-know-you packet that arrived after my application was accepted. It listed different furniture styles and we were to check our top three favorites. Along with furniture, there was a section on favorite foods and alcohol. Oddly enough, my choices were all in my welcome basket.

"I know, right?" Chad grinned. "My choice was nautical; you should see my room! It's epic," he grinned and began singing *a pirates' life for me*. I busted out laughing and walked back into the main room. "Wow, that was fast."

"Do I look bad?" I asked.

"Not at all," he answered. "If I were straight, I'd go after you."

"That is quiet the compliment, thank you," I grinned.

Winking, he offered his arm to me, "Shall we?" he asked.

"Aye, matey," I teased. Just as I was about to take his arm, I thought better of it and went to the desk at the bay window pulling out my iPad. Having told Chad about my writer's block last night after the second glass of champagne, his amused gaze followed me. "What?" I questioned. He shrugged innocently. "Wishful thinking."

The breakfast room was as ornate as the rest of the castle. The all-you-can-eat buffet was set out on one side of the room and the coffee, tea and juice bar was on the other side. Chad and I picked a seat with two other authors, a paranormal and an historical.

"Have you seen an upswing in sales given the recent upsets in the Middle East?" the paranormal writer asked her companion, her accent was German.

The historical author nodded his head.

"I do not know why," René answered, French by his accent, "but the American market is always so fickle."

Chad and I, the only two Americans at the table, looked at each other but said nothing.

"And you, Jilliana? That whole vampire movement... did it boost your sales?" he asked.

Jilliana shrugged. "I was doing pretty well before all of that. There's always some love-struck teenager waiting to meet a mysterious stranger with secrets of his own. Vampire, Werewolf, Zombie, it matters little. There are no men like that."

"Oh I beg to differ," René said. "We men may be monotonous creatures but there are some good ones still out there," he winked at her.

"I have yet to meet any man who could truly be considered mysterious and I am sure my friend here will agree with me." Jilliana looked over at me expectantly.

"Tell us, *mademoiselle*, any mysterious strangers in your life?" René asked.

"Well," I started, catching Ross's eye as he walked over to our table behind René and Jilliana. "There is one. I met him in Heathrow airport. I missed my plane you see and as I was sitting at the bar having a glass of wine, this man came up to me, having heard my self-degradation and offered a seat on his private jet. He and his three friends were heading to Edinburgh and asked if I needed to get there as soon as possible. He was gorgeous, mysterious, and obviously generous but I didn't even know the names of his friends. Anyway, he bought my drink and food and told me the gate number if I changed my mind. I realized if I went I would be taking a huge risk but he was very sweet and insanely good looking." The side of Ross's lip ticked up but he never said anything. "He left and I finished my wine. After a moment, I realized what kind of a risk I was taking not taking him up on the offer so I convinced the bartender to sell me a bottle of his favorite scotch and I raced across the airport to meet him."

"What happened?" Jilliana gasped.

"I reached the gate in time and joined him on the flight," I explained. "And had the best time of my life."

"Honey, was he gay?" Chad asked.

"What?" I looked over at him confused.

"Well, clearly you two didn't join the Mile High Club which is crazy if he was as insanely gorgeous as you've said. So, I need to know, was he gay? Because as much as I love my boyfriend, I wouldn't mind taking one for the team."

I laughed but looked up at Ross still standing behind René and Jilliana.

"Not that I'm aware of," I said. "Maybe he didn't think I was as attractive." Ross's eyes narrowed.

"Or maybe he was being a gentleman," René offered.

"Or maybe he'll ask you to pay him back later," Jilliana said. "Most men have only one thing on the mind."

"Maybe," I said. "But with him... I don't think I would have complained much."

Ross laughed out loud then and the table turned to see him.

"I'm sorry, Ms. Thompson, but I could nae help and overhear," he began. "Believe me, the man was constantly thinking of taking you to the back room and having his wicked way with you but you said there were three others on the trip with you? Maybe he didn't feel like sharing."

Chad looked back at me, his eyes wide. I should have known he would figure it out.

"Maybe," I shrugged. "But I guess I'll never know."

"You don't have a way to contact him?" René asked.

"Slipped my mind," I replied.

"If he's interested, he'll find a way to contact you, of that I'm certain," Ross stated.

"Maybe he already has," Chad replied. "I love a good romantic mystery."

After staring at each other for a long moment, Ross broke the silence with a sigh and leaned forward, placing his hands on René's and Jilliana's chairs. "All work and no play?"

"The effect of too much free booze, Mr. Ross," Chad said.

"Just Ross will do, Chad," Ross replied. "I like to make sure my guests enjoy their stay. How are your accommodations?"

"Oh wonderful!" Jilliana said. "Thank you."

"Good, that's what I like to hear. You know, Chad, I hadn't gotten a chance to tell you, I read your latest novel, *Picture Perfect.* I have to say it was a work of art," Ross praised.

"Oh my, thank you thank you so much!" Chad gushed. "That means so much and your latest one is wonderful."

"Ah cheers," Ross smiled. "Jilliana, your latest *Darkness of the Night* I have to say was my favorite so far."

"You are too kind," Jilliana smiled softly.

"Not at all, the characters were so real and it was tightly plotted, brava," he replied. "And of course, René, truly I did not realize France played such a crucial role in the American Revolution. It was quite exciting to read."

"Thank you, *Monsieur*," René babbled. "That is quite the compliment."

"Ms. Thompson," Ross looked at me. "Sounds like this mysterious character might make a good story."

"Maybe," I agreed. "But there are enough romance novels out there with half naked men in kilts on the cover. Now if there's a ghost... that might spice things up a bit."

"Don't forget Castle MacCulloch is supposed to be haunted," he said.

"I'll need to look into that," I replied.

"Do, he is quiet an interesting character."

"I've meet a ghost," Jilliana interjected.

"Have you?" I asked.

"Indeed, my grandmother appeared to me as a little girl told me about a piece of jewelry she wanted me to have."

"How did she appear to you?" I asked.

"Solid form as if I could reach out and touch her," she reached up and clasped the locket she wore. "I sometimes wish she would appear to me again. Since then I have been looking for a deeper experience. Perhaps I have found one."

"Perhaps," Ross agreed. "But I have taken up too much

of your time already. I'm glad you are all making friends. Remember if you need anything, the libraries and my staff are at your disposal. If you need me, I am available to you but I do ask, you go through my assistant with any non-urgent matters. Some forget I am a writer too," he nodded to us and left to another table of authors.

"Excuse us, would you?" I heard, then felt Chad's hand grasp mine as he hauled me outside to the patio and down the stairs.

"Chad?" I laughed. "What the hell is wrong with you?"

"Okay, what was that?" He turned around, his eyes alight with mischief.

"What?" I asked.

"The mysterious stranger? The airplane? Spill, sister and I don't mean no milk," he crossed his arms over his lean chest and stared down at me.

Sighing but agreeing, I led us to a bench and we sat. I started from the beginning but still kept Ross's secret of his real name.

"How did you not know it was him?" Chad asked stunned.

"Um, well there's never been a picture of him and he only introduced himself to me as Ross nothing else," I said.

"Still..." he groaned and leaned back against the bench. "How did you handle it? Being cooped up inside a jet with the most gorgeous man in the world?"

"How does your boyfriend like you asking that question?" I teased.

"Frank knows I like to flirt, but trust me the only one I want is my man," he smiled. "Have I shown you his picture?"

"Not yet, you haven't," I said and leaned in close when he took out his phone.

Later that afternoon, I left Chad at the pool to take a walk through the grounds. Skyping with Dad to show him how beautiful it was, I promised to call him again later, but as soon as I hung up the call I realized I stood at the entrance to the maze garden and, curious as to what it looked like at eye level, I walked toward it. Before I could get inside, a cold gust of wind hit me directly in the face. Turning my back, an old water pump stood in front of me just at the tree line. The wind still blew fiercely at my back and I closed my eyes against the cold. Once the wind died down, I looked up and my breath caught in my throat.

The same man I had seen yesterday stood before that pump again. He wore a wool cap on his mop of light brown hair and pants instead of a kilt. Again, he was looking at me with that strange expression on his face. I was more intrigued by him than ever.

"Hello?" I called out. He didn't respond. "I'm Nikki, what's your name?"

He said something then, but it wasn't English.

"I'm sorry, I don't know Gaelic," I said. He looked at me more intently then.

"Do ye hae it?" his voice rang out in a thick highland brogue but it sounded odd, almost hollow.

"Have what?" I asked.

"The Highland Pride," he said.

"The what?" I asked confused. That was the name of Elliot Ross' latest book. Of course I had it. Were Ross's sales so low he had to hire an actor to dress up as his hero and go around asking if his guests had bought his book? Somehow, I doubted it.

The man looked sharply toward one of the turrets in the castle. My eyes followed his just in time to see a curtain fall back into place on the third floor. When I looked back, the man was gone. I wrapped my arms around me as a chill ran down my spine.

Turning, I ran right into Ross Sutherland. "There you are," he grinned. "You distracted me with all your talk about a handsome stranger this morning, I didn't get a chance to see how you like your accommodations."

"*I* distracted *you*?" I asked. "More like you interrupted a very interesting conversation."

"Och aye it was a verra interesting conversation, lass," he replied.

"Most of it made up of course," I teased trying to be

serious.

"Oh of course," he agreed. "We authors tend to embellish."

"Absolutely, completely exaggerated," I replied.

"No truth in it whatsoever," Ross answered.

"None at all," I said.

We were silent for a long moment, but the heated look in his eyes mirrored mine. In one swift movement, he grabbed my hand and pulled me into the tree line away from the castle. Pushing me against the trunk of an old oak, he pressed his body against me.

"Exaggerate this," he whispered then lowered his lips to mine. Throwing my arms around his neck, I pulled him closer to me and deepened the kiss. Our teeth clicked against each other's in our haste.

Velvety, smooth and warm. Ross curled my toes and caused goosebumps to rise along my arms in mere moments. Even the most incredible night with Daren was a dim flickering candle in the brilliant sunlight that was Ross Sutherland. His hand slipped passed my waist and hooked around my thigh pulling my leg up to wrap around his hip without breaking our kiss. I wasn't sure how long we stayed like that, but soon voices nearby had us breaking apart almost as quickly as we had come together. Straightening his shirt and hair, he cleared his throat as two authors walked by. They waved to us but continued on their walk through the woods.

"It looks like everyone is looking for a secret place," I breathed.

"Aye," Ross answered. "I'm sorry for breaking away, I did nae want anyone to see us, no' that I'm ashamed of you, of us I just..." I placed a finger over his lips to stop him from digging an even deeper hole than the one he was already in.

"I get it," I replied. "But that's going to have to happen again."

"Och aye, and soon," he said. "Have dinner with me tonight."

"What?" I breathed.

"Have dinner with me," he repeated.

"Oh god, Ross, I can't," I said. "Not tonight, I promised

Chad I'd keep him sober and I was going to call my best friend. I kinda left without telling her."

"Of course," he answered. "Ehm, tomorrow night?"

"Definitely," I agreed. "Just know this, okay, I went through a really bad break up three months ago and I don't want you to be a rebound but I also don't want to miss out on this. I am short tempered and irresponsible, jealous and downright stubborn. I have stretchmarks from when I gained a ton of weight in high school and lost it in college and a bad knee from an old injury during softball practice. I don't wear fake nails, have fake boobs, or wear a ton of makeup. I'm a daddy's girl and an American woman. I'm kinda new at this single thing and definitely new to a no strings attached relationship."

Ross stared at me fighting the smirk that threatened to lift his lips. "Pleased to meet you. Now shut up and kiss me again."

# Chapter Five

I hadn't seen Ross since we parted in the woods. God, could that man kiss. I had to admit a part of me was ecstatic about our date tomorrow night the other part of me was petrified. I didn't think I was over Daren and I didn't want to put that on Ross. But for the first time in my entire life I was by myself in a foreign country and a deliciously hot man was kissing me and asking me out. I booked a couple hours at the spa for after lunch, complete with waxing, facial, and a massage. Chad and I had lunch with three other authors and parted ways when he wanted to join a small group going into the village. I promised to join the next time but had only twenty minutes until my spa time.

Wanting to take in some fresh air on the beautiful day, I went back out to the garden and walked through the maze finding my way to the middle where a small stone fountain featuring a lion's head stood surrounded by stone benches. One other author sat in the center, nose deep in a notebook, a fountain pen flying across the page.

I was about to turn around and leave her to her story, when she called me back. "Hooey!" She was waving the small notebook at me. Finally getting a good look at her, I recognized the face from the back of mom's collection of romance novels. Marilyn Tucker, Romance Queen, gathered her things and rushed over to me, her unruly white hair billowed in the wind. "Beautiful day!" She called. "Marilyn Tucker," she introduced herself once she was close enough.

"Yes, I know," I answered standing. "Nikki Thompson."

"Ooh, Nikki Thompson, how splendid! You must sign my book! I absolutely loved it!" She gushed.

"Thank you," I replied, her compliments and British accent making me smile.

"Now don't you be telling anyone but I just can't bring myself to read those sappy romances anymore. I do love a good thriller. Gets the blood going, I must say and at my age... *phew*, it takes quite a bit," she grinned and started using the notebook as a hand fan. I couldn't help but laugh, she reminded me of my mom. "So, what are you working on right now?"

"Um, this and that," I answered, not wanting to admit I was having the worst writer's block of my career.

"You poor dear... writer's block got you?" she asked tenderly touching my arm.

"Is it that obvious?" I replied.

"Only to those of us who know and have been there. Don't you worry, dear, this place is filled with stories. I'm sure one will pop its way into your head," she encouraged.

"Has one found you?" I asked.

"With all these kilted hotties walking around? Rather!" she grinned. "I have always been a sucker for a man's bare knees under that kilt. But I have to say I am more interested in a romance blooming right under my nose."

"Oh?" I asked. "Whose?"

She stopped and looked me straight in the eye. Understanding finally dawned on me.

"Mine?" I asked shocked.

"Oh, come now," she reasoned. "I've seen you with Elliot Ross. You walk into the room and the temperature goes up. And this morning? Oh my, that is the sort of thing a writer dreams of seeing."

"Oh, Ms. Tucker—"

"Marilyn, dear," she ordered.

"Marilyn," I obliged. "I'm afraid you're mistaken. Ross that is, *Mr.* Ross and I are not... I mean, we are colleagues, nothing more."

"You can't lie to me, Sweetie," she said. "I write this for a living. I know passion when I see it."

"I'm sorry to disappoint you, but there is nothing going on between me and Elliot Ross," I stated firmly. *Not a lie,* I heard Ross's voice in my head. *There isn't anything going on between me and* Elliot *Ross...*

Marilyn said something more but movement caught my eye. A fleeting figure rushed passed the entrance to the center of the maze garden. I caught a glimpse of a kilt and brown hair. It was him again!

"Marilyn, I need you to come with me, quickly," I interrupted her.

"Why, dear, whatever is it?" She asked. Not answering her, I grabbed her hand and we raced after the image. Only a few moments had past but I had lost him. Cursing in frustration, I scanned the area for any sign.

"What's wrong, dear?" Marilyn asked. "You look like you've seen a ghost."

"No, no," I dismissed the idea. "I've been plagued by this guy ever since I arrived. He's been appearing randomly and then when I go after him, he's gone."

"What man?" She asked looking around.

"I don't know, some guy in a kilt," I said.

Marilyn laughed, a tinkling sound. "Oh dear, look around you, practically everyone is in a kilt."

We had made it to another opening in the maze garden, this one coming in off the pool area. Servers passed champagne and cocktails to authors sitting beneath the shade of an umbrella, a man walked through the garden with a tennis racket over his shoulder, another with a ringing telephone and another carrying a toy poodle under his arm headed toward another author; all wore kilts of varying plaids. Everyone wore a kilt, so why was I so fascinated by one guy?

"I'm sorry," I said. "I just want to know who this guy is. He's a pest and I don't think he's staff."

"Have you spoken to Elliot about it?" she asked.

"No," I shook my head. "I don't want to bother him. And besides like you said, I'm sure there's a logical explanation." I sighed and jumped when my phone's alarm rang. "Shit," I silenced it. "I'm sorry, Marilyn, I have a spa time booked but I would love to talk with you more."

"Of course, dear, I'll be around. Don't hesitate to come talk to me," she offered and headed to another romance author who waved her over as she sat by the pool, leaving me alone with my thoughts.

Ever since the movie *Psycho,* women have been afraid to take a shower when they are alone in a creepy place. Not that Castle MacCulloch was creepy but it was strange.

As I stood in the claw footed tub, rinsing off from a luxurious bubble bath after my wonderful day at the spa, my thoughts drifted to Ross. It was nearly dinner time and my heart raced with the idea I might see him. I was Chad's conscience that evening, his boyfriend, the doctor, was miffed he was so drunk he couldn't remember much of the previous night. All I caught of that conversation was something about his liver and how he wasn't as young as he once was.

Ross had business to deal with in Edinburgh that day so I hadn't seen him at all since our kiss. It gave me time to think about the man I kept meeting in the woods. Marilyn was right, the staff were kilted and I doubted Ross would hire an actor to terrorize his guests demanding if they had bought his latest book, but in a small way I could. His libraries were filled with research books of every topic, the kilted staff were encouraged to flirt with the romance writers, could this mystery man be set up for us suspense writers?

Sighing, I turned off the water and grabbed the towel I had hung on the railing beside the tub.

Wiping my face, chest and arms, I pulled back the shower curtain to step out and immediately screamed. The same man was in my bathroom! Covering my naked body as best I could, I heard him speak.

"Get outta here!" he ordered me harshly. "She'll see ya!"

"Who the hell are you?" I demanded.

"Go!" he commanded and then dissipated right before my eyes.

The next thing I remember, I was in Ross's lap and Chad stood nearby on the phone with a bottle of whisky in his hand, the stinging taste was on my lips. I looked down, suddenly self-conscious I was in a towel and not sure if I was fully covered.

"You're fine," Ross eased my fears. "Donnae be moving that head too much before we have you looked at."

"Ow," I groaned feeling like a thousand drums were beating away at my temple.

"You've managed to get yourself a nice goose egg," Ross said.

"Not intentionally," I answered attempting to sit up. Ross had to help me.

"He's on his way," Chad turned back to us and handed Ross the phone. I looked at both of them confused.

"Who?" I asked.

"Our French companion at breakfast this morning; René, moonlights as a doctor," Chad explained. He sat on his ankles before me and took my hand. "I'm so glad I was in my room at the time, honey. I heard you scream. What happened?"

I groaned when Ross shifted his arm from behind me, my whole body aching.

"There was someone in the bathroom." I suddenly remembered.

"How the hell did someone get in here? Is there another master key?" Chad demanded Ross.

"Aye," Ross replied. "I have one and the other is kept under lock and key below stairs. We used mine to get in and it has nae left my possession. Can you describe this person, Nikki?" He looked at me. Of course I could, but how could I explain the bit about him vanishing into thin air without sounding like I should be committed? I shook my head. "Did he or she say anything? Anything at all?" Ross asked. Again, I shook my head.

"*Monsieur* Ross?" A heavily French accented voice rang out from the main door.

"In the bathroom, René," Ross called, his voice near to

my ear caused my head to pound even more.

The tall, lanky Frenchman I had met earlier sauntered into the room.

"Oh, *mon dieu*," he exclaimed seeing me in Ross's arms.

"She's coherent and understands what's going on around her. We found her face down on the tile floor about five minutes ago," Chad began explaining. "She said there was an intruder in the room."

René knelt before me and Ross reluctantly gave me over to the doctor. He got up and went to Chad. They both stepped out of the room. I watched them, their conversation getting fairly heated at one point with Chad jamming his finger into Ross's chest. Ross did not back down and I could only imagine what they were saying.

"I think it is just the one bump," René said. "Your eyes are dilating well. Take it easy for the next twenty-four hours and if the headache persists call for me at once. I will give you some medicine for the pain."

Having had a concussion before as a child, I knew the rule; no sleeping, but I was so tired.

"Can I call it a night, doc?" I asked. René looked at me confused. "Can I go to sleep?" I clarified.

"Oh *oui*, yes," he confirmed. "But I would suggest someone stays with you, not just for security but also to make sure you are cognizant when you wake."

"Already ahead of you, René," Ross walked back inside. "Chad and I will not leave her."

"Oh no, there's really no reason for you guys to stay with me," I hurried to say.

"Yes, there is," Ross replied and his tone showed he would not hear any more about it.

"*Bon*," René said and began packing his things.

"I just heard!" Marilyn's voice came from the main door as she rushed to me. "It's so terrible, are you all right?"

"Yeah, I'm fine, just a mild headache," I reassured.

"How about a nice cup of tea? Hmm?" She offered.

"Just like the English," Ross snorted. "A cup of tea'll fix everything in their minds."

"You mind your manners, Elliot Ross," Marilyn snapped.

The way she spoke to him, made me think she was more than just a writer staying at his castle.

"A cup of tea does sound good," I admitted. "And I am fair to starving."

"I will be sure something is sent up if I have to do it myself, dear," she replied. Once she reached the door, she turned back to me. "I knew you should have told Elliot everything earlier. This whole thing could have been avoided. Be sure to tell him now."

*Gee thanks, Marilyn...*

Ross's eyes flashed back to mine.

"What is she talking about?" He demanded.

"Let me get dressed first," I complained holding my arm across my chest.

"I don't know..." he started seriously then that devil smirk quirked one side of his mouth. "I rather like you clad in a bath towel."

"Ugh, Neanderthal!" I cried grinning from ear to ear.

"Here, honey," Chad brought me some clothes. "Let us, more evolved creatures, help you." Chad shut the door on Ross and helped me dress.

As I lay propped up in bed with a tray of food over my lap, the men sat in the wingback chairs by the bedroom fireplace sipping whisky.

"Do you know about this guy, Elliot?" Chad asked.

"I wish you had come to me," Ross said. "I have no idea who this person is. None of my staff are allowed in the guests' rooms unless given prior approval by the guest and myself or my assistant. This man doesn't sound familiar but I swear I will ask around. Maybe Lorna knowns something. I'll text her and see." He pulled out his phone and sent a quick text. "You've only seen him at the tree line?"

"Near it, except last time he was in the garden and here of course," I offered.

"I will figure out who this is, Nikki, I promise you."

"Hey, I know you will," I said softly. He looked worried.

Setting the food tray aside, I pulled off the sheets and comforter, swung my legs over the edge and tried to stand to go over to him. Immediately, the world spun and I fell back. Chad and Ross were at my side. My head fell back as I looked up at them, then over their shoulder to the painting above the fireplace.

"Of course..." I breathed.

There in the painting of the man and woman, was the man who had been following me. In the painting, he wore a black doublet over a white shirt and tight tan pants. His mop of light brown hair curled around his ears and collar and the light eyes I had seen before, stared down at me. Sitting before him was an exquisite woman with raven black hair upswept to the top of her head. Her blood red gown hugged her bodice and flared out pooling at her feet. Her dark eyes caused a chill run down my spine.

All of the sudden, grey mist swirled before my eyes. I blinked it away and when I opened them again, I was still in the same room but I had a distinct understanding I was in a different time. The woman from the painting sat at the settee by the window where my desk should have been and the man paced before the fireplace.

"What are ye sayin', Elizabeth?" he demanded of the raven haired beauty. I recognized his voice and appearance. It was my kilted stranger.

"I'm saying I am leaving you, Angus," the woman replied slowly as if he was having a hard time understanding. Oddly, her voice had an English accent.

Angus stopped dead in his tracks and turned to stare at her.

"Why?" He breathed.

"I think I made myself perfectly clear," she answered.

"Hae I no' taken care of ye, lass?" he demanded. "Hae I no' given ye everythin' I hae?"

"You are a brute. I wish Father had never agreed to this marriage," Elizabeth answered.

"Ye were the one who wanted it!" he shouted. She seemed unfazed and kept embroidering. "Ye'd shame me by leavin' my house?" he asked softer. "Ye've already shamed me by taking another to your bed."

"I have never loved you, Angus," she said. "This should come as no surprise to you."

"Ye gut me, woman," he uttered. "Ye're my wife, before God and man. I'll no' be havin' ye leave my house."

"You knew I was no blushing bride when I married you, Angus," she replied. His eyes narrowed on her face.

"Ye were the one who seduced me!" Angus cried.

"Well, that should have told you right there I was no bonnie wee lassie," she mocked.

"Ye demanded yer father marry us!" he growled.

"Of course, you were but a pawn in my game," she grinned. I had never seen a witch grin but if I could have guessed what it looked like, Elizabeth's grin would have been the perfect embodiment of it. "It was so easy. You were pining for your dear dead wife. All I had to do was throw you a few little looks and get to your bedchamber. Tell me, did your wife take care of you like I did that night?"

Angus's face grew red with rage. He stormed over to her and raised his hand to her. She put aside her needlepoint and stood up to face him defiantly.

"Go ahead, Angus," she taunted. "Do it. It will give me the proof I need of your brutality."

He froze, hand still raised, shaking with rage. After a moment, he calmed and lowered his hand.

"I have always tried to be a good husband to ye, Elizabeth," he finally whispered. "I hae ne'er hurt ye. I hae ne'er forced ye."

"I do not care what you call it," she said. "I only had you for my own pleasure. I am able to pick the men who have the potential to please me. You happened to be one of them. But now, you have failed. England will rule you and your precious Scotland for generations. You will never find the Highland Pride. I will make sure of it."

He took a foreboding step toward her. "Tha' is my family's property. Ye hae no right to it," he grasped her shoulders.

"What are you going to do, Angus? Kill me for it?" she demanded.

"If I hae to," his voice was low. Her eyes grew wide with

fear but only for a moment, then her features relaxed into a practiced Mata Hari. "I hae ne'er raised hand nor whip to a woman apart from this day. I will nae abide an English spy in me midst. Nae me own wife," he said. She did not react. "Och, aye, yer secret was nae well kept. I kenned when ye seduced me ye were working for Cumberland. Did ye think I was daft to no' ken what ye were doin'? Ye donnae become laird of yer clan by being taken in by a pretty face."

Elizabeth let his words sink in; her ruse was up and she knew it. As realization dawned on her, she struggled to get free of him but his grip on her arms increased.

"Ye will nae shame me, lass. No English will e'er shame me. Ye ken the name I am kenned by. Take another to yer bed again and ye will both feel my wrath. I swear it, on me own grave, I will nae rest until I have had my revenge on ye. Ye stole something that belonged to me. I am a Highlander, lass, perhaps I should acquaint you with what that really means. As God is my witness, I will nae rest until the Pride is in my clan's hands once more."

"Nikki!" Ross's voice and shaking roused me. Chad and Ross were leaning over the bed. "Nikki, wake up!"

"I'm up, I'm up," I replied. "What just happened?"

"You scared the living shit out of us, that's what happened," Chad answered soothing my hair back.

"Did you guys see that?" I asked.

"See what?" Ross demanded.

"Angus and Elizabeth," I said indicating the painting.

Both men looked behind them, confused. Looking back at each other, then to me, Ross squeezed my hand.

"Tell me what happened?" he whispered.

"I don't know," I replied. "I saw..."

"What, honey?" Chad pressed.

"You'll both think I'm crazy," I said. "Hell, I think I'm crazy!"

"Tell me what you saw," Ross all but ordered me.

"I saw... them," again I motioned to the painting.

"Laird MacPherson?" Ross asked surprised.

"*That's* Fearsome MacPherson?" I replied.

"Aye, lass," Ross answered. His hand trembled as he passed it over my brow. "Tell me what ye saw."

Hoping, but somehow knowing, they wouldn't think I was crazy, I told them the vision I had and how Angus MacPherson was the mysterious man I had met earlier. They both sat on the edge of the bed on either side of me. Chad had taken my hand in his and Ross had his hand comfortingly on my knee.

"I know you guys probably think I'm crazy," I said after I had finished. "But I swear that's what I saw."

"Ross," Chad said after a moment. "Your latest book is named The Highland Pride, what does it all mean?" I couldn't prevent my smile and squeezing his hand thanking him for believing me.

"Honestly, I donnae know," Ross replied. "I had heard about the Pride when I bought this place." I sighed thankful he believed me too. "But I only found it mentioned in a couple of references. The rest of my research was from the old lads at the pub. I came across the name and thought it sounded interesting. I have no idea what it is or the significance of it. But if what Nikki was shown in her vision is correct, it obviously is something very important to the MacPherson Clan."

"You bought this place?" I questioned. "I thought it was a family home. Isn't that what you do in Scotland?"

"About eleven years ago with the proceeds of my first novel," he explained. "It had been empty since the thirties. Angus MacPherson bought it in 1750 after Culloden. When he died, his family left the place. I had heard about the ghost and the legend but nothing this concrete."

"Thank you, for believing me," I clarified.

"Of course," he answered soothing my hair back from my face. My head followed his hand and tucked it against my cheek and shoulder. Ross's light smile mesmerized me but it was gone shortly after and replaced with a frown and furrowed brows. "But I donnae like how he seems to have attached himself to you."

"I'll be okay. What about the Pride?" I asked.

"Legend has it that MacPherson's second wife, Elizabeth was an English spy working for King George the Second's son; Lord Cumberland. He wanted the crown for himself and Bonnie Prince Charlie, a direct descendent of James the sixth of Scotland the first of England, stood in his way. The English have a long and convoluted history," he said with such Scottish arrogance I had to smile. "Basically, everyone wanted the crown and Angus' wife, Elizabeth sided with the Butcher Cumberland. Neither of the two men sat on the throne but, hey one's English, if they're no' fighting to take over something they're no' happy. Anyway, Elizabeth stole the Pride from Angus's vaults. It was supposedly a good luck talisman of some sort dating back to William Wallace and Robert the Bruce. When Angus found Elizabeth in bed with her step brother, he became enraged and killed them before turning the pistol on himself. No one knows what happened to the Highland Pride after that."

"Hang on," Chad interrupted. "Correct me if I'm wrong, but... this isn't the Highlands."

"No, you're right," Ross replied. "These are the lowlands but MacPherson held two castles. This one and one near Pitlochry that was taken after Culloden. Years after his first wife died in childbirth with his only child, he married Elizabeth. She wanted to be closer to England apparently to be able to send information. Angus MacPherson was a respected Jacobite and one of the most feared in all of Scotland but he was a known figure in the English Court after Culloden. Many believed he had become a turncoat and sided with the British after his lands were confiscated by the crown."

"We have to find the Pride," I stated.

"Lass, no one has been able to find it since it disappeared nearly three centuries ago," Ross reasoned.

"Ross, please," I pleaded. "Help me find it. He needs it."

He sighed heavily but replied, "Aye, lass. I'll help ya."

"Me too," Chad piped up. "Don't think you're gonna get rid of me that easily. What's a little ghost to me, eh?"

"Let's go then," I said attempting to get up. Ross pressed his hand gently to my shoulder preventing me from getting up.

"You're not going anywhere tonight," he replied. "First thing in the morning, I promise. But not now. You need to rest."

Huffing, I knew he was right. But I didn't want to fall asleep yet. Grabbing the remote, I turned on the TV.

"Any decent channels over here?" I asked.

# Chapter Six

## *Ross*

She was asleep, and dear god how I wanted to hold her to me. After our kiss in the woods, all I could think about was her. It didn't help my business negotiating skills when I was constantly reminded of our date the next evening. I needed the flat in Edinburgh and it was a steal. Thankfully Graeme was there to keep me focused but his constant talking in the car after and when we went to The Last Drop Pub in Grassmarket rubbed me raw. All I wanted was to get back to MacCulloch and see Nikki. Eight and a half hours after I left her at the doorway of the library bar, I arrived back at the castle with the express purpose of showering, changing, and going down to dinner with my guests and especially Nikki. Little did I expect as soon as I reached the top of the stairs to hear a screamed *who the hell are you?* Then see Chad race out of his room and pound on Nikki's door.

Watching her now, asleep with the bruise on her forehead, I clenched my hand around the whisky tumbler. Never in my life had I ever allowed a woman to get under my skin like Nikki had. I had been with many women in my thirty-two years but none of them caused me to feel this way.

I was always one to love 'em, never leave 'em wanting, and when dawn came, we both knew it was over. That was how it was since I was with my first at sixteen. But now… When I read *Secret Revenge*, I knew I needed to get Nikki Thompson to Scotland. Her book sang to me in a way few had. Lorna tried to convince me she wasn't our preferred type for Fellow. Meaning she didn't have sixteen books out and three movie deals. I didn't care. The castle and retreat paid for itself. All expenses were paid unless the authors wanted to go out to the village, that was on them, but everything from food, to spa service, to drinks, was all taken care of. All I asked in return was one percent of the book deal and movie or TV deal they received from their publishers and producers for the book they wrote while they stayed there. It wasn't in the fine print, it was the very first thing they had to agree to. Surprisingly, I hardly ever got push back on that. Lorna wasn't pleased with my decision especially when I cut another author whose book was about to be a TV show.

"Ross," she moaned from the bed. I turned to look at her and my heart nearly stopped. She was so beautiful. Chad had fallen asleep on the sofa in the main room giving me a chance to keep watch. "Ross." She said again and this time she writhed on the bed as if in pain. Standing quickly, I pulled off my jeans and slipped into the sweats I grabbed from my room. Padding over to the other side of the bed, I pulled the sheets down and slid in next to her. Immediately, she rolled over to face me and snuggled her head into the crook of my neck, her leg flung possessively over mine. I didn't mind one bit, but this was not how I expected to sleep with her the first time.

"Mm," she sighed and placed her hand over my chest. Kissing her hair, I settled into the bed and relaxed.

"I'm here," I whispered. She cried out but didn't wake. "Shh, shh, it's all right."

*Nikki*

I didn't know where I was, all I knew was I was running. Running for my life. My lungs burned, my heart pounded fiercely and yet I still ran. It was dark, night, there was no moon and still I kept running. I held something in my hands. I didn't know what it was but it was important. I had to keep it safe. Passing tree after tree, all looked the same.

Voices.

Voices were behind me. Someone was following me. Dogs howled. Oh, Heaven help me, I couldn't stop. My foot caught a tree root sticking out of the ground and I fell face first into mud.

I tried to get up but my ankle hurt too much. Looking back, it was bent at a terrible angle. It couldn't be broken, it just couldn't be.

"Get up, lass, ye must hurry," a voice ordered.

"Help me!" I cried.

With the little strength I had, I stood, tested my ankle, I thanked my lucky stars I could put weight on it. Limping, I kept going. Tears ran down my cheeks as I walked on. I still carried the precious object clutched to my chest, hiding it. The voices were getting closer. I rounded the bend and nearly collapsed with relief. Castle MacCulloch. I would be safe there if I could just get to Ross.

Looking over to the rusted old water pump, the man from my visions; Fearsome MacPherson, Angus, stood there. He rushed to me when I stumbled. I went limp in his arms. Picking me up, he cradled me like a child. His massive chest was strangely comfortable. I felt safe, secure. He said nothing as we went around the side of the castle to the stables.

"Ross?" I called looking for him.

"Shh, lass," Angus said. "Ye donnae want to be giving away our position." I looked up at him as he lay me down in a pile of hay and put a finger to his lips. "Hae ye got it?" he whispered.

I nodded my head and showed him the wrapped parcel.

"What is it?" I asked.

"Answers, lass, answers for ye," he said.

Unwrapping it, he held it out to me. It was a key in the shape of a thistle.

"Angus?" I asked, looking up at him.

"Aye, lass," he answered.

"What's going on?" I asked.

"Let me guide ye," he passed a gentle hand over my face and pushed some hair back. "I am so sorry I scared ye. I am no' used to being seen but you being here has awoken a terrible beast. She will hurt ye to get to me. Trust me, it will nae be easy, but... do ye trust me, lass?"

"I don't even know you."

"Aye, but ye will," he said. "I'll show ye. Let me into yer heart and I will be able to come to you on the earthly plane as well."

"How?" I breathed.

"Nikki," Angus went on. "No' many will understand. There's only two you can trust."

"Ross and Chad," I said.

"Aye," he replied. "Ross is a good man. Chad does nae want anything but yer friendship. Trust no other, swear it, lass."

"I swear, Angus," I said.

His big hand cupped the back of my head as he leaned in and kissed my forehead. When he did, I saw a vision of him sneaking out of my room through a glass door, down a poorly lit stairwell and through another door. He walked to a shelf of books. Picking one, he opened it to the two hundred and fifth page, then slid something into the gap of the binding. Closing it, he put it back on the shelf and looked around the room, a large fireplace flanked by two leather chairs and bookcases lined the walls.

Angus pulled back from kissing my forehead, looked me straight in the eye and smiled. I had a distinct impression I had seen that smile before but I did not know where.

"Save me, lass, ye're the only one who can," he said standing.

"I don't understand, why me?" I called after him. He turned from the door to the stables.

"O fortune I wad you favor me," he said.

"I still don't understand," I said.

"Ye will, lass," he replied and turned to the stable doors. I heard a loud bang, the loudest sound I'd ever heard, almost like an explosion. Angus stumbled backwards but he didn't fall. Turning to me, he cupped his chest with his hands as blood seeped through his fingers and stained his white shirt. "Forgive me, lass," he choked on blood seeping out of his mouth. I screamed as he fell forward.

"Shh, shh, it's all right," a voice whispered in my ear. I clung to the comfort of the body lying beside me. My breathing was ragged and my pulse was beating so hard I was sure my heart would explode. A soothing hand passed up and down my arm and soon I was drifting back to sleep. Knowing my comforter would be with me all through the night, I snuggled deeper into their heat and sighed.

*Whoever you are, you are very comfortable,* I thought as I nuzzled my head into the crook of their neck. Prickly spikes speared my cheek, but I didn't care if my comforter had warts as well as spikes, I was more relaxed than I'd ever been. Blissful sleep claimed me once more.

The sun shone down through the windows and streamed across my face, but it wasn't the only source of heat. I was pressed tightly against something hot, strong, and entirely comfortable. I hadn't felt that in... well, ever really. My hand rested on a broad chest covered in a white t-shirt and an iron-like vise was around me. My head lay in a crook of a warm, prickly neck.

Moving a little, trying to see who my wonderful stranger was, I was greeted by brown curly hair, a rugged, defined jaw with a five o'clock shadow, closed eyes and full lips.

"Ross," I whispered smiling. He moaned softly in his sleep and pulled me even tighter against him, not that I minded.

Slipping my hand up his chest, I outlined his lips, shivering as I remember our kiss. Leaning up as much as I could, I placed a small kiss on his warm lips. Pulling back, I was surprised and slightly embarrassed to see his eyes open, dancing as he watched me.

"Good morning to you too, lass."

A blush crept up my face as I looked down. "Hi," I

whispered.

He slid his hand under my chin and gently pulled my face up to his.

"You call tha' a kiss?" he asked before pressing his lips to mine in another heart stopping kiss. When he pulled back his eyes were cloudy and his breathing was quick. "*Tha'* is a good morning kiss," he breathed.

"Mm, I could get used to that," I said before I could stop myself. Ross kept me firmly pressed to his side and leaned in, gently brushing his lips against mine.

"Me too, lass," he whispered. I turned away from him, unsure if I was ready for another relationship so soon, but he pulled on my chin forcing me to look back at him. "I know the wounds are still fresh, Nikki, but I really would like to get to know you. Will you let me?" he whispered clutching the back of my neck and pulling me to him.

"Kiss me again and I'll tell you," I offered. Grinning, he leaned forward and pushed me to my back. Hovering over me, encapsulating me in his arms, he leaned down.

"I can do that," he breathed and lowered his head but just before he kissed me, someone cleared their throat at the doorway. We both looked over to see Chad standing there, one eye brow raised.

"Should I come back?" he asked.

"Yes," Ross teased.

"No," I said at the same time.

"Och, ye gut me, woman," Ross rolled to his back but those words brought Angus back to my mind with full force. "What is it?" he asked seeing the change in my face.

"I had another vision," I revealed.

Chad walked all the way into the room and set the tray of food on a table by the window.

"Just for the record, I knew nothing about his wayward behavior," Chad beamed casting a look at Ross.

"I don't mind at all and at least I am still fully clothed," I teased.

Ross sat up and I saw he wore a white t-shirt that left none of his muscles to the imagination, and a pair of sweatpants.

"More's the pity," he said. "I've never been one to take

advantage of a lady. When we are together, I want you wide awake. I saw you were fitful and well... ye did call out my name," he smirked. "What's a gentleman to do? I need to step in here a minute..." he indicated the bathroom. "Donnae say anything important before I get back," he had the gall to wink at us before disappearing into the bathroom.

Chad looked at me beaming from ear to ear.

"So..." he pressed.

"So... what?" I asked.

He rolled his eyes. "So, I mean you slept with Elliot Ross, I need details!" he pressed.

"Chad," I laughed. "We didn't *do* anything."

"Right, so when I walked in that kiss was nothing? Honey, *I* was over heated," he said.

"Slut," I teased. He grinned and nodded emphatically. "All I know is I woke up to find him lying beside me, could you fill in the details?" I asked.

"We were in the bedroom until you fell asleep," Chad revealed. "Didn't want to wake you so we turned off the TV and I went to the sitting room. We were gonna crash on the sofas. When I got up, he wasn't there but I thought he had just gone to freshen up. I went to get you some breakfast."

"It's not really important I guess," I said as the bathroom door opened and Ross appeared drying his hands.

"You can stop talking about me," he said. Laughing, I made room for him to sit beside me. "So, tell us about your dream."

I told them as much of it as I could remember and then waited.

"You're saying there is a secret passageway from here to a library?" Chad asked.

"That's what I saw," I said. "I don't know which library it is. I hadn't seen it before."

"Makes sense," Ross nodded. "Most old castles have a Laird's Lug, a secret place behind the walls where the Laird could listen to his guests without them knowing. It was a useful way to sniff out any assassination plots or treason. There normally was a maze of passageways starting in the master's chambers and connecting to his lady's."

"I'm in the lady of the keep's bedroom?" I asked.

"Aye," he answered. "And," he leaned in close as if to tell me a secret. "I'm in the master's." Shaking my head and laughing I was too tired to think of a flirtatious response so I closed the gap and kissed him.

"Seriously," Chad groaned. "If I have to watch you guys being all whatever you are, I'm going to need my boyfriend flown out here."

"No relatives or significant others until the end of the retreat," Ross quoted from the guidelines. "But I might be able to make an exception."

"Guys, magic door, secret passageway, old curse to solve, let's focus," I said.

"So says the lady who kissed me," Ross replied.

"Let's find that door," Chad said standing. "You said it was a window?"

"It looked like one," I replied. "A glass door of some sort."

Chad went over to my windows and began pushing on the stones nearby.

"I better help him before he pulls my entire house down," Ross teased.

"Good idea," I answered. As the men went to work trying to find the entrance, I walked around the room coming to a stop before the fireplace and looked up at Angus's and Elizabeth's portrait. "Where, Angus?" I breathed.

"Lass," I heard his voice to my right. Looking over, I saw his image projected in the floor to ceiling mirror. He had his hand outstretched to me, wearing only his kilt and a white shirt. Mesmerized, I walked toward him. His eyes never left mine and almost instinctually I raised my hand to one of the thistles decorating the corners of the mirror. Touching the round part of Scotland's national flower, it sunk in and the mirror popped open.

Angus gave me a proud smile and vanished. Chad and Ross walked up beside me.

"How in the hell?" Chad began. I shrugged. Ross grasped the edge of the mirror and slowly pulled it back, the hinges groaned but eventually loosened. The passage before us was pitch black. "I'll get my flashlight," Chad said and scurried out of the room.

"Ross," I whispered, too mesmerized to speak louder.

"Aye, lass," his voice matched mine. I took his hand and together we stepped forward into complete darkness.

# Chapter Seven

Once when I was a little girl, I got lost in the woods behind our house. I was playing and fell asleep. When I woke, it was complete darkness and I didn't know where I was. My dad found me and after making sure I was okay, he carried me back to the house. I had never felt such peace in a scary situation since, until the moment Ross took my hand and we stepped into the passageway together.

Ross's breathing, slow and steady, resounded in the silence, comforting me. There was nothing to be scared of as long as he was there. The stone stair was a straight shot down and when we reached the bottom there was an old locked door.

"We're in the old part of the house," Ross said softly beside me.

"How do you know?" I asked.

"The architecture," he said, our eyes having adjusted to the darkness and the small sliver of light in front of us. "There was a fire in the late thirties, nineteen thirties, and all of the west wing was condemned but the east wing was only smoke damaged. Still livable but reconditioned. When I bought this place, I had the main construction centered on repairing the east wing. This area, I had planned to restore later this year. But I was still getting quotes for structural soundness."

"Is it safe?" I asked suddenly worried. If he was talking structural integrity, I would be getting the hell out of there.

"Just mind your step," he replied. "No one I've spoken to says it's unsound. No' many people have been in here since the fire."

"Where is that light coming from?" I asked looking back.

"It would nae surprise me," Ross started. "If there is no' a window nearby. You can smell the dampness from the rain the other night," I took a deep breath of the musky and rainy scent. "Did this vision of yours show ye how to open the door?"

I looked around and saw the sconce beside the door. Mirroring what I saw Angus do, I reached up and pulled it down. Metal on stone grated our ears as the door slowly swung open.

The room was dark and dust hung in the air. The smell of smoke still clung to every item but it looked like nothing had changed for nearly three hundred years; a massive desk stood before a boarded up window, two bookcases, whose glass doors had been broken, stood against a wall and a large fireplace to the right with two old wingback chairs.

"This must have been the Laird's Solar," Ross said in awe. "Books are still on the shelves. How could this have been untouched for so long?"

"Maybe no one could get to it after the fire," I offered.

"Socrates, Shakespeare, John Knox, Malory, Chaucer, do you know how old some of these are?" Ross breathed. "How much they're worth?"

"I'm guessing a lot," I said.

"Oh my god, a first edition of Paradise Lost," Ross reverently took the book from the shelf. "I would love to have these in my library."

"It is your castle. You bought it all," I reminded him. "Including these."

"They technically belong to Macpherson's heirs," he said. "I only bought the structure."

"I'm sure they wouldn't mind you having them," I replied. "After all, how are you going to find them?"

He placed it back on the shelf and nodded.

"True," he said. "But still. I would nae feel right about it. Now where did you see him go?"

I indicated the bookcase to the left. Carefully, we walked over to it.

"Do you remember the book?" he asked scanning the titles.

"I couldn't see the title," I answered. "I just know something is in the binding."

Ross nodded and turned his attention to the books on the shelf.

"You guys!" Chad's voice and a blinding beam of light came from the secret passageway. "You didn't wait for me!"

"Sorry, hon," I called. "It's my fault."

"Wow, this is amazing!" Chad said as he walked in.

"Watch your step," Ross called to him. "I cannae vouch for the integrity of the structure."

"Any idea what we're looking for?" Chad asked walking daintily toward us.

"Nikki didn't get a good look at the book," Ross said.

"Okay well," Chad reached forward and picked up the first one. "Desperate times."

Both Chad and Ross picked out books and began examining them. I scanned the titles as Angus's words again came back to me.

"O fortune I wad you favor me." I didn't realize I had spoken the words out loud until silence engulfed the room. I looked over at Ross and Chad. They were both staring at me. "What?" I asked.

"What did you just say?" Ross questioned.

"It's something Angus said to me," I explained.

"When?" Ross asked.

"In the dream," I replied. "Why? Is it important?"

Ross was back at the bookcase before I finished speaking.

"Chad, bring your light," he said. Chad pointed the beam toward the books.

"What are you looking for?" I asked. Ross didn't answer me. When he found the book he was looking for, he gently pulled it out and opened to the table of contents. His finger slid down the page until it stopped on something in particular. He then flipped through the book.

"Here, Nikki, listen," he started. "Page two-oh-five. 'Nae mair I'll hear wi' pleasure sing, the cheerfu' lav'rock in the Spring, but sad in grief now I maun mourn, far, far frae her, o'er Logan-burn. O fortune I wad you favor me, in some snug corner her to see. My heart I wad to her reveal, an' in her arms my pardon seal.'" Ross looked up at me but I couldn't focus; my eyes misted and I blacked out.

"Charlie is a fool," I heard a gruff voice say. "He led our men to slaughter and all ye say to me is we need to join with the English?"

"Aye, MacPherson that's what I be saying," another Scottish voice said. "To say anything else would be treason." Slowly, I opened my eyes.

"Och," Angus replied. "I will nae follow a boy who cannae lead his own people. Nor a pretender to the throne. The Hanovers are nae legitimate heirs. No' when there's a Stuart to be had. Be it treason or no' I stand for Scotland and her people."

"What are ye saying, MacPherson?" the man asked.

"I'm saying that Bonnie Prince Charlie led our men to slaughter," Angus repeated.

Two men, Angus and another, were in the room. Angus paced before the fire while the other sat in one of the chairs.

"We lost too many good men at Culloden," Angus's voice choked for a moment. "And with all the new regulations, we are nae longer Scotsmen. We have nae identity. It's been stripped from us and our children will suffer for it. So much death could hae been avoided."

"It's been years since Culloden, Angus," the man said. "What are yer plans?"

"I donnae ken," he answered. "But whatever I do, it'll be for Scotland."

"Well, the Sutherland clan is wit ye, MacPherson," the man said.

"Aye, and I'm grateful," Angus replied.

"Where is your bonnie wee girl?" the man asked.

"Riona's wit her nursemaid right now," Angus answered.

"She's what nearly thirteen, aye?" the man asked.

"Aye, she is tha', and the spitting image of her mother, God rest her," Angus answered.

"Hae ye given anymore thought to me offer?" he asked. Angus paused before the fire.

"Aye, and I donnae want to come across as ungrateful," Angus started. "Since me brother died ye hae been like family."

"Grief united us," he answered. "Have ye forgotten I lost a brother, too?"

"Nay, and I grieve his loss every day. 'Tis just, Riona's a wee girl. She cannae be betrothed until the proper time and even then, I would hae her in a love match no' an arrangement. I hope ye understand."

"Aye, so we get them together every summer and see wha' happens," the other man said. "Ye need a man to take over when you're gone, Angus. Unless you will marry again and produce an heir..."

"Nay," he snapped. "I will nae marry again. My wife was everything to me. I honor her request to no' blame myself but I cannae marry another."

"'Tis surprised I am ye hae such a loving manner to yer daughter, Angus. After all it was her birth that claimed Riona's life."

"Nay, and I'll ask ye kindly never to speak such shite in my presence again," Angus replied heatedly. "It is nae Riona's fault her mother died and a more loving child, I'll ne'er meet."

"Forgive me," the man backed down. "I hae nae wish to offend ye." Angus nodded and took a seat opposite the man. "So your answer has no' changed?" he asked.

"Nae, Keith," he answered. "I cannae. Understand, I ask ye."

"She will nae be a child forever," he said. "Me brother's boy Farlane is only five years older."

"Aye and a strong lad," Angus answered.

"And his forth son, he may have limited prospects in our clan, but if he were to marry into another," Keith's voice trailed off.

"Aye, jus' give me more time," Angus replied. "Let me foster him for a year and we will see."

"Aye," Keith answered and I could hear his pleasure even though I could not see him. "I agree to that."

"Good," Angus replied. "Now, we must consider what's to be done to free Scotland from England's tyranny. I will nae have my child and grandchildren grow up without identity."

"I'll drink to that," Keith said standing and raising his glass.

"O fortune I wad you favor me," Angus toasted. They tossed back the drink and Keith turned so I could see his face. It was a face I knew; even though it was in its mid to late forties.

Graeme Fergus.

"Ross!" I felt my scream before I heard it.

"Easy!" Ross barked. I clutched his arm feeling him supporting me. I was on the floor of the same study, the leather chairs the men sat in, to my left.

"You need to stop scaring the life out of me," Chad said. "I don't need to go prematurely gray."

"I'm sorry," I gasped. "That poem. What is it?"

"It's by Thomson," Ross answered helping me sit up. "He's a Scottish poet before Burns."

"I saw Angus and another man. They were here in this room talking about Bonnie Prince Charlie and Culloden Battle," I said.

"Angus MacPherson was a strong advocate for the Jacobite's. He fought against the English," Ross explained.

"They were talking about how Charlie screwed up the battle," I went on.

"It's no secret Prince Charlie chose the wrong location and landscape for the battle," Ross said. "My own ancestors lost a lot of men that day."

"Your ancestors?" I asked. "Are you and Graeme related?"

I felt him stiffen beside me. His eyes searched mine.

"Why?" he asked.

"The was the other man in the room," I said. "He was trying to convince Angus to agree to a marriage between Angus' daughter, Riona and Keith's nephew, Farlane. He looked like Graeme."

"Nope not getting it," Chad shook his head dramatically. "What's going on?"

"The Fergus clan was never an ally or a threat to Sutherland and we never had an alliance through marriage with MacPhersons. We were always friendly," Ross said as if Chad hadn't asked his question.

"Huh?" Chad asked.

Ross sighed. "Keith Sutherland is my great uncle many times removed. He disgraced the family by selling out his friends to the crown for coin," he said. "He was a spy sent by King George to weed out those loyal to the Stuart. Though we have no proof, it is believed Keith killed his brother, Iain on Culloden Moor. Farlane was not the son I am descended from but there were five. There was no known alliance between the MacPhersons and the Sutherlands."

"Hang on," Chad said. "Your name is Elliot *Ross* not Sutherland."

"Elliot Ross is a pseudonym," he explained. "My real name is Ross Sutherland."

Chad's brows raised and he looked at me, "hence the *Ross* and not *Elliot* you keep saying." I nodded.

"I don't want everyone knowing so I keep it Elliot Ross while I'm here," he went on. "I introduced myself to Nikki as Ross Sutherland."

"I can keep a secret," Chad replied.

"Aye, thank you. But this is interesting to me," Ross said. "My ancestor was sitting in this room?"

"All I can say is they were sitting together there by the fireplace talking," I indicated. "Who did Farlane end up marrying?"

"I have no idea," Ross answered. "But I know someone who might, let's get you up." My legs were wobbly and I was suddenly light headed; a massive pounding at my temples made me want to cry. "Those visions have to stop," Ross exclaimed.

"Not until I help Angus," I replied. "He needs me."

"Look at this!" Ross cried and gently wiped my nose with the back of his hand. Blood coated the skin.

"Oh, god," I pressed my fingers to it. It didn't hurt. "Did I hit it on something?"

"No, that's just what this is doing to you. Nikki, it's gotta stop," Ross said.

"Soon," I promised. "Did you check the binding of the book?"

Ross and Chad sighed. "Aye," Ross gave in, knowing I wouldn't give up. "There is something but I cannae get it out. I need some tweezers."

"Whatever it is, it's important," I said. "I have some in my room."

"Let's go back and see about getting the paper out," Ross said taking my arm, handing Chad the book and winding his other arm around my waist.

# Chapter Eight

I watched as Ross meticulously picked at the binding of the book. It seemed such a sacrilege to hurt an old book like that but we needed to see what was inside. In my sitting room, where there was the most natural light, Ross bent over the desk.

"I got it," he whispered. Both men had donned white gloves before handling the book any more.

"Easy," Chad breathed.

"Ya think?" Ross whispered.

Slowly, he pulled out a piece of paper that had been wrapped up as a scroll then flattened when the book was closed. Ross set the parchment on the wax paper we had pillaged from the kitchen. Sitting back for a second, Ross wiped his forehead and took a deep breath.

"Okay," he breathed, then went about unrolling the old paper. It was actually a much longer document than we at first thought. Folded once, the words, in flowy handwriting across the front, were in black faded ink.

*To my heirs...*

A cold gust of wind tunneled toward us. Chad wrapped his arms around himself and Ross covered the paper as best he could.

“Angus?” I called.

“No’ yet, lass,” I heard his voice say. “Donnae open that yet.”

“Why?” I asked.

“She’ll see it,” he answered. I looked around the room but couldn’t see him.

“Who?”

“Keep it safe,” his voice said.

I grasped Ross’s shoulder to stop him. Both of the men were looking at me oddly, they clearly could not hear Angus.

“I want to help you,” I called out.

“And ye are,” Angus replied. “Jus’ by believing. Come out to the pump. Hide the document. I’ll be waiting.”

“All of us?” I asked.

“No, jus’ ye,” he answered.

“I don’t think they’ll let me,” I said.

“They can come, but they hae to stay back.”

“Okay,” I replied. “What’s going on, Angus?”

“Ah, lass, more than you ken,” he said as the air died down and the heat returned.

It took some convincing but Ross and Chad agreed to stay on the brick courtyard patio as I walked through the grounds to the pump toward Angus.

“Ye came,” Angus said.

“And I can see you,” I replied. “Why can’t they?” I indicated Ross and Chad.

“Because ye opened yer heart to me and allowed me to show you. You are the only one who heard me that first moment you arrived,” he said.

“That was you?” I asked. “Saying hello?”

He nodded. “I spoke to everyone as they arrived and only you heard me but ye could nae see me yet.”

I was intrigued by him and felt an overwhelming urge to touch him. Slowly, I reached out and he didn’t move. We locked eyes and even in that fearsome face, I saw gentleness and was not afraid. He was a very handsome man and closer to Daren's forty-two than Ross's thirty-three.

"Will I be able to touch you?" I asked.

Angus stood there not moving. I surged ahead and grasped his upper arm. It was difficult to explain the feeling; his arm felt like a normal man's arm, but it was ice cold and a bolt of electricity went straight through me.

"What did it feel like to you?" I asked pulling back.

"Warm," he answered and it tugged at my heart. "So verra warm, lass. Thank ye."

A torrent of tears rolled down my cheeks. He reached up and wiped them away, the same feeling jolting through me.

"What can I do, Angus?" I begged.

"Find the Pride," he replied.

"Where is it?"

"No one knows, lass," he revealed.

"Is that why you're tied here?" I asked.

"Aye, I could nae find it while I was alive. I vowed I would nae rest until it was safe in the hands of my kin," he explained. "My wife stole it and hid it somewhere."

"I heard that," I said.

"Ye've been verra close to this from the beginning," he said cupping my face. I covered his hand with mine and leaned into his touch.

"I don't know why," I said. "I'm just a girl from Chicago."

"Och, lass, ye're so much more than that," he stressed. "So much."

"What's in that paper we found?" I asked.

His eyes trailed up to the third floor turret window and whispered, "My confession."

"Confession?" I asked.

"Aye, lass," he answered. "I turned my back on Prince Charlie and fought for Scotland when he abandoned her."

"From the little I know of Bonnie Prince Charlie he has the blood of thousands of Scots on his hands," I said.

"Aye, he led our lads to slaughter. Me own..." he paused and cleared his throat. "Me own little brother was killed at Culloden. But he would ne'er hae wanted me to seek revenge. He would hae said he gave his blood proudly for king and country but he was only nineteen."

Reaching for him, I rested my hand on his arm and squeezed.

"I am so very sorry," I said. Nodding once he refused to say anything. "Keith Sutherland wanted an alliance with you through marriage," I changed the subject. "Did you agree?"

"Nay," he answered. "My Riona, named for her mother, chose her own husband."

"I wondered. You see, Ross," I turned to look back at him still on the patio. "Is Keith's family's descendant. A friend of his looks just like him."

"Aye, I've seen Graeme Fergus," he replied. "But Ross is descended from Iain Sutherland, a man as dear to me as a father. He and his son died on Culloden leaving behind a unborn heir. I was pleased when Ross bought this place. He's a fine man. Donnae close your heart like I did mine." About to say something, he stopped me and continued. "A broken heart kens another like an animal kens its sire, instinctively," he paused. "What happened to ye, lass?"

"A man I thought I loved, never loved me," I replied simply.

"Then he's a fool," he said his thumb stroking the apple of my cheek.

"He was too old for me," I answered.

"'Tis a sad business when a man leads a woman to believe he loves her," he said. "'Tis terrible when a woman does the same to a man."

"Wars have been started over that," I replied.

"Aye, that they have, lass," he agreed. We were quiet for a moment. "When you read my confession, think of me with kindness. There are some things I would change if I could go back. Betraying my king is one of them."

"Is that why you need to find the Pride?" I asked. "You feel like you need to redeem yourself?"

"I need to see Scotland free again," he said.

"They're having a vote," I replied. "A vote to see if Scotland wants to be free."

"Then I pray they hear the blood of the countless souls who died on this verra ground. Listen to them cry out with their last breath. *Alba gu brath;* Scotland forever. I went through life known as Fearsome MacPherson because I fought for Scotland's freedom. There are things you will nae understand. But ken this, my heart, my life's blood flows in Scotland's soil. I lived and died for my country. The Pride is not mine. It belongs to every freeborn Scot from Edinburgh to Sutherland, from Aberdeen to Skye. It is a symbol of our Pride in our country and our heritage. Remember that, lass. I'll be here for ye. All ye need to do is call and I'll come to ye."

"I will find the Pride for you, Angus," I promised. "And you will be able to be at peace."

"Peace?" he scoffed. "I hardly ken what that is anymore. There is more you need to know but Ross is right, it is hurting you."

"I am not afraid," I stated.

"Nay, I ken," he smiled at me. "Ye're a fearsome lass... But now go."

"Go where?" I asked.

"To yer fate," he nodded toward Ross. I looked back at him then turned to Angus but he was gone.

# Chapter Nine

Chad ordered us all two fingers of Famous Grouse Scotch whisky saying he needed a drink and didn't want to drink alone. We were quiet at the lunch table in the conservatory when Ross finally leaned back in his seat, tossed down the remaining liquor and spoke.

"I donnae want you to get any more involved," he said.

My eyes snapped up to his. "What?" I asked.

"It's no' safe and I donnae want you to do anymore," he amended.

"I'm finishing this," I stated. "You can't tell me what to do."

"Aye, I can," he answered. "I own this place and I'm telling you this is killing you. You have to stop."

"What are you going to do, Ross? Kick me out?" I asked.

"If I have to," ice dripped from his words. Just as he said those words, Lorna, his assistant conveniently tripped over an invisible cord and dropped the pitcher of ice water she carried down the front of my shirt.

Ross immediately stood. "What the hell, Lorna?"

"I'm sorry, sir," she said, her tone showing she was

anything but sorry. "I tripped."

"The hell you did," he gritted. "Nikki, let me help you."

"I'm fine," I snapped.

"Go and get Ms. Thompson a towel," he snapped.

"There's a napkin on the table, sir," she replied.

"Lorna," his tone was sharp and his eyes hard. "Now."

"Excuse me, I need to fix my shirt and I guess I should go pack," I said.

Before I heard anything more, I left the room and hurried to the elevators. After a minute waiting, I saw the sign for the stairs. Heading that way, I walked down a lonely hallway.

"He's not what you think he is," a voice said nearby. Turning, I saw Lorna carrying a white towel.

"Excuse me?" I asked.

"Ross," she clarified. "He's not what you think he is. He always has a woman. You're just one in a long line of star struck bimbos to crawl into his bed."

"And you are an arrogant, spiteful woman who can't keep her claws out of other people's business," I stepped down one stair. "What's wrong with you, Lorna? Screw you and leave you? This little stunt you pulled?" I gestured to my sopping shirt. "Just proved how much of a vindictive witch you are."

"Many have come and gone," she took a step closer. "Many of you Americans have been notches on his bedpost but trust me when all this is over, Ross and I will be happy together."

"You couldn't make him happy if your life depended on it," I said. Without another word, I turned and walked up the stairs and to my bedroom. I locked the door and rushed to the bathroom. Grasping the edge of the sink, I took deep shaky breaths calming my racing heartbeat. Looking up into my refection in the mirror, I was pale and my wet t-shirt clung to me causing a chill. Pulling it off, I ran some hot water and stood in my bra and jeans staring at my reflection.

I wasn't going to let him get away with it. There was no way in hell I was going to let him kick me out. I would come back and finish this with or without him. Either way I wasn't going to hide from him or the issue at hand.

"Nikki, listen," I heard. Spinning around to see Ross walking toward the doorway of the bathroom, his eyes grew large and lowered to my bra but I wasn't having it. Picking up the closest thing to me, my hair brush, I chucked it at him. He dodged, so I picked up my plastic bottle of body spray and threw that next. Again, he dodged but it caught him in the leg. "Bloody hell, woman!" He cried. "Stop throwin' stuff and listen tae me!"

"You've made yourself perfectly clear," I said. "And I'm not going anywhere! You can't force me to leave! I have every right to be here! And I don't care what you say, I will use every weapon I have to stop you from kicking me out!"

Before I knew it, he had dashed forward, grabbed me and fused his lips to mine. Reaching up I hit his chest he wouldn't let me go, I gave up the struggle and kissed him back. His lips were bruising and unforgiving, our teeth knocked against each other as I reached into his hair and yanked. He groaned and pulled my leg up to hook around his hip. Pushing away from him, I threw him against the wall of the bathroom but he pulled me with him and we crashed together knocking a frame off the wall.

"I cannae lose you, don't ye get it?" he gasped out as I bit his lower lip. "I cannae. It scares me to death," his hands were driving me crazy. "I cannae lose you."

"I'm a grown woman, you can damn well let me take care of myself," I rasped.

"I want ye," he growled. Sliding my hands up his shirt, I ripped it open and pulled off his white t-shirt touching his hot skin.

"Then what are you waiting for?" I challenged.

*Alistair needed me. He was wounded already. Running as fast as I could, I saw another damned English Redcoat race to my friend. Blood, from the pistol shot he had nae ducked away from fast enough, dripped off his fingertips. A front kick straight to Alistair's gut had him falling onto his back but I was there before the Red could do anything more than sneer.*

*Thrusting my sword home through the English before him, the bloody bastard fell with a womanly scream.*

*"I had it handled, MacPherson," Alistair stated from his*

*place on the ground.*

*"Aye, thought I'd take a wee bit of yer glory, Sutherland. Too much'll go to yer head," I said offering my hand and helping him up. "How bad?" I asked seeing the blood continue to drip from his right arm.*

*"I'll live," he grunted squeezing his hand around the hilt of his basket sword as if getting the feel of it in a hand he did not usually favor. "How does the battle fare?"*

*"Charlie's a fool. Angus was right," I said. "A fool and a coward. He fled."*

Opening my eyes to complete darkness, I felt Ross's body lying beside me, his arm wrapped snuggly around my shoulders. Smiling slightly, I pulled away gently and sat up. Running my fingers through my hair, I held the sheets around my chest and took a deep breath. The same dream I had back home haunted me. Who were the men? I still could not remember their faces just their clothing. Ross's soft breathing was the only sound in the room. Looking over at the desk by the window, I wondered.

Rolling out of bed, I found Ross's ruined shirt on the floor, most of the buttons had scattered in the bathroom when I had ripped it off of him. Pulling it on, I buttoned the two buttons that had survived. Tiptoeing to the desk, I switched on the lamp grateful it wasn't very bright and pulled out the chair. The notebooks emblazoned with the league's logo sat stacked and empty beside my elbow. Grabbing one, I flipped it open and smiled. This was the part I loved the most. The empty notebook just waiting to tell me the story it wants me to write inside it. A box of black and blue ink pens were in the top drawer of the desk. Clicking one, I pressed it to the paper and lost myself in the story unfolding in my mind.

It was hours before I heard a groggy voice from the bed call my name. Looking back, I grinned at Ross. He looked so rakish. His eyes glowed with lust and sleep. His hair was messed up and the lopsided grin on his lips rushed my body into a tailspin. "What are you doing?"

"Writing," I shrugged.

"Writer's block gone?" he asked smugly. "Inspired again?"

"Maybe," I answered coyly.

"Come back to bed," he ordered eyeing me. "It'll keep and right now I want you."

"And what if I don't want to stop, Mr. Sutherland?" I teased.

"Then I'll convince you," he answered.

"Hmm," I looked between him and my notebook and the two others already filled beside me. "I suppose I could take an hour out of my night."

"One hour?" he asked pretending shock. "You definitely underestimate me."

"Maybe I do," I bit my lower lip.

"Get your arse in my bed, woman. You look so unbelievably sexy in my shirt."

A smile spread across my lips as I felt what those words did to me. Setting the pen down, I stood and accepted the hand he offered. Pulling me down I straddled him for a second before he flipped me over and proved my one-hour deadline was not going to be met.

# Chapter Ten

*Ross*

"Good morning," I said when I felt her move in my arms. Nikki looked up at me and smiled tiredly.

"Hi," she answered. "How did you sleep?"

"Oh, you know," I teased. "Got interrupted around three am. This sexy goddess found her way into my bed. Kept me awake."

"Hmm," she hummed. "Sounds like you had an interesting night."

"And amazing one," I answered. Then her face shadowed and she looked away from me. Damn her ex, he must have never stayed over.

"Listen, about last night…" she started and it made me want to beat that man's arse from here to New York.

"Isn't that usually the man's line?" I stopped her.

Her body stiffened in my arms. "Yeah, I guess I'm used to the man saying that line." If I ever saw that jackanapes bastard I would kill him. Gently, I slipped my hand under her chin.

"I'm no' him," I said and kissed her softly. "But if it makes you feel better, let's just have fun, hmm? Nothing stopping us, nothing hindering, no expectations... just a good time."

"I'd really appreciate it," she lied.

I didn't answer as her head rested on my chest again, she played with my chest hair.

"Tell me about America," I said.

"Have you ever been?" she asked.

"To New York, but nowhere else," I said. "You're from Chicago, aye?"

"Yes," she answered. "It's pretty much right in the middle east to west but really far north."

"Is it cold?" I asked.

"Sometimes," she answered. "But it's such an amazing city."

"Your parents live there too?"

"My dad," she clarified. "He basically raised me when my mom left us."

"I'm sorry," I said.

"No no, it's okay, I made peace with it and she realized her errors and came back to ask forgiveness but my parents divorced when I was twelve. My dad was a single dad for a long time. Poor guy had to have the sex talk and the puberty talk."

"Tough," I winced I couldn't imagine having to have *that* conversation with my twelve year old daughter. I would just lock her in her room until she was thirty.

"He was amazing," she praised. "I really miss him. You know every Thursday night we have dad-daughter date nights."

"What do you do?"

"It's always the same, we go to this little hole in the wall Chicago pizza place order a deep-dish Sicilian and a bottle of Cabernet. It's always so much fun and we usually close the place down." She grew quiet for a moment. When she spoke again her voice was soft and sad. "Thursday will be the first time I've missed our dates in about three years."

"I'm sorry, lass," I said, a plan forming in my mind.

"It's okay," she replied with more joy than I know she felt. She raised herself up on her elbow and looked down at me. "Hey, I really want to work on the story I began last night, do you think I could take a break from treasure hunting?"

"Maybe," I stated. "Depends on if you wrote me correctly

in said book."

"What makes you think I wrote about you at all?" She questioned.

"Oh, I don't know, maybe it's because I helped with the writer's block," I shrugged.

Slapping my shoulder in feigned indignation, she gasped through her grin, but leaned down to kiss me.

"You may make an appearance," she said.

"Then aye, I'll keep the wolves at bay," I replied.

"I need to run to the restroom and then I need breakfast."

"I'll be here," I said. Slipping out of bed, she took my white t-shirt and slipped it over her head.

As soon as she shut the bathroom door behind her, I reached over and grabbed my phone, quickly dialing my assistant's number.

"Good morning, Ross," she cooed but I wasn't having it, not after the stunt she pulled with the water.

"Excuse me?" I stated.

"Mr. Sutherland, I'm sorry," her voice was back to the professional coolness I require of all my staff.

"Better," I said. "I need you to have Ms. Thompson's file on my desk as soon as possible."

"Is everything all right?" Her voice betrayed the glimmer of hope I had mistakenly given her.

"Yes, I needed to see if she wrote down her food preferences so I can take her out to dinner. I will tell you where to make the reservation for tomorrow night as well as the hotel room we will need. I expect you to carry out my orders to the letter." I was being harsh. I already knew where I was going to take her so her preferences didn't matter. I needed to get her father's number from her emergency contact.

"Yes, sir," she replied. "I will have it on your desk and await your instructions.

"Good, and Lorna? Don't ever do that again. This is your only warning. You pull a stunt like that again, your arse is out of a job. Do I make myself clear?"

"Yes, sir, I'm sorry," she replied, her voice small.

Hanging up the phone, I looked up to see Nikki coming

out of the bathroom still wearing my white t-shirt, her hair hanging about her in soft brushed layers.

"Who was that?" she asked.

"Lorna," I answered.

Her eyes narrowed slightly but she quickly hid it behind that damn cool look I hated. She didn't have to hide from me.

Shrugging, she came over to the side of the bed, I lay back giving her a full view of my chest. Her fingers toyed with my chest hair, her gaze lasered at the planes and dips. I didn't say anything, enjoying her touch.

"Did you sleep with Lorna?" she finally asked.

Of all the things I thought, hoped and expected her to say that was the last thing. It wasn't even on the list of things I thought she would say.

"Did she say something to you?" I demanded. Her gaze never left my chest. "Nikki?"

"She said I'm just the next in a long line of bimbos that are notches on your bedpost," her voice was soft.

"Damn her," I breathed. She was out of a job as soon as I could get downstairs.

"Did you?" she looked up at me and for the first time, I could see a scared insecure woman behind the fiery beauty I had taken to bed.

"Once," I admitted. She looked away. "It was a long time ago and we were both very drunk."

She said nothing for the longest two minutes of my life.

"I don't like her," she whispered. "And I don't think she likes me either. I'm sorry. I know we agreed no strings but I like you too much and I don't know how to do that."

I cupped her jaw and forced her to look at me. "There's no need to be sorry. I'm glad. I never wanted no strings. I care about you too much too and I know you've been through hell recently but let me prove I'm no' him? You have no reason to trust me, but I hope you do."

"I do," she admitted but I could see tears in her eyes.

"Donnae cry," I said. I couldn't bear to see a woman cry.

"Don't fire her," she stated.

"What?" I breathed.

"Lorna, don't fire her," she clarified. "She was just trying to protect what she thought was hers."

"I'm not hers," I was adamant.

"I know," she answered. "So let's prove it to her."

"I've been trying to for the past year," I replied.

"You haven't had me for the past year," she reminded me. "I'll be happy to help. But don't fire her."

"That would make you happy?"

"You make me happy," she answered. "But yes that too."

"All right," I finally huffed. That didn't mean I couldn't have a strict talking to with her. "Kiss me?" I asked.

She smiled and leaned down, her tears, a salty taste on her lips.

"Breakfast!" Chad's voice rang out as he burst into the bedroom.

# Chapter Eleven

*Nikki*

I scrambled to cover with Ross's shirt when I heard Chad's voice. "Uh… Oops," Chad stopped dead in his tracks when he saw our clothes on the ground and my face which had flamed hotter than ever before. "I'm guessing I should come back?"

"Yes," Ross teased.

"No," I said at the same time then giggled as Ross's hand tried to tickle me and pulled me down onto the bed. "No, it's okay," I slapped his hand away and looked over at Chad. "Just let me get dressed."

Chad grinned but tactfully left the room. I looked over at Ross, his eyes gazing down at me. He looked so young with his floppy hair messed up and hanging in his eyes. So completely different from Daren, I ran a hand through his brown locks. Kissing my forehead, he grinned.

"Breakfast came to us," he said. "I know you're hungry."

"Cheeky bastard," I teased. He laughed but lowered his lips to my collarbone and sucked.

Shaking, I pushed at his head and glanced at the door. Chad was in the living area and here we were acting like a randy couple.

"My turn to use the facilities, lass," he said. "Try not to talk too much about me to poor Chad I'll have to pay for his boyfriend to come here just to stop him from fantasizing about him."

"I heard that," Chad's voice rang from the other room.

"Stop eavesdropping," Ross called back.

"I can't help it, your voice carries," he said.

"Go to our friend, but I'll be sure to keep the wolves away so you can work later."

"Then dinner? We never did get our dinner date," I reminded him.

"No, we didn't, did we," he tsked but nodded. "I'll make it up to you."

With a final kiss, he got out of bed and closed the bathroom door behind him.

Flopping back down on the bed, I couldn't help but giggle as he started humming a song. Covering my face with my hands, I shook my head and reveled in the joy.

"Oh my god, you have a hickey!" Chad cried as I walked out of the bedroom still wearing Ross's shirt but I pulled on my capri leggings. Reaching up to my neck, I covered the small bruise but after a second, I shook my head, shrugged and dropped my hand.

"So what if I do," I replied biting my lower lip.

"Okay, so," he egged me on.

"So… what?" I teased heading over to the platter of fruit and pastries Chad had brought. I popped a grape in to my mouth and got a plate.

"Oh don't give me that," Chad teased. "You're positively glowing and *he's* humming!"

"Don't you have your own love life?" I asked.

"He's like your fantasy come true, right?" Chad asked as I sat down on the sofa and tucked my legs under me. "Elliot Ross just took you to bed."

"How was I supposed to know Elliot Ross was some Highlander god? He could have been an eighty year old, overweight, troll," I said.

"Have you *read* his sex scenes?" Chad asked as if that justified how hot Ross was.

I grinned and couldn't help myself. "No need," I said. "I've lived through one."

Chad grasped his chest where his heart beat, pretending shock. I giggled.

"That good, huh?" We both heard Ross say from the doorway.

Looking over, I groaned. "You shouldn't be allowed to look that sexy," I said. His jeans fit far too well, he wore another white undershirt that may as well have been nonexistent for all the covering up it did, barefoot and perfect hair. He grinned as he pushed off the door frame.

"Lucky for you I'm no eighty year old, over weight troll, then," he teased dropping a kiss on my lips. Chad did not attempt to cover his jealous moan. Ross sent him a wink then went to get his breakfast.

Once Ross's back was turned, Chad mouthed *oh my god!* to me. I bit my lower lip and nodded. After Ross got his plate of food, he took a seat beside me. His arm lined the back of the sofa and I leaned into him as his arm came around my shoulder.

"So, I'm guessing all of that shit about you leaving is yesterday's news?" Chad asked.

"Ross shared with me his concerns and I explained I wasn't leaving and I was my own person," I said. "We came to an understanding."

"Hot," Chad replied. "What's the plan today? Or are you guys gonna stay in bed all day?"

"As much as I would love that," I started. "Didn't you say you know someone who might help? Know about your family's history?" I asked Ross. Even though Angus had assured me his daughter Riona did not marry Ross's ancestor – though if he looked anything like Ross, she would have had to have been a nun – I wanted to learn more about the Sutherlands and maybe figure out my dream.

"Yep," Ross answered. "I texted her while I was in the bathroom."

"Who is her, Sutherland?" I replied. He merely smirked at me.

"Jealous much?" he teased. "She is someone I would like you to meet, someone... very special to me." Pursing my lips together, he laughed and kissed me. "Relax would ya?"

"After our conversation?" I reminded him about Lorna.

"Nothing like that," he assured me.

"Right, well," Chad spoke up. "I think a day at the spa is in order. Wanna join me?"

I shook my head. "Can't babe," I said.

"Nikki's writer's block is gone," Ross replied a bit too arrogantly for my taste. "She wants to work."

"Well, that's all well and good, honey, but with this ghost hunting, I think we all must have some *me* time," Chad said.

"You guys go," I urged. "I do want to get some work done."

"I need to catch up on some things too," Ross said.

"I'm on my own?" Chad pouted.

"Just for today, promise," I said.

"I'm gonna head back to my room and shower," Ross said. "If you need me, my office is behind the check-in desk." Dropping a kiss on my head, he left the room.

Chad waited until the door shut behind him before he turned to me and said, "Stop it now."

"What?" I asked confused.

"Overthinking," he replied. "Mr. Sexy may not be able to see it, but you can't fool me."

"Chad, I honestly don't have any idea what you're talking about," I said.

"You are overthinking everything. I know *asshole ex* broke your heart and you are scared, but trust me, it's okay to live again. Oh, and the someone he wants you to meet? It's his mother, honey," Chad revealed.

"How do you know?" I demanded.

"Because, you should see the way he looks at you," he said. "He was talking about his mom. Trust me, he cares about you. He is not Daren." He stressed every word.

Ross wanted me to meet his mom? Would she like me? What was she like? One of those straight laced older women who would look down in disgust on our activities last night? Or would she be the carefree woman my mom is. The kind who goes traipsing off around the world with her acting troupe... What should I wear? Princess Kate or Lady Gaga?

"There's that smile," Chad beamed. "Now if you're still sure you don't want to join me."

"As tempting as a couple's massage with Ross sounds, I need to work. My writing was interrupted earlier this morning," I said.

"Ugh, I need to call Frank," Chad teased. "Be safe, yeah?"

"I will, love ya," I replied, watching him head to the door.

Once he left the room and I was alone, I stood and went to my bedroom. Staring up at the painting of Angus and Elizabeth, I softly called to him.

"Angus? Are you here?" When he didn't respond, I wrapped my arms around myself and looked around the room. "Where are you?" I whispered.

*Ross*

Heading downstairs I clicked open the gate behind the check-in desk. My small office was there in the back. Without speaking to Lorna who stood behind the counter, I closed the office door behind me.

As requested, Nikki's file was on my desk. Sitting in my plush chair, I opened it, immediately smiling when I saw the author photo she submitted with her application. Usually I would take my time but I reviewed her file personally when it first came in and knew it well. Flipping through the file to the part I needed, I saw her father's name, number and address. Glancing at the clock, I quickly did a time change calculation trying to remember if Chicago was on the same time as New York. Too early to call. Instead, I turned on my laptop computer and opened the email from my editor. He had finished the first round of edits on my next novel; *Highlander's Bounty* part of my *Highlander's Heaven* series.

Sifting through the usual banter on the sex scenes and the overall impression on the plot, he explained certain passages he didn't understand or wanted me to rewrite. Knowing it would take a couple hours to do the rewrites and read through his edits, I hunkered down and promised to call

Mr. Thompson closer to noon, my time.

The alarm on my phone startled me as I typed up a new section my editor wanted me to fix. Noon glared at me. Wiping my eyes, I leaned back in my chair wincing when my back popped. Saving my progress, I reached for the desk phone and Nikki's file to dial the appropriate number.

"Travis Thompson," a man answered on the fourth ring.

"Ah, good morning, sir. My name is Ross Sutherland, I'm the President of the League of Extraordinary Writers here in Scotland."

"Is Nikki okay?" his voice was immediately panicked.

"Oh, yes, sir, yes, no I'm sorry to worry you, she's perfectly fine," I assured him kicking myself for worrying him.

"Oh, okay, uh... what can I do for you?" he asked.

"Well, sir, I was speaking with Nikki and she mentioned your Thursday night date nights. Pizza and wine. She misses you and said it would be the first time in about three years she would miss the evening with you."

Mr. Thompson was quiet so I went on.

"I was wondering if I could set something up for you both. She tells me you Skype?"

"We do," he answered.

"Grand, would you be willing to Skype in with her if I can get my chef to prepare the meal?"

Again Mr. Thompson was quiet. My nerves were getting the best of me.

"I'm sorry, what did you say your name and title was?" He asked.

"Ross Sutherland," I answered. "I'm the President and Founder."

"I thought another guy was the founder. Elliot something or other."

"Elliot Ross is my pseudonym," I explained.

"Ross Sutherland... wait a minute, did you help my daughter get to Edinburgh?"

"I did, sir," I admitted. "I met her at the airport restaurant and I couldn't let her berate herself for just being herself."

"She does that far too often," he sighed.

"I'm hoping to do this for her, sir. It's something that would mean a lot to her."

Again, he was quiet and I had a distinct impression I had over tipped my hand.

"Tell me what you're thinking, son," he said and I leaned back in my chair, silently letting out my breath.

*Nikki*

It was about an hour later, as I furiously typed on my laptop transcribing my work from that evening when I felt Angus's comforting hand on my cheek. I leaned into it.

"There you are," I whispered. Turning, I saw him crouching down before me in his traditional kilt and white shirt.

"I'm sorry, lass," he said. "I could nae come to you when you called."

"Why?" I asked.

"Yer heart was nae open to me," he said. "It was only open to one."

"You must think me a whore," I replied.

"Nay, lass," he sounded offended by the suggestion. "I think many things when I think of ye but ne'er a *hoor*."

His world was so different from mine, what else could he think?

"But Ross and I are not married," I went on.

"Aye, I ken," he replied, then paused. "Ah, lass I ken what yer thinking. Ye think, in my time, a woman was considered a *hoor* if she bedded a man who was no' her husband. Am I right?" I nodded. "Well," he started. "That may have been other's views. But… May I tell ye a secret?" I nodded again. "My wife and I loved each other far too much to wait. We were married before God before we were married before man and I ne'er considered her a *hoor*."

I stared at him. I couldn't believe what he was saying. Growing up, my mother was a free spirit, still is, and she would tell me all about men and their desires. My dad would try to tell her not to go into such detail with a ten-year-old but she would simply wave him off saying, I'll need to learn about it sooner or later.

"Did I shock ye, lass?" Angus asked mortified, bringing me back to the present.

"No," I answered quickly and saw the relief in his eyes. "Not really. Just... I was always told that to do that before marriage in your time was a scandal."

"It would have been, had we been caught," he clarified. "Lass, I need to show you so many things, but Sutherland is right, it's hurting you."

"Ross is not my protector, Angus. He does not tell me what to do," I stated.

"Nay, I ken," Angus chuckled. "Ye're just as fierce as a Highland Lass."

"I am partly Scottish, Angus, on my mother's side. Grandpa Brodie used to sing me songs and tell me tales of Scotland."

"Did he?" Angus smiled softly. "I'm glad. What was his favorite?"

"Loch Lomond," I said.

A soft smile lifted his lips and he began to sing my favorite verse. "'But the broken heart it kens, nae second spring again, though the waeful may cease frae their greetin'. 'Tis a beautiful song." I did not realize I had been crying until he reached up and wiped my cheek. "Nay, donnae cry, lass," he whispered.

"I'm sorry," I said sniffling. "I don't know why I'm crying. How do you know that song? It was written many years after you..."

"Died?" he supplied. I nodded. "I may no' be able to speak to people, lass but I can always hear. I have heard that song many times."

"Have you sung that to me before?" I asked, unfamiliar joy and yet sorrow filled my heart hearing him sing those words. "You can't have."

"Nay," Angus breathed a laugh, but there was no humor in it. "We had a very similar song in my day and I used to love to sing to my wife and our child as she carried her." His voice trailed off and he looked passed me out the window.

"Show me," I said. His eyes turned back to mine but there was such sadness rimming them I couldn't catch my breath.

"I cannae," he replied. "It could..."

"Please," I breathed.

He nodded finally and offered his hand. "Forgive me for showing ye something so private, but the only time I sang to my wife and child was in our bedchamber."

"I understand and it does not bother me, Angus," I said. Grasping his hand in mine, I stood and stared up into his eyes.

I don't remember much of what happened next. All I remember was feeling like I was drowning but I never let go of Angus's hand.

"Now lass, open your eyes," he said softly.

Obeying, I looked around a room I had never seen before. "Where are we?" I asked seeing the furs lining the window, and a fire blazing in the massive fireplace. "*When* are we?" I amended.

"Castle Eachthighearn, in the highlands," Angus explained. "You are in MacPherson Keep in the Laird's chambers. As far as *when*, look."

Turning, I saw two people lying on the bed together, a man's back was to me and I couldn't see his face but I could see he was shirtless and gently stroking a woman's swollen stomach. The man softly hummed a tune as he trailed kisses down the woman's shoulder and arm. She laughed and swatted him away when his hand slipped under the bedsheet.

"Angus," she giggled. "Stop, tis nae good for our child."

"The healer said you need to stay active, *mo chridhe* what better way?" I could hear the grin in his voice. Looking over at my Angus, still holding my hand, I saw the glistening tear streaks on his cheeks. My heart hurt for him. I wanted to wrap my arms around him and hold him to me so tightly, but I couldn't. I squeezed his hand instead. This was Riona, his first wife and the love of his life.

Riona's hand reached up and caressed his face. I had yet to see her face.

"*Mo ghaol,*" she said. "I must speak with you. I need to have your solemn oath."

"What is it?" He asked.

"If something were to happen to me during the birth," she started. "If I am nae strong enough—"

"Nay, do no' say it," he interrupted.

"Angus, please, listen," she stressed. "If I die, I need your solemn oath you would ne'er blame our child. It would no' be his or her fault."

"Of course no'," he declared.

"And, my love, it is no' *your* fault either," she expressed. "Do no' blame yourself."

"As that is no' going to happen," Angus answered. "I give you my vow."

"Anything could happen, *mo ghoal,*" she replied. "But I do no' want to discuss this anymore. Make love to me, Angus."

"With pleasure, my love," he said turning to hover over her, her pregnant belly in the way between them, but she giggled and turned her head toward us.

My blood ran cold.

It was me.

# Chapter Twelve

I woke in Ross's arms and could read the fear in his eyes as he breathed my name.

"Ross, it was me, oh god it was me," I heard myself say as I tasted my tears on my lips.

"What? What are you saying, Nikki?" his voice was strained as his arms tightened around me.

"Riona, was me," I knew I was babbling. "Angus?" I tried to sit up.

"Easy," Ross ordered as he cradled me in his arms. "What happened?"

My head was pounding, I couldn't focus and my nose felt wet. Reaching up to wipe it away, I pulled my hand back and saw a fresh coat of blood. Ross quickly pulled out his handkerchief and gently pressed it to my nose.

"This has to stop!" Ross sounded so desperate. "It's killing you!"

"I'll be okay," I said.

"The hell you will," he replied. "I'm taking you away from here." He slid his arm beneath my legs and lifted me.

"No," I answered. "No, Ross, I have to finish this. I will be fine."

"Nikki," he breathed.

"Kiss me, I need you," I said wrapping my arms around his neck.

"No, Nikki, you need to get looked at," he pulled back.

"I need you more," I replied.

"Nikki," he breathed. Cupping his face, I forced him to look at me. Finally, he let out a harsh sigh and walked me to the bed, "Tell me what happened." He lay me down and crawled in beside me.

Snuggling against him, I told him what Angus showed me.

"What does it all mean?" I asked him.

He took a deep breath, "I'm not sure," he answered. "How do you feel about it?"

"I'm scared," I admitted.

"I am too," he stated. "But together, we'll figure this out. I'm here. You donnae have to deal with this alone."

"Thank you," I sighed. It was nice to have him there. Odd since it had only been a few days since I met him but the connection I felt was deeper than five years with Daren.

"How's the book coming?" he whispered changing the subject.

"Not bad," I replied. Unsure if I wanted to sleep or work, I turned my head to look out the window. The sun was still high.

Taking a deep breath, I sat up.

"I need to keep working," I said.

"Okay," he replied kissing my hair. "Then dinner?"

"Sure, our date?" I teased.

"About that..." he said. "I want to do something special, so can we plan for it on Sunday and just have a regular dinner tonight?"

"Of course," I replied. "If it ends like last night, I'm guaranteed to love it."

"Oh trust me, it will," he answered.

After a moment of silence, I pulled away and looked down at him, my headache gone.

"Do you want to stay? Work on your latest with me?"

"Sure," he said. "I need to get my laptop from my office.

Do you want me to bring up anything? A bottle of wine?"

"That would be amazing," I said.

"Red or white?"

"Chilled white? Dry?" I said.

"I think I can find a bottle somewhere. Elliot Ross spends most of the budget on alcohol or so I'm told."

"It's not like you wouldn't know… you have known him your whole life," I teased.

"We're pretty close," he winked. "I'll be back in ten."

*Ross*

I headed down the stairs and across the hall to the lobby. Lorna stood at her post behind the counter. I knew I needed to speak with her and now was as good a time as any.

"A word," I said. Her eyes widened but she nodded and followed me into the office. "Shut the door," I ordered as I walked around my desk to sit. I never considered myself an intimidating person but I could be tough when needed. I suppose being six-two had its perks. At the moment, I sat at my desk chair and rested my ankle on my knee.

Lorna fidgeted as she stood before me.

"Is it true you spoke to Ms. Thompson after spilling the water on her?" I asked.

Her chest heaved. I had my answer but I wanted to hear it from her.

"Yes," she said.

"What did you say?" I asked but my tone was icy.

She swallowed audibly. "I… I said things I regret," she tried to dodge but I wouldn't be put off.

"What exactly did you say?" I asked.

Her eyes rose and pleaded with me.

"Are you firing me?" she asked softly.

"I want to. Ms. Thompson told me a little of what you said but besides the line about being one in a long line of American Bimbos to be notches on my bedpost, she didn't say anymore. I want you gone, Lorna. This has gotten out of hand

and I do blame myself for your... connection to me. But let me tell you this, sleeping with you was a mistake, one I regret utterly. It gave you delusions we shared a connection deeper than a onetime moment of drunken weakness. I wanted to fire you but Ms. Thompson begged me not to. She said you were just trying to protect what you thought was yours. Remember her hand in this the next time you feel like dumping water on her. Now, I've let it go but I will tell you this, if you do anything like this again, if you so much as look at Ms. Thompson cross-eyed, you will relieved of your position here. If you decide you cannae work under these conditions and decide to seek employment elsewhere, I will write you a good letter of recommendation as your work as an employee has been exemplary. Do I make myself clear?"

"Yes, sir," she answered softly.

"Good, now, I need you to make a reservation for two at the Tower Restaurant for Sunday and make sure the table is outside with their best view of the castle. Be sure to have a chilled bottle of their best champagne on ice waiting for Ms. Thompson and me. Also, I want the apartment on the Royal Mile prepped for our evening. Do you have an issue with doing any of that?"

"No, sir," she wouldn't look at me.

"Good," I reached forward and disconnected my laptop. Stuffing it into its protective pouch, I headed for the door. "I will be occupied but send me an email once everything is confirmed."

"Yes, sir," she said.

Without another word, I walked out of my office and to one of the bars that kept chilled wine. The bottle and two glasses in my hand along with my laptop, I started climbing the stairs to Nikki's room.

As much as I wanted to keep Nikki locked away, naked in my bed, she needed to get out with the other authors. Seeing several of them milling about outside, at the pool, or under the umbrellas with their computers, tablets or notebooks, ordering drinks, I couldn't help but smile. The retreat was my dream come true and every year was better than the last. The authors became lifelong friends and the best part was, my staff at the castle would sometimes receive requests for reservations with several of the previous authors' names listed, almost like a reunion. Castle MacCulloch was a working hotel, ten months out of the year and every month but January we sold out of the fifty working rooms. Knowing I could easily double the occupancy as soon as the other wing was completed, made me itch to call Gerard to see if he had scheduled the repairs.

My best friends were just as much a part of this hotel as I was. Though it was in my name, they assisted with the overarching running of the castle. Gerard knew several handymen who had helped with getting the farm back up and running and Graeme's ability to charm anything had helped immensely with my business negotiations.

Taking the final few steps to Nikki's and my floor, I thought about offering the outside as a work location. Maybe the busier she was with the book and mingling the less Angus will contact her. The nose bleeds had to stop.

"I worry about her just as much as you," Angus appeared in front of me.

"Shite," I breathed calming my heart that jumped higher than ever before.

"Sorry, lad," he said.

"How can I see you?" I questioned. "I thought only Nikki could."

"You and she are one. Your love of her gives me the ability to speak with you."

My heart still racing from the suddenness of seeing him, I looked down the hall then back at the ghost haunting my castle.

"She will nae stop this," I said.

"Aye, I ken," Angus replied.

"But it's killing her, Angus," I said. "And I donnae want to lose her. No' when..."

"Aye," he stopped me from unmanning myself completely. "I have felt the same love. But she will nae stop."

"What can I do?" I asked. "Those nosebleeds are hurting her."

"Aye, but there is so much more she needs to see. The only thing we can do with a stubborn Highland Lass is work with her and no' against her."

"And if the worst should happen?"

"I lost my wife, my love, I will never allow another man to feel that pain. Trust me, lad, I will keep her safe."

Slowly, I nodded. "No' tomorrow night," I said.

"Aye, I heard your conversation with her father. I can tell you, lad, if she were my daughter and you called to do something that important to us both, I would be encouraging the lass to keep you."

"I am nae sure why, I have such a connection to her. I cannae and will nae fight it."

"Good," he smirked. "Now I may see how she is later but hear me, lad, you hurt her and you will have me haunting you for eternity."

I knew he wasn't joking. "I never want to," I promised.

"Good, I'll be around if needed."

"I'm sorry I never took the reports seriously," I needed to apologize for ignoring him for ten years.

"I was pleased when you purchased this place and restored it. It looks better than it ever has. Ye have respected the history and I thank ye. Now go to our lass, her story is a good one, one I hope will have a good ending."

*Nikki*

Ross and I worked for hours, the white wine he had brought had been finished long ago and Ross ordered a room service lunch and another bottle.

Finally, my fingers aching and my back stiff, I turned when I heard Ross close his laptop and stand.

"Where are you going?" I asked.

"It's dinner time, love," he grinned. "I need to make an appearance and most of the authors are already down there. My staff have been asked where I was. Instead of telling them you've kept me hostage, I thought it would be best to show up."

"Ooh, I want to come too. That BLT was divine, but I have my eye on the Shephard's Pie."

"Excellent choice," he said. "Come then, love. Let's give

the romance writer's some inspiration."

"Will you wear your kilt?" I asked.

"I just might," he replied

Ross's hand in mine as we walked down the stairs to the dining room, all eyes turned to us as we entered. Meeting Marilyn's gaze across the room, she grinned and winked at me. I looked around for Chad but found him, grinning, sitting with three other authors.

"I do believe I hear the scape of pen on paper," I teased as Ross led me to a table for two beside the fireplace. "All the romance writers are taking notes."

"I best make it good then," he said as he pulled out my chair. Before I could breathe he grabbed my waist and drew me flush against him. Our eyes sparkled as we heard gasps around us and he leaned down, kissing me.

Finally sitting, he waved the waiter over and ordering a bottle of red wine and an ahi tuna appetizer. "So, this manuscript you're working on, what's it about?" He asked as soon as the waiter left.

"Something," I grinned.

"Oh, grand," he teased right back. "I have a very vivid picture of what it is," I laughed. "You know, I was talking to my agent the other day," he started. "I… mentioned you."

"Oh?" I asked.

"Yeah," he went on then stopped as the waiter returned with the bottle of wine. Popping the cork, he poured a little into Ross's glass, waiting as Ross swirled the contents and tasted it. Smiling, Ross nodded and the waiter filled our wine glasses. We toasted each other and I took a drink. "He purchased your novel."

"Who?" I asked.

"My agent," he reminded me.

"Oh? And?"

"He loved it," he stated excitedly. "In fact, he said if you have any other work, no' to go to anyone but him. He wants it, Nikki."

"Seriously?" I asked shocked.

"Seriously," he replied. "Now, I donnae ken what kind of relationship or contract you have with your current agent but…"

"No, I need a new one, my agent for *Secret Revenge* was a friend of Daren's and it's gotten… awkward. This is fantastic."

"He wants to meet you before the retreat ends."

"Ends?" I questioned. That's right… this retreat was going to end. After the confrontation with Lorna, I couldn't very much imagine either of us would be good at a long-distance relationship. She was right. Our time together was merely a fling. But that didn't sit right with me. I didn't have much experience with love but I had never felt this way about Daren. Before I was able to say anything more, my phone rang a ringtone I hadn't heard in more than three months. Grabbing my phone, I stared at the screen.

*Daren*

What. The. Hell?

"Nik?" Ross called to me. I looked up at him, hit ignore and put my phone away. "Don't over think it," he said. "I promise he's a great agent."

"No, it wasn't that, honestly thank you."

"You donnae mind I talked about you?"

"Mind? Of course not!" I cried. "Thank you, Ross," I reached across and took his hand in mine. Sifting our gaze to the ahi tuna appetizer, we put in our orders for two Shephard's Pies, ate and drank in silence for a little while. Our Shephard's Pie arrived soon after.

"Who was that on the phone?" Ross asked. "Sorry," he said when I looked up at him. "It looked like you were surprised then angry."

"My ex," I admitted. "The jerk hasn't returned any of my calls for months but now he calls me?"

Ross's eyes narrowed. "Bastard," he muttered. "I'm sorry I did nae mean to bring up bad memories."

"You didn't," I was quick to assure him.

Just as I was about to say more, a strange gust of air blew through the dining room. The gusts grew in intensity. Tables started to rattle and the women's hair whipped around them. It felt like a tornado was coming through. Ross held on to my hand but his eyes scanned the area trying to figure out what was going on. The wind picked up even more and people were being pushed and pulled across the room. Screams were heard all around us, then the temperature dropped drastically.

"Angus!" I screamed as Ross pulled me down to the floor and shielded me from the moving tables. "Angus!"

"Nikki!" I heard Chad yell from across the room.

The wind died down and black smoke appeared in the center of the room. I held my breath as I watched the smoke begin to form into a figure. Suddenly the blackness rushed toward Chad and to my horror, Chad reached up to his throat as if he was being strangled. The poor man was lifted off the ground in a Darth Vader-like move.

Twisting out of Ross's arms, I stood and screamed. "Leave him alone!" Chad was released almost immediately and the smoke, if it had a face, turned to me. "You're not welcome! Leave us alone! Go!" I didn't realize until after I had spoken, it hadn't been in English. The harsh guttural words surprised me.

The smoke rushed at me but I held up my hands and screamed, "*Creag Dhubh!*"

When I opened my eyes, not realizing I had closed them, I saw – and from the faces of the other authors surrounding me, they saw too – Angus standing before me, his hands holding the smoke as if it were a person.

"Who opened the west wing?" Angus demanded. "Someone let her out! Go, lass, get outta here!" Then the smoke vanished and Angus along with it.

# Chapter Thirteen

"Chad!" I screamed. Trying to get to him as fast as I could, my body aching as if I had been through a battle. I crawled on my hands and knees.

"What the hell was that?" Chad coughed and rubbed his neck.

"I have no idea," I said. Ross came up beside him and helped us both up. "Where's the west wing?" I asked Ross.

"It's off limits, no one can go," he explained.

"Well, clearly," Chad coughed. "Someone went there. I don't think Angus would be so upset if it wasn't so bad."

"I want to know who *she* is," I said, an odd form of anger rising in me.

"In time, you're no' running over there, that was the wing that had the most fire damage," Ross elaborated. "The solar was as far as we can go. At least until I get a sound report on the building."

"What the hell was that about, Elliot?" René demanded helping Jilliana back to her feet.

"All part of the show, nothing to worry about," Ross turned to them and smoothly raised both hands in a gesture for everyone to keep calm. "You all came here for inspiration, right? Well, you just got another taste of the things my staff and I put together. I want to thank Mr. Neugan for being such a good sport."

As everyone began to nod and accept Ross's explanation, he turned to me and motioned subtly with his head to Chad. Nodding, I grabbed Chad's elbow and helped him to the elevators. He still coughed and rubbed his neck where I saw a red handprint begin to form.

"Are you okay?" I asked.

He reached over, grabbed my hand that rested on his arm, helping him remain upright and gave it a squeeze.

"I'm fine, honey," he said. "A little sore and my head is pounding, but I'm good. Could use an aspirin... but more a tequila shot."

"We're heading up to my room," I replied. "We'll bust open the mini bar."

The elevator dinged and we walked in. As the doors closed, I watched him in the reflection of the mirrored walls. He was badly shaken by what happened. I wanted to know, now more than ever, who she was and why the hell she attacked him.

*Ross*

After calming the situation and assisting my staff with fixing the dining room, I ordered the bar to pass around shots of whisky and push the movie we were showing in the theater. Hoping Angus had the situation under control, I called my security head and gave him a rundown on what happened, of course without mentioning the ghost. Having him call our on-call doctor asking him to be on standby, I headed up to Nikki's room.

When I heard her call for me to come in, I entered and shut the door behind me.

"How are you feeling, Chad?" I asked walking over to where they sat beside the fireplace.

"Better after the tequila," he replied. Some color had

returned to his face but there was a clear impression of a hand print on his throat.

"I want to apologize to you on behalf of the league for what happened," I said. "I've had our on-call doctor notified and he is more than willing to come over and check on you."

Chad waved me off. "Maybe you should, honey," Nikki said leaning forward and squeezing his hand.

He took a deep breath, he was scared. "I…" he cut off and we both saw the fear and tears in eyes. "I just need to talk to Frank and I'll be okay."

"Absolutely," Nikki said.

"Chad, I truly am sorry, the league will assist you in any way."

"Don't give me any of that HR bullshit," Chad answered. "We both know I'm not going to run to the press or report any of this. I'm in this with you guys. Just tell me what we're going to do about it." He cleared his throat and sat up a little more.

"I don't know yet," I replied sitting beside Nikki in a huff.

"We'll go to the west wing and see what the hell happened," Nikki offered.

"Absolutely not," I stated. "No one is to go there. Under no circumstances are either of you permitted to go there."

"Ross," Nikki started.

"No, Nikki," I said forcefully seeing the marks on Chad's neck. I couldn't imagine marks like that on her beautiful neck. "I'll no' let that thing, whatever it is, hurt you, all right? End of discussion." I stood and stalked out of the room. No matter what, I couldn't let Nikki be hurt. I got to my room, poured a large glass of whisky and called Angus's name. He and I were going to have a wee chat.

*Nikki*

Chad looked at me with a look I can only explain as a bromance agreement as Ross stalked out of the room.

"What?" I asked. "I can take care of myself."

"That's not in question, honey," he reached forward and

took my hand. "I know you're not used to guys wanting to take care of you but he's under so much stress right now and he really cares for you. You should let a guy be a guy. If I could say one thing to my girlfriends after watching them with their men, after a while the men let them do whatever they want but the girls don't understand why he doesn't take care of them or worry about them like they want. My main answer is 'it's your fault, sweetie. You prevented your man from the very beginning to not look after you. You trained him to not offer his protection and help.' They lose the guy and don't understand why. That's why. A guy by nature is protective, dominate and constant. But when he's with someone who doesn't allow him to be like that he gets bored or he accepts it and becomes a shell. Don't do that to Ross, you will lose him."

Chad's words rang in my ears. Caring for him and letting him care for me and take care of me, did not prevent me from taking care of myself and being who I am. He was not Daren.

"Go," he said smiling. I nodded and got up nearly running to Ross's room.

Knocking softly, I didn't hear an answer. Trying the door, it was unlocked and swung open. My jaw dropped. I had never seen a more beautiful room.

Mahogany.

Masculinity.

Awe inspiring.

The layout was the same as mine with a sitting room and a bedroom. A large marble fireplace was the focal point of the room flanked by two wingback worn leather chairs with a cherry wood table carved with lion's heads between them.

Ross stood with his face staring down into the fire, one hand on the mantle the other holding a cut crystal tumbler containing a shot of amber gold liquor. If he hadn't worn jeans and a green Aran sweater, I would have sworn I had stepped through time.

He didn't look at me as I walked in and closed the door. He didn't look at me again when I softly called his name. Only when I stepped toward him and placed a hand on his arm did he move; and it was only to toss back the contents of his glass.

"Ross, I'm sorry," I said softly. "You are right, please. I know you're only wanting to help and protect me, but, baby, you can't always protect me. Help, yes, I'm just not used to it. Daren never tried. He never wanted to do either unless it suited him."

"Damn him," Ross muttered. "Am I to always live in his shadow?"

"No," I shook my head. "Just understand, he's all I know. There are so many unanswered questions between us and I can only hope to move on. I know I'll never get closure."

"I'm falling in love with you, Nikki," he confessed. "No," he sighed harshly. "The hell with it… I love you."

My breath caught in my throat. I wasn't sure I had heard him correctly. The last man to say those words to me ripped my heart out and I had never been the same. But I figured it was about time I stopped thinking all men were like Daren. I needed to start living again.

"Shut up and kiss me," I breathed.

"Good morning, Sleeping Beauty," Ross whispered. "I know you're up." His lips tickled my nose. "Your breathing changes when you wake up."

"My Prince Charming wakes me so gently," I replied my eyes still closed. He leaned down and kissed me. "Mmm," I hummed. "I could get used to that."

"Me too," he murmured against my lips. Finally opening my eyes, I gazed up into his crystal blue depths. He grinned, gripped me tightly and twisted laying me on my back. He had just managed to make me a quivering mess when the main door to his room burst open.

"Hooey!" A woman's voice cried. Never had I moved so quickly but this woman, who I had never seen before, burst into Ross's room before we had a chance to fully cover ourselves. "Darling!" She grinned looking at Ross.

"Mother!" Ross shouted pulling the sheets tighter around us. "What the hell? I'm thirty-three years old! You cannae come bursting into my room without knocking!"

"Oh nonsense," she waved him off. "Jacqueline Sutherland, dear," she said to me. I couldn't help but notice her distinctly English accented voice.

Attempting to salvage the first impression I was making on Ross's mother, I wrapped the sheets around me and nodded. "It's very nice to meet you, Mrs. Sutherland," I said.

"Lady," Ross volunteered.

"Lady Sutherland," I corrected then paused realizing what I had said. My eyes grew wide as I looked over at him. "Lady?" I asked. He shrugged.

"Oh tosh, *Jacqueline* will do," she said hurrying over to the bed.

"Uh… Nikki Thompson," I replied.

"Oh yes!" she cried. "Ross gave me your book to read! The women and I loved it! It was on our reading list. If I had known you two were together I would have asked you to come to the meeting! Ross, why didn't you tell me?" She asked. Before Ross could say anything, she went on. "Now tell me," she pulled over an ottoman and sat beside the bed. "Is my son treating you well? Is he satisfying you?"

"Mother!" Ross shouted.

"Hush, Ross," she said. "I know you must be, you are your father's son after all. Now tell me, Nikki, may I call you Nikki?" At my nod, she continued. "Is he treating you well?"

I couldn't help but laugh. The devilishness in me made me grin as I answered, "Actually, Lady Sutherland," I started.

"Jacqueline, dear," she interrupted.

"Jacqueline," I conceded. "Yes, he is taking *very* good care of me."

"I am *very* glad to hear it," she giggled.

"Mum, seriously, how did you get in here?" Ross asked.

"You gave me a key remember?" She replied.

"I knew I would regret that," he mumbled.

"Now does she know your secret? Or is it like with all the others?" She asked.

"Mother!" he cried.

"Yes, Jacqueline, I know he is Elliot Ross," I said.

"Oh! You're American," she smiled. I nodded. "Oh! How

wonderful! Marilyn Monroe, Katherine Hepburn, Rock Hudson, Clark Gable! Oh! Ross's father was just as handsome as Clark Gable!"

"I can see that," I said looked down at Ross.

"Oohhoo!" She laughed.

"Mum, why are you here?" Ross questioned.

"You asked me here, love," she said innocently.

"Och," Ross groaned. "I forgot."

Suddenly I remembered, too. Ross had asked his mother to come to the castle to answer questions we had about Ross's ancestry.

"Now what questions did you have of me, love?" She asked.

"If you'll excuse me, Jacqueline, I'll get dressed," I said.

"Oh go right ahead, dear," she said unmoving.

"Mum," Ross intervened. "She was subtly trying to ask you to leave."

"Oh nonsense," she said. "It's not like I've never seen it before. Besides I have two as well," she motioned to her chest indicating her breasts.

"Mother!" Ross cried.

"Oh, very well," she stood. "Is Marilyn here?"

"Yeah," he said. "She's probably having breakfast."

"Oh good! Nikki, you and I must have tea," she invited. I nodded. "Good, find me once you're done," she singed and left the room. I buried my head into Ross's chest and shook with laughter.

"Not exactly how I wanted you to meet my mother," Ross said.

"I like her," I replied.

"Good," he said kissing the top of my head. "Come on, let's take a shower."

He stood and picked up his shirt. Turning back to me, still lounging in bed watching him, he grinned. "What?" he asked.

"You're pretty amazing, you know that?" I asked.

"Ms. Thompson are you trying to seduce me?" He teased.

"Always, *Sir* Ross," I tried the title to see what he did.

Ross merely laughed and ripped the sheets off of me.

"Are you going to get into my shower, lassie or am I supposed to throw you over my shoulder like my Highland ancestors?" He asked. I squealed and raced to the bathroom.

# Chapter Fourteen

Checking in on Chad, he was on the phone with his boyfriend and his laptop was on his desk with the beginnings of a novel. The hand mark on his neck fortunately looked much better but he was still clearly shaken. Ross and I let ourselves out hearing him confirm to Frank he was all right.

Marilyn and Ross's mother, Jacqueline were easy to spot by the brightly colored scarves they wore and Marilyn's Bohemian wardrobe stuck out among the classic features of the breakfast room. Waving us over, Ross acknowledged them but turned to me.

"Let me get us some coffee, they can be quite a handful when they've had caffeine," he admitted.

I nodded and couldn't resist giving him a quick peck on the lips. Smirking, he headed to the side table and I ambled to the ladies watching us, whispering like two old biddies though they looked far from old. Jacqueline's hair, though streaked with grey, was still a vibrant shade of dark auburn and her crystal blue eyes – Ross's eyes – were shining in the morning sunlight that streamed through the windows. Easily two inches taller than me, her figure was one any woman between twenty-three and fifty would kill for. And I couldn't help but notice how the kilted waiters lingered a little too long beside her after offering to fill her water glass.

"I see you've recovered from your fall, my dear," Marilyn said as I took a seat. "Enough to make your man worship you?"

I laughed. The last time Marilyn and I had spoken of Ross, I had told her there was nothing going on between us.

"Fall? Did you get hurt, love?" Jacqueline asked concerned.

"It's nothing, I thought I saw something in my bathroom, a trick of the light," I covered. "And fell, hitting my head."

"Ross and the other one, Chance? Chuck?" Marilyn guessed.

"Chad," I confirmed.

"That's right, Chad, stayed with her," Marilyn explained.

Jacqueline reached over and covered my hand. "Oh, I'm so sorry, my dear. How terrible for you."

"I'm really perfectly all right," I put her mind at ease.

"Well, good," she answered.

"Have you two been friends long?" I asked curious.

"Oh, eternity," Jacqueline laughed.

"And Connor said *I* was the dramatic one?" Marilyn asked. Fits of laughter came from both women.

*Who was Connor?* I wondered, storing the name away.

"We've been best friends since we were school girls," Jacqueline went on. "Even had crushes on the same men."

"Men? They were merely boys then," Marilyn teased.

Ross came over and placed a mug of steaming coffee in front of me and winked. He knew I did not take cream in my coffee and yet it was as pale as Marilyn's hair. Curious, I looked over, his coffee was the same. Watching him raise it to his lips and close his eyes for a moment, I decided I'd give mine a try.

The ladies began talking to Ross but I didn't hear them as I raised the coffee mug to my lips and took a small sip.

Heaven... in the form of Irish Cream hit my tongue.

It wasn't until everything around me went quiet, that I realized my eyes were closed. Guiltily, I looked around the table.

"I think she may need a moment alone with her coffee," Marilyn teased.

"Sorry," I replied taking another sip. "This is an amazing cup."

"I'm sure," Jacqueline grinned and looked at Ross. "Did you use your father's recipe?"

"It's a cold morning," Ross justified.

"Not from what I saw," Jacqueline teased.

The alcohol had started warming and relaxing me. I couldn't stop the giggle bursting from my lips.

"Well, Jacqueline, as you said, he is his father's son," I answered.

The women laughed as Ross shook his head and covered his face in embarrassment.

"Oh, look how cute he is when his English blood comes to life," Jacqueline beamed.

"Mother, please," Ross attempted to stop her.

"Oh and he's so Scottish he hates it when I mention he's half English," she said.

"A quarter," he corrected. "Remember your father was a MacGregor."

She waved him off. "Now, Nikki, dear, tell me all about yourself," she said.

"Not much to tell," I replied.

"Oh nonsense," she answered.

"Tosh," Marilyn said at the same time. "Did she tell you about the ghost she encountered?"

"You met Fearsome MacPherson?" Jacqueline's eyes grew large with excitement. "Is he as fierce as everyone thinks? Is he handsome?"

"Mother!" Ross shook his head, then leaned back in his seat and downed his coffee.

"What?" She asked innocently. "You know I have a soft spot for you Scots."

"Mm, who doesn't?" I teased placing my hand on Ross's thigh. "And he does wear a kilt."

"Nothing sexier than a man in a kilt, right, Mari?" Jacqueline questioned.

"Mmhmm," Marilyn replied dreamily. "I remember the first time we met Connor. His bare knees showing beneath that kilt and heaven only knows what he was wearing under it."

"Oh, I know," Jacqueline beamed.

"Oh god, if you're going to start talking about yours and da's sex life, I'm leaving," Ross said. "I'm starting to feel this conversation is no' meant for a son's ears."

So, Connor Sutherland was Ross's father… I kinda like that name. Very Scottish, very dreamy and the father of the man I lov - cared deeply for. Shaking my head, I took a sip of coffee.

"You have to admit, Ross," I started. "You do look hot in a kilt."

"Only if you say so, love," his endearment sent a shiver up my spine. I didn't miss the not-too-subtle elbow Jacqueline nudged into Marilyn's side.

"So how long have you two been together?" Jacqueline asked.

"Not long," Ross replied.

"Your son saved me," I answered.

"Saved you?" Jacqueline asked surprised.

"Like a knight in shining armor," I continued stroking his leg. "I was stranded in Heathrow and Ross came to my aid offering his jet for my use."

"Ross Alexander MacGregor Sutherland, you were in London and you didn't come see me?" His mother cried.

Ross cringed. I gulped. *Shit,* I thought giving Ross a sullen look. *Sorry,* I mouthed.

"Mother," he started. "It was a quick trip finishing up some details with my agent and I had to get back here. I had no time to pop over for a chinwag. You know I would have if I could have."

"I'm not so sure," she sniffed. "I have seen you a grand total of ten times since your father died last year."

My eyes snapped to him. His father died? But if Jacqueline is a Lady, then that would mean Ross…

"Mum, you know how busy I've been since da's death. I have the estate to take care of," *Estate?!* My mind cried. "Not to mention my agent and writing."

"And you know how I support you, love, I just miss my only son," she said genuinely.

"I know, Mum, and I'll always want to see you. You're my mum and I love you," he replied.

"I love you too, Ross," she said sweetly.

Ross touched two fingers to his lips, kissed them and extended them toward her. Looking back toward Jacqueline, my eyes passed her and went to the window to see Angus standing out by the old pump.

Ross's eyes followed mine and I felt his hand take mine off his thigh and hold on. Glancing over at him, it was obvious he could see Angus too.

"I'm sorry, would you excuse me?" I asked standing. Both Jacqueline and Marilyn nodded.

"Mum, I'll be right back," Ross said standing as well.

We left through one of the glass doors. Ross's hand still held mine. Once we reached a close enough spot, Ross stopped. "I'll be right here," he said. I nodded and walked on toward Angus.

"How are ye, lass?" Angus asked concerned.

"I'm all right," I answered. "What was that last night, Angus? What happened?"

"The man she attacked, he's doing well, aye?" He asked.

"Chad?" I confirmed. He nodded. "He's okay, he has hand prints on his throat, and he's a little frightened."

"With reason," he said.

"What the hell was that, Angus?" I demanded. His eyes grew wide when he heard the word I said. Clearly women of his time did not curse. "Tell me!"

"Elizabeth," he hung his head.

"Your wife?" I asked.

"Aye," Angus sighed.

"What's going on?" I demanded.

His eyes drifted passed me to Ross. "It's no' something I can tell ye," he said. "'Tis something I hae to show ye."

"Then show me," I stated.

"I cannae, you'll be hurt," he replied.

"Stop, I need to know," I declared then felt Ross's hand slip into mine and I looked up at him.

"Not tonight," Ross said. "Tomorrow, aye, but I have something planned that cannae be rescheduled."

"What?" I asked.

"Nothing you need to know right now," he replied then

turned to Angus. "Where were you last night? I called to you and you were not there."

"I had to bind Elizabeth in the tower," Angus justified.

"You have spoken before?" I looked from one to the other.

"Aye," Angus replied. "Because you are one, I was able to speak with him last afternoon."

"What did you want to talk to him about?" I asked.

"Who it was and why they attacked Chad and what they want with you," Ross confided.

"We know who now," I turned back to Angus. "Why Chad?"

"I donnae ken," he answered. "All I can say is when he called to you she must have thought he was someone important to you."

"He is," I defended.

"I mean in a different way," he replied.

"What do you mean?"

"He means she must have thought he was me," Ross said.

"Aye," Angus agreed.

"Poor Chad," I sighed and looked over Angus's shoulder to the trees, remembering the night before. "What can we do?"

"Nothing at the moment," Ross replied. "I'm sorry, Nikki but tonight cannae be changed and I think for now, it would be best if we joined the others and Mum for the rest of the day. You haven't had a chance to meet everyone."

"That is a grand idea," Angus said. "I promise you, lass, I will come to you again and will be able to share what needs to be shown."

"But you?" I asked.

"It's been two centuries for me, lass," he answered. "What's a couple more hours?"

"Elliot?" A voice behind us made me jump. "Who are you talking to?" It was René and another author I knew by sight but hadn't been introduced to yet.

"René, James, good to see you," Ross didn't miss a beat. I looked back and Angus was gone.

"And you," René said. "But who were you talking to?"

"Oh," Ross chuckled. "Ms. Thompson and I were play

acting a part in her new novel."

I nodded. "It's about a ghost," I explained.

"Well, you have enough inspiration here," James said. "I say, Elliot, what was that last night? My wife and I couldn't sleep a wink."

His wife, the great mistress of thrill and macabre boasted the distinction of being somehow related to Edgar Allan Poe. I had only seen her in passing and didn't dare approach her as she was nose deep in an iPad typing away.

"Och, you know how these retreats are, James," Ross said. "Have to keep you guessing somehow."

"But we are safe, *oui*?" René asked.

"Absolutely," Ross replied.

James nodded slowly then his eyes were on me. "My wife and I read your book," he said. "I have to say, Ms. Thompson, a page turner if ever there was one."

"Thank you," I said excitedly. I couldn't believe it. The King of Spy Thrillers married to the Mistress of Thrills and Chills had read my book and liked it, that was something I would have to tell my dad. The moment I thought about Dad, I had to shake off the sadness of missing our date night that night.

"Haven't seen you for a little while, Mademoiselle," René said. "Has this Scottish Rogue been keeping you to himself?"

Ross chuckled and draped his arm around me. "Do you blame me?" he teased.

"Not in the least," René grinned.

"It's more me keeping him prisoner," I winked.

"Don't give my wife ideas," James answered laughing. "Maybe we could have tea on the terrace? I know Jen would love to meet you."

"I would love that," I said.

*Ross*

Leaving Nikki to meet with James and his wife Jennifer, I went back to my office and checked for an email I was waiting for. Seeing Mr. Thompson's name in the sender line, I opened the message and read. Wanting to make everything perfect for tonight's dinner for Nikki, I had asked Travis to get a recipe from a Chicago Italian man named Vincent Morelli. Apparently, Nikki loved his pizzas. Mr. Thompson's message said the Italian didn't want to give up his secret recipe but when he knew it was for Nikki he agreed to share at least some of the secret with my chef.

Unsure how Marcus would react when I asked him to make a deep dish Sicilian pizza for Nikki tonight, I printed the email off and sought out my chef. Following the directions of his Sous-Chef, I found him standing near the abandoned servants houses near the west wing of the house. The plan was to renovate those as well and make small cottages for overflow or the off season. Marcus snuffed out his cigarette when he saw me, not that I cared if he smoked, but he was considerate enough to not let me smell it. My father had died of lung cancer.

"I'm sorry to bother you on your break, Marcus," I said.

"No bother at all, Sir," he replied. "How can I assist you?"

"I was wondering if you knew how to make a deep-dish Sicilian pizza," I said.

Marcus looked at me and raised an eyebrow. I offered him the email I had print out with the recipe. He reviewed the paper and looked up at me.

"Can I ask why?" he asked. "It's not traditional fare."

"No, you're right and I would only need it to feed one person," I explained.

He nodded slowly. "Well, I would be willing to give it a try. I haven't made a deep dish in a long time, usually Chicago style isn't my favorite but I'll work on it. When would you need the final product?"

"Tonight by seven," I said. He nodded again. "I hope you didn't have plans for the evening."

"No," he replied. "And my sous-chef would be able to handle dinner."

"I appreciate it, Marcus, truly," I said.

"I appreciate you taking a chance on me," he answered.

"How long are you going to be using that?" I chuckled. "It's been years."

"Still, I'm grateful," he said. I smacked his arm thanking him and turned to go. "Oh, sir?" he called me back. "Any idea where I can find *Morelli's famous Italian spices* mix?"

I chuckled. "A hole in the wall pizza place in Chicago," I offered. "Just do your best, Marcus. It'll be grand."

# Chapter Fifteen

*Nikki*

Ross led me to a different guest room on the second floor later that evening. Before I entered the dining room he found me and ushered me away. Unsure where we were going and only knowing my stomach was about to turn on itself, I called to him.

"Ross, what's going on? I thought we were going to dinner," I asked.

"We are, or at least you are," he said.

"What's going on?"

Without another word, he opened the door to a guest room and I was greeted by a table for two covered in a red and white checkered poly-plastic table cloth, red small vases with lit tea candles, wood framed black and white pictures of Chicago's skyline, wooden chairs and the smells of Italian spices and cooked dough.

A man stood dressed in black slacks, a crisp white button up shirt and skinny black tie with a short black apron wrapped around his lean hips.

"Good evening, Ms. Thompson, party of one?" he asked.

I looked back at Ross who smiled but stepped back. The

man pulled out the chair and I sat, instinctively placing the red cloth napkin on my lap.

"Oh, I'm sorry," the waiter said. "Table for two," he reached down to the seat of the opposite chair, pulled out Ross's iPad, and a stand. Unmuting the audio, he turned the iPad over and set it in the stand. I gasped when I saw dad on the screen.

"Hey, darling!" he called. "I'm here at Morelli's. Ready for our date night?"

I covered my mouth as a sob escaped and tears instantly pooled in my eyes. Looking back at Ross who hung back by the door, I turned to dad who grinned. "All his idea," dad said. I stood and rushed to Ross, throwing my arms around his neck. I kissed him full on the lips causing Dad and the waiter to chuckle.

"Go and enjoy your evening," Ross said quietly. "That pizza is making me hungry."

"I'll save you a couple slices," I promised. "Thank you so much."

"You are welcome," Ross replied then turned to look at the iPad. "Enjoy, sir."

"Thank you, Ross," Dad said. "It means a lot to us both."

"My pleasure," he answered. Turning back to me, his thumb gently stroked the apple of my cheek and gently pressed his lips to my forehead. "I love you."

I wanted to say the words back to him, but the sound of Vincent Morelli's voice over the iPad stopped me. I thanked Ross once more and watched as he slipped out of the room. Walking back to the table, the waiter uncovered the pizza on the table; a deep-dish Sicilian and popped the cork on a cabernet.

"Hey, Vinny," I waved.

"*Cara mia*!" the Italian American cried. "We miss you, but when your papa asked us to set this up, we had to agree. Even if it meant sending over my secret ingredient."

"You didn't!" I gasped.

"I did, for you, *cara*," he said. "But tell me, am I going to have to give up on us? That Scottish Rogue has stolen you from me?"

I giggled. Vinny was nearing sixty with a wife of forty years, ten children and fifteen grandchildren.

"Sorry, Vinny," I said. "But he will never compare to you,

you know that."

Vinny and dad laughed but soon dad and I were alone apart from the waiter waiting for me to dismiss him. After I thanked him for the wine and promised to tell Ross how attentive he was, he bowed, waved to dad and left the room, promising to come back and check on me.

"Ross set this all up, sweetheart," Dad said when we were finally alone. "He called me and asked if I could do my end of things. I miss you but I know you're having a wonderful time."

"Oh dad," I felt tears prick my eyes. "I miss you so much."

"I know, hey shh, it's all right, sweetheart, come on," he lifted his wine glass and raised it out to the camera. "Cheers."

Picking up mine and raising it as if to clink glasses, "cheers," I repeated.

Immediately, we fell into our comfortable rhythm, talking and laughing the night away. The pizza was amazing, even though it wasn't quite like Vinny's. Whoever made it had done an excellent imitation.

After a while, our conversation died down and dad took another sip of wine. "Tell me about Ross," he said. "From what I've talked to him, he's a very interesting man."

"He is," I said. "Daddy... how did you know mom was *the one*?"

Dad's face went blank as he leaned back in his chair. He adjusted his glasses and took a deep breath. "Well, as you know sweetheart, your mother and I divorced fifteen years ago so I wouldn't say we were the best marriage to base anything on but I did love your mother."

"I know you did, that's why I wonder. You know the fiasco of my love life. I don't know if what I feel is love or something else. I haven't felt this way before."

Dad took a deep breath and drank a large gulp of wine. "It's hard for a father to know his little girl is interested in men, but I will tell you this, when I first spoke with Ross, I was worried it was too soon, that boy was horrible at covering his true feelings toward you. But I was never more worried about you than when I met Daren. Honey, he was your choice and I love you so I respected your decision but I knew he would hurt you. Ross on the other hand scares me even more."

"What? Why?" I asked anxious.

"Because he is exactly what I hoped for my little girl. And that scares the hell out of me."

I was quiet for a while thinking everything through.

"I think I love him," I whispered.

Dad's eyes glistened but he nodded. "Good, sweetheart, because that boy loves you. But promise me one thing?"

"Anything, Daddy," I swore.

"Don't leave me alone? If he is who you want, I want to be in your life. If that means moving to Scotland, I will."

"Oh Daddy," my tears fell. "It's way too soon, but you will always be with me and I will always want you to be here."

"That's all I needed to hear, sweetheart. Now let's talk about something else, okay?"

"Okay," I wiped my eyes.

*Ross*

Nikki's face had been worth everything. Marcus was able to work his magic on the pizza and had even made me a few slices. The deep-dish was a lot to eat but I could see why Nikki loved it so much. Several of the American authors came into the dining room and took a deep sniff. It was a success in my book if the Americans wanted the pizza. Seeing the waiter I asked to get everything started, come into the dining room, he smiled and nodded at me. Nikki was settled and it was time for me to enjoy my dinner.

Without her, the evening was uneventful, but I enjoyed a glass of Laphroaig with Chad, James and René along with two other men. The women milled about enjoying their drinks but every time I looked up to see Nikki she wasn't there.

"I say, you do have it bad," James said. Looking over at the English author I claimed as a friend I raised an eyebrow. "For the American girl. You've been mooning about her all evening."

"You have, *monsieur*," René stated lighting a cigar and puffing out the smoke. Waiting for the clench in my stomach anytime I smelled tobacco smoke, the feeling never arrived. My father was a chain smoker but he never smelled badly, his tobacco of choice was a cigar or pipe but the doctor attributed the cancer to his daily cigarettes. Graeme, Gerard and I swore off smoking when he was diagnosed.

"I donnae moon," I replied.

"You moon, honey," Chad said. "It's all over your face."

"Is it mooning to make sure all of my authors have a good time?" I asked.

"Not at all," James replied. "It's the light you get in your eyes when the doors open and the disappointment when you see it isn't her."

"James," I shook my head.

"You can't deny it, I've been watching you all evening," he said. "Where is the pretty little thing anyway?"

"Having dinner with her father back home in America," I explained.

"Has anyone seen Jilliana since dinner?" René asked.

"Talk about someone who has it bad," I said happy to divert the attention to him.

"She is a lovely lady," René defended. "Besides, it's been too long since I had a summer fling."

Rolling my eyes at him, he was clueless. Jilliana was not interested but he kept flirting. The door opened and I looked over, hoping it was Nikki and when she walked in, a bright smile on her face, but tears in her eyes I stood immediately, barely hearing James say something about how bad I truly had it and walked over to her.

"Are you all right?" I asked.

She nodded, wiped her eyes and framed my face. "Thank you," was all she said before she kissed me senseless.

*Nikki*

Ross and I waited for Angus in my room. The morning was overcast and dreary but I needed to let Angus show me the next part of the story. Finding the Highland Pride was the only thing that would give him peace and I meant to find it before the retreat was over. Ross had woken me with coffee and a small breakfast unsure if I would be hungry. I thanked him but hardly touched the food. Feeling his arms wrap around me from behind as I stared out at the darkening clouds, I leaned back into him holding my coffee mug in my hands.

"I'll be right here," he whispered.

"I know you will," I replied. "I won't lie. I am a little scared. But it needs to be done."

"I know," he kissed the top of my hair and rested his chin on my head. "Just promise me one thing... come back to me."

Turning in his arms, I gazed up at him and nodded. "I want to and I promise I will."

"Are you ready, lass?" Angus's voice startled me but seeing him over Ross's shoulder, I nodded. Setting my coffee mug on the desk, Ross guided me to the bed and I sat down.

"What will happen, Angus?" I asked.

"You will see my life as a stranger on the outside looking in. Only the parts I was there for, I cannae show you something I donnae ken myself," he explained.

"Like a movie," I said.

"Aye," Angus replied. "Is that those moving picture things?"

"Yes," I said.

"Then exactly like that," he confirmed. "Lie down, lass and when you're ready, take my hand."

Complying, I lay on my back and looked over at Ross. He kissed my forehead and took my other hand.

"Be careful," he whispered.

"I will." Looking over at Angus, I nodded and took his hand.

"Relax, lass," Angus said. "And donnae let go of me hand. Hold on to yer love for Sutherland. It will ground ye to the land of the living. Are ye ready?"

"Aye, Angus, I am," I didn't realize my voice had a Scottish accent until it echoed in my ears. Ross's grip on my hand increased but soon all went black.

# Chapter Sixteen

I was drowning. Clutching Angus's hand, I gasped for air when it was over. Finally, I looked over at Angus. He grounded me and I knew as long as I felt his hand in mine, I was safe.

"Welcome to Eachthighearn Castle, lass," he said. "Home of MacPherson Keep."

We were inside the bailey and a large keep loomed before me. Mountains filled the view behind the building and the castle was surrounded by trees. My eyes turned to two men, swords clashing, curses flying, and sweat pouring from their foreheads. I was shocked when I saw Angus about twenty years younger than the one holding my hand fighting a younger man, about eighteen, with stark black hair hanging down beyond his shoulders. They were both shirtless, wearing kilts and leather boots.

They parried and danced together as they fought. The young man's sword tip swung dangerously close to Angus's neck but he dodged and blocked the strike with his Targe. Rushing forward to stop them, Angus held me back.

"We're no' fightin', lass," Angus whispered. "'Tis me brother; Niall. We're training."

I watched Angus knock the sword out of his brother's hand, catch it and hold both to the younger man's throat.

"Damnation, Angus!" Niall yelled. "Gie it back!"

Angus threw his head back and laughed. Clapping his brother on the back, he handed him his sword.

"Keep training, little brother," Angus grinned. "Perhaps one day you'll best me."

They both laughed and embraced before Angus pulled back and called out, "Now, who's for a swim in the loch?"

The warriors cheered and as they walked toward the gate, a young woman ran out of the keep and rushed across the courtyard.

"Me Laird!" She cried and Angus turned quickly. "'Tis my lady," the lass screamed. "Something is wrong!"

Blanching, Angus raced to the keep and disappeared inside. I wanted to follow but my Angus pulled me back.

"'Tis sorry I am, lass," he whispered. "But I cannae." Turning back to him, I saw tears rolling down his cheeks. "My love, my Riona, died in an hours' time."

I squeezed his hand and nodded. "Then show me something else, Angus," I said.

He nodded and transported us to another time. Once the darkness lifted, we were in a field, somewhere near the keep, the same mountains were in the distance. Turning to see the keep behind us, I watched as a small smile lifted Angus's lips. My eyes followed his gaze to see him, his dark brown hair streaked with grey and his eyes much heavier than when he was playing with his brother in the last vision. But seeing the baby dressed in a pale pink frock it could only have been a year's time between visions. His wife's death changed him.

"Tha's it, lassie," he coaxed the baby with his arms outstretched. "Come to yer da'," the baby squealed and took a few shaky steps toward him. She fell but Angus caught her up in his arms and spun her around, kissing her cute plump cheeks causing the baby to squeal as only babies can. "Did ya see her, Niall? Did ya see yer niece?"

"Aye, Angus I saw the wee lass," Niall called from his spot resting against a boulder. "She's growin' into a fine lass. She'll be just as strong as ye are."

"What do ya say to tha', Ree?" Angus cradled the baby on his hip. "Do ya wanna be as strong as yer da' and knock yer uncle on his bum?"

"Och, ye can try, ol' man," Niall called. Angus chuckled but spun around the next second, a warrior at the ready as horses' hooves pounded the ground inside the woods. Niall, in one swift movement, had gotten to his feet and drew his sword. Angus passed Riona to her nursemaid and grabbed his own sword beside the blanket. The brothers stood side by side protecting Riona.

The next moment, the largest, most frightening horses I have ever seen, broke through the tree line.

"Dammit, Sutherland!" Angus yelled sheathing his sword. Niall did the same. "Ye nearly got yerself killed." The man on the largest horse laughed once and dismounted. I could see the resemblance between him and the one I had seen earlier in the Laird's Solar but it was not the same man. This was Iain Sutherland, Ross's direct ancestor.

The men shook each other's arm in a warrior's greeting and Niall greeted the other warrior who had dismounted beside Iain.

"Good to see ye, Alistair," Niall smiled. I stared. The man in my dream stood before me. Alistair Sutherland; the man I had protected by killing the Redcoat in the recurring dream was Ross's ancestor.

"Aye, and ye, Niall," Alistair said. "When da' mentioned he needed to speak with yer brother I kenned it would be ill form no' to come and see ye."

"I'm glad ye did, 'tis been too long," Niall replied.

"To what do I owe this honor?" Angus asked Iain.

"I must speak with ye," Iain replied in hushed tones.

"Yer welcome to MacPherson Keep, Iain," Angus replied.

"I thank ye," Iain answered. "'Tis been a long journey."

"From where have ye journeyed?" Niall asked.

"South, near Edinburgh," he replied.

"Edinburgh?" Angus stated surprised.

"Aye, there is much to tell ye," Iain said.

The next second we were in the Laird's solar. Angus, Niall, Iain and Alastair all sat together beside the fireplace not speaking until the butler passing whisky, had left the room. Alastair began to speak but Angus raised his hand to stop him. Standing silently, Angus walked to the door and opened it. The butler jumped and looked up guiltily.

"That will be all, Robert," Angus said.

"Aye, my laird, thank ye," he bowed and backed up, disappearing down the hall. Once Angus was sure he was gone, he shut the door and returned to his seat.

"Not all Scots are loyal to the Stuart," Angus explained.

"Aye, I was nae thinking, forgive me, Angus," Alastair stated.

Angus waved him off, raised his glass and spoke in Gaelic. My Angus beside me leaned over.

"Long live the Stuart," he translated. I nodded, knowing somehow that was what it meant.

"The Stuart has chosen the location for the battle," Iain Sutherland stated without preamble.

"Where's it to be?" Niall asked sitting up straighter. Angus glanced at his brother.

"Culloden Moor," Iain replied.

"Is he mad?" Angus demanded. "Culloden Moor is a bog land, a flatland. 'Tis a slaughter waiting to happen."

"Have you so little faith in your kinsmen?" Alastair demanded.

"Donnae play with me, lad," Angus said. "If the Young Pretender spent more time with his kin, he would ken Highlanders fight best on slopes no' a wasteland."

"Highlanders fight to the death," Alistair stated.

"Aye, and what good is a dead highlander?" Angus demanded.

"Angus," Niall breathed.

"We are in need of trained men," Iain broke in, sending his son a warning look. Alistair clenched his jaw but remained silent. "What say ye, MacPherson? Will ye join us?"

"I will nae leave my Riona an orphan," he stated. "Nay, I will nae."

"Ye'd turn yer back on yer king?" Alistair demanded.

"Nay, if the Bonnie Prince showed his face on MacPherson lands he would be more than welcome, but I will nae join him in a suicide battle," Angus said firmly.

"I kenned this would be your response, Angus," Iain replied. "And I am sorry for it. I will nae ask ye to change your mind. But would you spare some men? 'Tis well kenned throughout Scotland the MacPherson warriors are the best trained of all Highlanders."

"I will nae let my men be lead to slaughter," Angus said. "But I will nae prevent any of them from joinin' ye of their own free will."

"Then will ye permit us and my men to speak with those who you deem loyal to the Stuart?" Iain asked.

"Aye," Angus sighed harshly. "Under one condition."

"Name it," Iain replied.

"They are to be told everything," Angus said. "I will nae hae them thinking there is a chance at winning. But if they decide to join ye, I will nae stand in the way."

"Good," Niall said. "I'm wit ye, Sutherland."

"What?" Angus growled.

Niall looked at his brother. "What did ye just say, Angus?" Niall asked.

"Did ye no' hear what I said?" Angus demanded.

"Aye, you said you would allow any able-bodied Jacobite of your clan to fight as long as they ken the whole truth. Well," Niall said. "I hae been sitting here the whole time and I say again, I am wit ye, Sutherland."

"Niall, yer me brother," Angus countered. "Do ye honestly think I'll permit it?"

"Aye, because my brother does nae go back on his word," Niall replied. "I will return, Angus, ye have my word."

"Ye better, ye eejit," Angus stated.

The next scene Angus showed me was of Niall walking out of the keep. He paused to give baby Riona a kiss. The little one cried and reached for him.

"Och, come now, me wee lassie," he smiled at her. "Nae need for tha'. Yer ol' uncle'll be back afore ye take yer next step." Kissing her cheek again, he looked at the nursemaid who wiped her eyes. "Promise me ye'll take care of them."

"Aye, Master Niall, I'll look after them," she swore in a choked voice.

"I'm counting on it," he smiled sweetly to her.

The groom had stepped away from his horse standing at the entrance of the gate as Angus held the reins. Niall paused when he saw his brother and, taking a deep breath, he strode forward. Angus's jaw ticked and he blinked back the moisture in his eyes.

"I'll return, Angus," he whispered.

Angus said nothing only grabbed his brother's shoulder and held him tightly. Angus could not hold his tears back.

"I lost Riona, I cannae lose you, little brother," he whispered. Niall gripped his brother's back tighter.

"I hae to do what I feel is right, Angus," he stated. "Ye taught me tha'."

"Aye, I ken," Angus replied. "Just... promise me ye'll come back one way or the other."

"Aye," Niall vowed. "I promise, brother."

"I love ye, Niall," Angus whispered. Niall buried his head into Angus's shoulder.

"Aye, and I love ye, Angus," he said. "Ye're like a da' to me as well as a best friend and brother."

"And like our da', I am so proud of you," Angus replied.

"Take care of our lass," Niall said pulling away from him.

"Aye, I will," Angus answered.

"Tell her about me," Niall pleaded.

Angus took a deep breath as his throat pulsed. "Aye," Angus whispered. "I'll tell her. I'll tell the world what a brave man ye are. And how honored I am to be yer brother."

"I thank ye," he said as the horse danced from one foot to the other beside Angus. Niall took the reins and swung up. Situating his kilt, sword, and cap, Niall looked the true highland warrior sitting tall on his horse. His eyes scanned the bailey, his kin gathered to send him off. Several warriors sat atop their mounts behind him and waited.

"We are Scotsmen," Niall's voice rang out across the courtyard. "And Scotsmen we shall forever be. *Saor Alba*!" He raised his fist into the air as he shouted.

The clan around him, men and women, raised their fists toward him and shouted in unison, "*Creag Dhubh*!" Niall gazed down at his brother as Angus adjusted a strap on the saddle.

"The Pride will be your hope," Angus said.

"Aye, I ken," Niall replied. "Be well, Angus."

"God speed, Niall," Angus said goodbye.

Sitting taller, Niall turned his horse away and led the handful of men out of the gate and across the moor to meet with Sutherland.

"He didn't return, did he," I asked my Angus as my eyes trailed after him, his black hair flying behind him.

Angus was quiet beside me until Niall's form disappeared into the woods. "Nay. He was killed on Culloden Moor along with two thousand Scotsmen. His body is buried in my family crypt beside my parents, my wife, and all our kin. I suppose I should be thankful their resting place had been undisturbed after the English gained control."

"What do you mean?" I couldn't imagine grave robbing.

"The crypt is hidden and only those who know where to look could find it. King George took over Scotland, Prince Charles fled to Skye and everything that made us Scottish was taken from us. We could nae longer speak our language, we could nae longer wear our colors. Our kilts and lands were stripped from us. MacPherson Keep fell under the jurisdiction of Lord Crispin Blackbourne. It wasn't until my Riona was fifteen summers was I able to go to the English court in an attempt to regain my lands, but the English was no' agreeable. While I was in London I met Elizabeth Blackbourne, Crispin's step sister. His father married her mother after their spouses died. Elizabeth... as you saw was beautiful but deadly. She came to my chamber one evening promising to help me regain my lands. I was weak and in need of a woman's touch, ye ken? She convinced me the only way to regain my lands would be to marry her and gain title in the English court. So I did."

I squeezed his hand. "Show me," I said.

He nodded and darkness surrounded us again. This time

when I opened my eyes, a large banquet was before me. Angus stood from his place at the dais and took his goblet.

"On behalf of my wife and I, I want to thank you all for coming. I ask you to raise your glass and drink the health of a lady who has pulled me from the depths of despair. A lady whose beauty is unmatched. My wife, Lady Elizabeth MacPherson," he raised his glass and drank.

"Why did you marry her?" I asked him. "If you knew she was so evil."

"I kenned she was planning something. She promised to help me regain my lands and honestly she did. I bought MacCulloch castle to be closer to the border in order to be able to travel whenever court was in session. It proved a good lodging for us. Even though I got my lands back in the north, we spent most of our time here."

"Was that enough?" I asked. "If she's so evil?"

"I needed to know what she knew and after we were... intimate, it seemed like the best thing to do," he said. "Make an honest woman of her."

"Forgive me but she doesn't seem the type to need you to make an honest woman of. I'm sure she slept around," I said.

"Oh, I was under nae delusion I was her first, nor her last, but it suited us both," he explained.

"What next, Angus?" I asked.

"Forgive me for showing you this next part, lass," he said. "'Tis important or I would ne'er show something so intimate." I nodded. "Keep your eyes closed until I tell ye." Darkness over took me again and the sounds of love making were unmistakable. When the sounds ended, Angus whispered beside me, "'Tis all right now, lass. Ye can look."

I opened my eyes. We were in Ross's room in the castle but the decoration was minimal and the lighting sparse. I could just make out Angus's and Elizabeth's silhouettes in the bed. Angus gathered her to him and kissed her forehead. She said nothing, only pushed away from him and sat up; her nude body glimmering in the firelight. She pulled her housecoat around her and stood.

"Where are ye going?" Angus asked languidly from the bed.

"To my room," she answered in her crisp English accent.

"What?" Angus chuckled.

"To my room, Angus," she said again.

"'Tis our wedding night, lass," he stated beckoning her back. "Come back to bed. What will my men say if you leave my bed after only two hours?"

"I do not care at all what your debauched men think of your… prowess," she said heading for the door. "I have done my duty… you cannot get rid of me now." Angus's face darkened as she left.

"I'm going to be standing to dress in a moment, lass if ye want to avert yer eyes," my Angus said.

I nodded and looked away. Hearing the bed groan as he stood, I waited.

"'Tis all right now," Angus said. I looked back to see him wrapped in a robe. He poured a glass of whisky and stared into the fire. There was a knock on the door and Angus twirled around.

"Come in," he called gruffly.

The door opened and a young man with the most striking blue eyes looked in. His dark blonde hair was cut short circling his head laying shaggy around his ears.

"Laird," he said. "Is anything the matter?"

"Nay," Angus snapped. "What is it, Malcolm?"

"Nothing, Laird," he stated. "I was standing guard outside your door and I saw her ladyship leave. I wanted to make sure all was well."

Angus's eyes narrowed on the boy, no more than twenty. Exhaling harshly, Angus went on.

"All is well, Malcolm, thank ye," Angus said. "And thank ye for yer diligence. How fairs my daughter?"

Malcolm blushed and looked down. "Lady Riona is well. I saw her and her lady's maid retire to their rooms an hour ago," Malcolm answered.

"Thank ye," Angus said. "And Malcolm I want to thank ye for keeping an eye on her throughout this week but especially today."

"There is nothing I would have enjoyed more, my Laird… except protecting you, of course," Malcolm said.

Angus chuckled. He could take care of himself.

"Malcolm, my daughter is approaching marrying age," Angus began. "She is very fond of you. I would like to see her with an honorable man, but more importantly with a man who loves her." Malcolm swallowed audibly. "Think on it," Angus said. "I hope you will consider what I am saying." Malcolm nodded dumbly. "I will be in my solar if anyone needs me. I am relying on your ability to tell them I am still in my chamber and unavailable should they ask. And I do hope what you witnessed here today, lad will go unmentioned," Angus said.

"Of course, Laird," he swore.

"Ye're a good man, Malcolm Brodie," he said. I froze. Brodie was my Scottish grandfather's name; the one who always sang to me. My gaze flew to Malcolm. Those eyes. The brilliant blue. They were the same as my grandfather. My wonderfully sweet grandfather. Were my ancestors part of Angus's clan?

Before I could think any more about it, I was whirled away to the next scene. This time snow fell outside the window and the air was chilled. I wasn't sure if it was several months or years later until I saw Angus, the same age as when I first met him, creeping down the back stairs again. My Angus's hand was still in mine as voices came from one of the rooms near us. I watched as Angus inched forward and looked through a vent.

"He cannot find out, Crispin," Elizabeth said to a man I had ever seen before. "I have exactly what is needed. Tell the Cumberland I will have the Pride in a fortnight's time. The fool is transporting it but thinks I do not know."

"Have you ever seen it?" Crispin asked.

"Not yet, but I know where it is," she answered.

"Just be careful," the man said. His voice had the same clipped English accent as Elizabeth. Crispin reached forward and stroked her face. "I know we can never tell anyone, but you know how I feel," he went on. "Be careful."

"Soon, my love," she said. "Soon all will be behind us. The legacy of the Stuarts will be crushed. They were far too weakened by Culloden but Angus is too clever. He has kept the Pride safe and as soon as it is in the hands of the Hanover, we will be victorious and we will be together.

"I love you, Elizabeth," Crispin said. "Just the thought of

you giving yourself to that brute—"

Elizabeth silenced him with a kiss. I could feel the anger surge through Angus. Again, we were surrounded by darkness. Angus's voice came through the pitch black.

"The vision you saw of my confrontation with Elizabeth, lass, the first vision I was able to share with you? That happened next."

"Why are you showing this to me, Angus? What do I need to know?" I asked still in the darkness.

"Lass, you need to know what's happened," he said. "'Tis important to me."

The darkness abated and I saw Angus running down some stairs I had never seen before. When he threw open the door it crashed against the stone and I saw the MacPherson treasury. Gems, coins and precious stones gleamed but Angus didn't stop, he kept going to the back of the room to a bared door.

Unlocking a cell, barren except for a small chest on a pedestal, Angus's hands trembled as he unlocked the chest and he shuttered. It was empty. Angus's face turned red and his whole body shook. Racing out of the treasury, leaving everything still open, he took the stairs two at a time.

Angus rushed up more stairs and broke into my room in the castle, the painting was still over the fireplace but when he saw Elizabeth wasn't there, he shook even more and raced to the main door. We ended up at the west wing, but I had never seen that area before. Angus opening every door in his search until he stopped before another and we could hear it. The sounds of a woman crying out in sickening pleasure. Angus ripped the door open and nearly tore it off its hinges. Elizabeth and Crispin were together in an old bed as Ross's words came back to me.

*"When Angus found Elizabeth in bed with her step-brother, he became enraged and killed them before turning the pistol on himself."*

Everything happened so quickly. Angus launched himself at Crispin, knocking him off the bed and to the ground. They fought and wrestled as Elizabeth laughed.

"Shut the hell up!" I screamed.

"She cannae hear ye, lass," my Angus replied.

"It makes me feel better," I fumed.

"I ken," Angus replied. After Crispin, who was no match for Angus's brawn, was curled up in a ball on the floor, Angus turned to Elizabeth who had pulled on a robe. She was flicking her raven colored hair out from under the silk and it floated down her back.

"That's quite enough, Angus," she purred.

"I told ye what would happen if ye took another to yer bed," he bellowed. "And no' only that, but ye stole the Pride from me! I'll kill ye for this!"

Elizabeth's face paled. "The P-Pride is g-gone?" She stammered.

"Donnae play the innocent wee lass. I heard all. Ye and this whoreson scheming to take the Highland Pride from me. Where is it?" He roared. "By God in Heaven, I'll have it, even if I have to torture ye for it with me own hands, ye scheming cheating harlot!"

Elizabeth screamed when she saw Angus raise his hand to strike her. My Angus closed his eyes beside me and suddenly there was a terribly loud noise, smoke and a strange smell, like firecrackers on the Fourth of July. Angus stumbled forward.

I screeched as I saw blood coming out of Angus's chest. He pitched forward just as Elizabeth moved out of the way, falling flat on his face, a horrid gurgling noise coming from his body. Elizabeth looked over to where the shot had come from to see Crispin standing aiming a pistol.

"Crispin!" she shrieked. "What have you done? We needed him alive!"

"You lost the Pride, my dear," he said in a devilishly quiet tone and aimed the pistol at her. She backed up.

"Maybe he never had it!" She shrieked.

"Tsk, tsk, tsk," Crispin clucked. "He had it. You were sent to get it. You failed. I am sorry, Elizabeth," he sighed dramatically.

"What do you mean?" she questioned.

"The Butcher had a second plan. In case you could not fulfill your part of the agreement, I had another part to play," he went on.

"Crispin?" she gasped as he cocked the gun.

"I did so enjoy our times together, my dear, but... this is what happens to those who fail the Butcher Cumberland," he fired the gun, the same sound, the same odor and the same smoke swirled around. Elizabeth fell beside Angus, dead. Suddenly, Angus rolled over and fired his own pistol striking Crispin in the chest. Noise in the hallway drew my attention and Malcolm Brodie, a little older than when I first saw him, ran in, a young woman behind me. She screamed and ran to Angus.

"Papa!" she shrieked. My eyes were drawn to Riona, she was nearly twenty and though we looked similar it was not a perfect image like his first wife. Malcolm rushed to his Laird, sliding on his knees at his side. Angus was still alive but his body was convulsing, going into shock. "Papa!" Riona screamed again. "Nay!"

"What happened, Laird?" Malcolm demanded taking in the scene before him.

"I killed her," Angus said in staccato.

"Nay!" Riona and I both screamed.

"I donnae believe it, Papa!" Riona said, tears rolling down her cheeks. "Donnae leave me!"

Angus reached up and caressed her cheek. "I love ye, lass," he said. Tears rolled down my own cheeks.

"Papa, please!" she cried.

"Take care of her, Malcolm. I gave her to you in marriage a year ago, now you must take care of her," Angus said.

"I will, Laird, I swear," Malcolm swore wrapping his arms around Riona.

"Papa, you cannae die! You cannae!" she screamed taking his hands in hers.

"Ken I love ye, me wee lassie," Angus said.

"Papa! I need you! You cannae!" She was crying hysterically now. "Malcolm and I are going to have a baby. Your grandchild! I need you! My baby needs you! Please!"

Angus looked at her and a faint smile crossed his lips.

"I'll always be wit ye, me wee lass," he gasped out. "I love ye."

"Papa!" She screamed as he closed his eyes. He stopped moving and let out a breath. I knew in that instant he had died.

# Chapter Seventeen

"Nikki," Ross's soothing voice broke through my haze. Opening my eyes, I focused on Ross's face as he wiped my cheeks. My chest hurt with unshed tears bubbling to the surface.

"Ross," I whimpered. "He didn't do it. Angus didn't kill Elizabeth."

"Shh, shh," he soothed. I tried to get up but Ross held me down. "Take it easy," he warned. "You've been out for two days. I donnae think you should be getting up yet."

Looking over at him, he looked ragged; his face was covered by stubble I didn't remember. Reaching up, I stroked his face.

"Two days?" I asked.

"Aye, scared me to death," he replied. "'Tis Sunday."

"Oh, you're awake!" A voice from the door called. I looked passed Ross's shoulder to the door. His mother and Marilyn were there with a tray of tea.

"Thank god," Jacqueline said rushing forward after placing the tea tray on the desk. "Ross was so worried for you. He hasn't slept and barely touched two bites."

"Mother, please," Ross said. "What Nikki needs right

now is peace."

"Actually, what I need is food, I'm starving," I replied.

As I ate, we all sat together in the morning room and I told them what had happened.

"So what happened to the Pride?" Chad asked. "If Elizabeth didn't steal it..."

I shrugged. "Maybe someone else wanted it," I offered.

"That harpie!" Marilyn cried. "It's true the English and the Scottish have never gotten along, but still it's women like that who give us bad names."

"Now, now, Mari," Jacqueline patted her hand.

"I think it would be best if we find the Pride," Ross said. "Angus can rest in peace then."

"I want to clear his name too," I stated.

"That might be harder than we think, love," Ross replied. "We've grown up with the story he killed Elizabeth for generations."

"Ross," I said after a moment. "Do you still have that paper we found in the binding of the book?"

"Yeah, it's in my safe," he answered.

"I think the time has come to read it," I said.

"But didn't he say not to yet?" Chad asked. "And who attacked me?"

"Elizabeth," I stated.

Everyone stared at me, then Chad threw his hands up in the air.

"So we have *two* ghosts?" he demanded. I nodded.

"What I want to know," Marilyn began. "Is who let her out? Remember? Angus asked 'who opened the west wing?'"

"Oh, great question, Mari," Jacqueline said. "Does Angus know?" she turned to me.

"I don't think so," then an idea came to me. "Ross, you don't think... Lorna?"

He huffed and ran his hands through his hair. "It wouldn't surprise me. She's a vindictive woman."

"Who's Lorna?" His mother asked.

"My assistant," he answered.

"Why would she do this?" Marilyn asked. "She seems like such a nice girl."

"Because..." Ross sighed. "Because she's in love with me."

"Oh Ross," his mother breathed. "How many times do I have to tell you to never mix business with pleasure?"

"I know," he answered. "It was a mistake. I'll talk to her."

"Not without some supervision," Chad piped up. "I volunteer to put the broad in her place. You don't mess with my girl. I'm shipping you two so you better make some beautiful babies."

I laughed outright. "Well I can't say we don't love trying." Ross stared at me as his mother and Marilyn squealed with excitement. Touching his arm affectionately, I kissed his cheek but my eyes trailed outside to the pump.

Angus stood there staring at me. When he caught my eye, he motioned for me to join him. Sobering, I wiped my mouth and got up. "Excuse me," I said.

"Nikki?" Ross asked.

"I'm okay," I reassured.

Ross looked outside and stood, "Mum, I'll be right back," he said. We walked toward the pump together.

"How is she?" Angus asked Ross.

"*She* is right here," I said.

Angus looked at me. "If I thought you'd have told the truth, lass, I would have asked ye," he said.

I crossed my arms over my chest.

"She's better," Ross answered.

"Are ye any closer to findin' the Pride?" Angus asked.

"Right now my main concern is the safety of my guests," Ross went on. "Who let Elizabeth out?"

"I donnae ken," he said. "But she's locked back up," his eyes trailed up to the west wing third floor window. "Donnae permit anyone to go up there," Angus ordered.

"Aye, I will nae, but, Angus, yer no' the only Laird here," Ross said. "I will follow yer instructions but only because ye ken how to deal with her."

Ross's voice deepened and his accent increased as he

pulled himself up to his full height. I shivered. But then his words hit me. Ross was a Laird. All the romance novels I read, and trust me, I have read my fair share, came back full force. Ross was a Scottish Laird.

"Aye, I kenned yer ancestor Iain Sutherland," Angus did not back down. "But there are things going on that ye cannae possibly ken how to handle."

"Aye, yer right," Ross agreed. "And that is the only reason I'm allowing ye to dictate in my home."

Angus nodded slowly. "I respect that, and ye for saying it. I will figure out who let her out but I beg ye, help me find the Pride," Angus said. Ross nodded. Turning to me, he stroked my cheek. "Tis glad I am yer better, lass," he went on. "Ye gave me a fright."

"I did?" I asked.

"Aye, when ye saw me die, ye fainted and dropped me hand. As soon as ye fell I caught ye but ye disappeared before me eyes," Angus said.

"I'm fine, Angus," I replied. "Confused by a lot of what I saw, but I'm fine."

"Have the nose bleeds stopped?" he asked.

"Not entirely," I admitted. I had a bad one in the shower but I hid it from Ross.

"As you say," Ross addressed Angus. "She will not stop."

"Aye, I hope to heaven you are all right, lass," Angus said.

"When did you say that?" I asked.

"Angus came to me a couple days ago, just after..." Ross let the thought die seeing my blush.

"We spoke of you and how we can help you, no' to stop you but encourage and be there for you," Angus explained. "We worry about ye, lass. But now, I think it would be wise if I left for now. I will come to ye with more information. Please lass, find the Pride."

"I swore to you Angus the first time, I will find it and I will see you rest."

"Aye, and I love you for that," he said.

"I love you too, Angus, I don't know why, but I do," I replied.

"In time you will ken why," he promised, then with a nod

to Ross and a soft smile to me, he disappeared before our eyes.

*Ross*

With so many ideas in her mind, Nikki retired to her room to retrieve her laptop. Coming back out on to the patio to enjoy the surprisingly nice day, I couldn't help but smile as she walked out. Dressed in a Chicago Cubs sweatshirt, jeans that should have been illegal, and a baseball cap, I watched her get situated and smiled when James and Jennifer, two authors she had tea with the other day, came around to see how she was doing and asked to join her. Knowing as authors they would understand her need for silence to write, I found a couple other authors I needed to catch up with and took lunch in the bar.

After a couple hours, I went out to check on her. A glass of, what looked like, coffee and Irish Creme at her elbow and nose deep in her laptop, she was alone. I ached to go over to her and wrap my arms around her. Instead, I went into my office and worked on the second round of edits my editor needed to run by me.

Lorna knocked on my door and tentatively stepped inside.

"What is it, Lorna?" I asked in as cool a manner as I could muster.

"I'm sorry to bother you, sir," she replied. "But I received a confirmation call for your reservation tonight at the Tower Restaurant and wanted to confirm with you to make sure all was well."

*Sunday, shite,* I thought. I had forgotten I asked Lorna to make the reservations. Unsure of Nikki's response to our forgotten date, I picked up the phone to call one of my staff to take her the phone.

"Ms. Thompson is in her room, sir," she replied. "I saw her go up about twenty minutes ago."

"Thank you," I said. "Tell Tower Restaurant we plan on keeping that reservation," I said. "But stress we have other things on our plates and may need to postpone. I will tell you what happens as soon as I talk it over with Ms. Thompson."

"Yes, sir," she answered.

Saving my progress, I shut the laptop and finished the water in my glass. Passing Lorna, I went upstairs to Nikki's room, knocked softly but didn't hear her answer. Gently pushing the door open, I saw she was still hard at work at her laptop, this time at the desk by the window. She saved the file and gently massaged her hand, but still hadn't turned to look at me.

A thought entered my mind and leaning down, I wrapped my arms around her, resting my hands on the keyboard and started to type.

*Leaning down, he could smell the soft minty scent of her shampoo. He took a deep breath wanting nothing more than to bury his nose in its luscious locks and survive off of the smell alone. She leaned her head against his shoulder and he felt a pang of possession and lust rush through him. He knew he would do anything for her because he loved her...*

There was work that needed to be done, but she needed a break and I wanted to spoil her. As she lay unconscious I thought I lost her a thousand times and it made me sick with worry. Never had I worried about a woman the way I worried about Nikki Thompson. Kissing the shell of her ear, smiling when she shivered, I whispered softly, "I love you."

"Oh, Ross," she sighed. "I want to say it, I truly do, but I'm scared. The last man who said that to me broke my heart."

"I'm not Daren, Nikki," I said. "Let me prove it to you."

"I'm just not sure," she admitted and I felt a strange pang in my chest. "There are a lot of unanswered questions between us and I don't know if I'll ever get answers. I want to be with you. But you deserve someone who isn't as messed up or broken as I am."

"I want *you*," I answered. "And you are far from broken. Breakups can be nasty especially the first one who means something to you. I honestly don't know how you women do it. I don't mean it in a sexist way. But, you trust a man with the most intimate part of you, hoping he will hold you as something special. But most men don't. I'm guilty of it, as are most men I know. For someone to give what you gave to Daren and for him to throw it away like he did, hurt you more than I can ever know.

And aye, I ken he was your first," I clarified. She looked away from me as an ashamed look filled her eyes. "Don't you dare," I said. "He is the one who hurt you. What I mean is, it's going to take you time to trust again. You trusted me quickly with your body, but I want this," I tapped her chest where her heart beat and then cupped her cheek. "It will take this time to heal, but I am more than willing to wait. I have never felt this way about anyone. I love you, Nikki Thompson and when you say the words to me, I will cherish them as I cherish you."

Tears ran down her cheeks and for a moment I thought I had overstepped but when she framed my face and kissed me, I released a breath.

"Come to dinner with me tonight," I pleaded. "I have plans. But only if you want."

"What plans?" she asked.

"I want to take you to Edinburgh. There's a restaurant overlooking the castle. I have a bottle of champagne on ice and the chef standing by to make us the best meal you will have in Scotland. Then I'm going to spoon feed you dessert while we enjoy the fireworks from the Edinburgh Military Tattoo. I have a flat on the Royal Mile and it's been made ready for us to stay over if we want or I can have the cabbie drive us home. It all depends on you. But please come to dinner with me tonight."

"I would love to come to dinner with you on one condition," she said.

"Anything," I promised.

"Wear your kilt?" she prompted.

Laughing once, I kissed her gently. "Aye, I'll wear my kilt for ye lass, and I'll be sure to wear it the traditional way."

"No underwear?" she gasped.

"Aye, just like my Highland ancestors did," I teased.

"Could we skip dessert?" she questioned.

"Whatever you say, lass," I grinned.

"Then what time?"

"Be ready in an hour?" I said.

"Deal," she replied.

*Nikki*

I had just finished the last curl of my hair when I heard him knock on my door. I grinned. He was early. Eyeing myself in the mirror, my little red dress and my black Prada pumps made my legs even sexier. The red dress was my favorite purchase during retail therapy after Daren. It hugged my curves and the square neckline cut across my breasts pushed up by my one and only pushup Victoria Secret bra. I felt sexy and I couldn't wait to see Ross's face when I opened the door.

He knocked again. I sprayed some of my perfume just to make sure it was fresh, grabbed the chain of my small handbag off my bed and headed for the door as another knock rang out.

"Yeah yeah, I'm coming, baby. You know you don't have to knock," I said reaching the door. Opening it, I froze as all breath left my lungs when I stared at the man before me.

"Hi, Nikki," Daren said.

END OF PART ONE

# Part Two

# Chapter One

*Nikki*

"Daren?" I breathed.

"Hey," he said again. "Wow," his eyes looked me up and down. "You look amazing."

"What the hell are you doing here?" I demanded.

"I... I had to come see you," he replied. "No one would tell me where you were and when you didn't answer my phone call I was worried something had happened to you or you did something stupid. I remembered you always wanted to come here and when I found the number, I called. Spoke with a woman who told me you were here and I got on a flight. Please, Nik, I just flew seven hours. Can I come in? I really need to talk to you. I need to tell you I'm sorry."

"You're sorry?" I challenged. "Sorry for what, Daren? Stealing five years of my life without giving any of it back? Or maybe you're sorry for ripping my heart out three months ago? Oh no, I know, you're sorry I caused a scene. How's that tie? Did my coffee stain wash out?"

"Nik, please," Daren said, his voice strained. He looked pretty terrible, and I hated the part of me that felt sorry for it. "I'm sorry, baby, I just... I really want to talk to you. Please let me in?"

"Who told you where I was? Who did you speak to?" I demanded.

"I don't know, some woman," he replied.

"Lorna?" I questioned.

"Yeah, I think that was her name," he answered.

"Bitch," I breathed. "Look, I can't do this right now, okay. I have plans for the evening."

"What? You're going out?"

"Yes, what's it to you?" I demanded.

He raised his hands in defense. He wore his typical suit but his tie was stuffed into his inner pocket and his shirt was not the usual pristine crispness he always demanded from the drycleaners.

"I feel terrible," he started.

"Good," I replied.

His shoulders drooped. "My sisters aren't talking to me. My parents think I'm an idiot and our friends said I was a complete jackass for letting you go. And you know what, they're absolutely right."

"So you came here, why?" I demanded.

"I tried to call first, but you didn't answer," he said. "I was worried."

"So when I didn't answer your call, you got on a plane just to come and see me? What about all those times I tried to text you or call you to work things out?" I demanded.

"I know I know," he thrust his hand through his hair. "I'm a fool. Please, Nik, just let me explain. I want to make it up to you."

"You can't, Daren," I replied. "I've moved on."

"What?" His eyes flew to mine. "You're with someone?"

"I'm currently seeing someone, yeah," I answered.

"Are you sleeping with him?" he asked.

"That's none of your business," I replied. "And if I was, at least I now know what a true man is now."

Daren's face constricted. "I thought you were happy with me," his voice was low. "You never complained."

"I was a kid," I said. "You were all I had known."

His eyes searched my face. And after months of pain, I

couldn't stop my hand. I slapped him hard. I don't know why or what came over me, but I slapped him again. Closing his eyes, he didn't try and stop me.

"You took five years of my life, you took everything," I shouted.

"Nikki, can you ever forgive me?" he begged. "I wanna talk it out. Will you let me?"

"No, I want you to leave and take Lorna with you. You two deserve each other," I ordered.

"Nik, please," his voice broke and with it, my resolve.

Looking at him, I was struck by how completely different he was from Ross. Daren looked so much... older. He was still very handsome, but I couldn't really see what had me so enraptured with him for all those years. He was old enough to be my dad and for the first time, he looked it. Against my better judgment, I nodded and opened the door wider for him and shut it as soon as he stepped inside.

"Thanks," he visibly relaxed. "Do you have anything to drink around here?"

"On the table, there's scotch," I gestured.

"Sounds good," he answered. Just then, there was a knock on the door. I closed my eyes. "Who is that?"

"Probably Ross," I answered without explanation. Heading to the door, I took a deep breath. Opening, I was greeted by a bouquet of red roses and a smiling Ross. My heart hurt. I wanted him, not Daren in my room.

"Wow," Ross said. "I donnae know if you want to be wearin' that. I donnae think I'll want dinner, skip straight to dessert." He must have seen something in my eyes because his face changed. "What is it?" he asked.

"It's..." I started.

"Who is it, baby?" Daren's voice came from behind me. He walked up and dropped his arm around my shoulders which I promptly pushed off.

Ross's eyes narrowed on Daren. "Daren, I presume, the arsehole ex?"

"Who the hell are you?" Daren demanded.

"Nikki's *current* boyfriend," Ross answered and offered his hand to me. "Nikki and I have dinner plans." I took his hand, grateful for the confidence he helped me have.

"Actually," Daren replied tugging me back to him by the hip so hard it hurt. "Nikki and I were planning on staying in tonight. We have a lot to talk about. I'm sure there are others who would be interested in having dinner with you."

"No," I said pushing out of his hold and rubbing my hip where his fingers would no doubt leave bruises. "I'm with Ross now, I don't want you."

"What?" Daren demanded.

"I'm over you, Daren," I said. "Ross and I are together now and I don't want you here."

"What happened to talking to me?" his voice grew heated.

"There's nothing you could say that will change my mind," I said.

He looked from one to the other of us and laughed. "It's the accent, right? Because he is so not your type."

"What do you know about me?"

Daren chuckled and drained his drink. "Need I remind you, I was with you for five years, Nik," he said. "I know *everything* about you. The way you respond to me, the little gasp you do when I suck your skin right here," he touched my collarbone and I pulled back into Ross's side.

"You don't get to touch her," Ross said, pushing me behind him. "You are not welcome here. I don't know how you found this place but you are not welcome."

"Lorna," I whispered to him. Ross's back stiffened. "He called my agent and he told him where I was. He spoke with Lorna and she confirmed it." Daren hadn't said anything about my agent but they were friends from college it wasn't a hard jump to make.

"She was an interesting woman to speak with," Daren said.

"As interesting as this conversation is," Ross's tone was tight. "Nikki and I were going out. I'm sure a tight suit like you can find your way out."

"This isn't about you," Daren stated. "By the way, nice skirt," he gestured to Ross's kilt.

"Daren," I snapped. "Ross is twice, three times the man

you ever could hope to be."

"What do you expect from me? You've been cheating on me with this bastard!"

"Cheating on you?" I demanded. "In case you have forgotten, you were the one who broke up with me, Daren Boyle!"

"I never thought you'd go off to Scotland and get laid by a damn horny Highlander!" he cried.

"What?" I was stunned.

"I thought... god, Nikki, it was getting a little too mundane," he confessed. "I wanted to spice things up."

"Three months, Daren," I breathed. "Three *months!*" I shrieked stepping around Ross. "You left me for three months without phone call, text, email, or visit. What was I supposed to do? I couldn't write, I couldn't think straight, my world was turned upside down. And you say it was all because you got bored in bed?" I demanded. "Ever thought maybe it was *you* who needed to be a little more inventive?"

"You want inventive?" he challenged. "I'll show you inventive."

Rushing to me, Daren knocked Ross down and grabbed my arms so tightly I cried out. His eyes were wild and angry as he slammed me against the wall. His lips clashed against mine.

"Let go of me!" I screamed. Ross got to his feet and barreled into him knocking him away from me. But Daren elbowed him in the temple and Ross fell unconscious. Rushing over, Daren grabbed me before I could get to him.

"You wanted inventive," he bellowed as he pulled me into the room and slammed the door.

"*You* wanted inventive," I shouted. He pushed me down to the floor and was immediately over me. "Get off me!" I hit his chest, but he wouldn't budge.

"Shut up!" He roared. "I'll teach you to complain about me, you cheating whore. What does he have that I don't? Huh?" The back of his hand smacked across my face. Stunned and dazed, I shook my head.

This wasn't my Daren. This couldn't be my Daren. My Daren would never do this to me. He would never hurt me. Never force me. This wasn't right. Something was wrong.

"Where's the Pride?" Daren demanded.

*What?* I didn't know if I was delusional or if he was actually asking about the Pride? How could he know about that? Hitting him again, I reached forward and latched my teeth on his forearm. He reared back in pain and covered his arm. That gave me all I needed. Kneeing him between the legs, he doubled over and howled. Elbow to the side of the cheekbone, and fingers to the eyes. He cried out but gripped my wrists again. He had near superhuman strength as he forced my arms above my head.

"Ross!" I screamed at the top of my lungs. "Angus! Chad!"

Hoping one of them heard me. I was no match for him. If they didn't come to me soon, Daren would rape me and probably kill me. I closed my eyes and for the first time in a very long time, I prayed.

*Shout it, lass!* I heard my Grandpa Brodie, dead many years, scream at me. Without another thought, the same phrase I had said earlier in Gaelic came to me and it thundered from my lips.

"*Creag Dhubh!*"

Daren flew backwards hitting his head against the wall across from me. I tried to catch my breath and rolling to my side just in time to see him get to his feet, I screamed again. Just then the door burst open and Ross and Chad ran in.

"Nikki!" Ross and Chad yelled running to me as Ross barreled into Daren. They fought on the ground for a couple heart-stopping moments. Chad grabbed me and held me to his chest.

"Ross," I panted clutching at Chad. "Ross."

"Are you okay?" Chad gasped.

"No," I replied but immediately felt something was wrong. Looking over, I saw Daren on top of Ross, his hands around his throat. Ross's hands clawed at Daren's grip. "No!" I screamed.

"Elizabeth, get outta him!" Angus appeared and reached into Daren's neck, his hand disappearing for a moment but when he pulled back, he clutched black smoke. That thing had been inside Daren. Possessing him. Elizabeth. Daren slumped on top of Ross. "I told ye to leave her alone!"

"Angus!" I cried.

He looked at me then disappeared, taking Elizabeth's black smoke form with him.

Ross coughed and grunted as he tried to shift Daren off him. Daren wasn't moving and his eyes were closed. *Oh god, is he dead?*Leaving Chad's embrace, we rushed to Ross and helped him sit up.

"Are you okay?" Ross asked as I hugged him tightly to me.

"I'm fine, are you?" I asked framing his face. He coughed but nodded. "Are you sure?" I asked, his temple beginning to bruise from Daren's first hit. "I'm so sorry," I cried.

Ross held me to his chest, his breathing ragged but he held me. Reaching up to his face, I cried when I saw blood from his busted lip.

"I'm all right," Ross stressed. "Are you?"

I nodded but still tears streamed down my cheeks. Ross had been there, he had tried to save me, protect me and I had gotten him hurt. But all I could think to say was what was in my heart.

"I love you," I said. Ross stared into my eyes, finally a smile crossed his lips and he kissed me quickly.

"I love you," he replied.

A groan broke us from the moment and we looked over to where Chad was tapping Daren's face.

"Is he alive?" I asked.

"Yes," Chad answered. "But not for long if he doesn't answer my questions. I'm all for peace but I want to kill this bastard."

"Nikki?" Daren groaned.

"Yeah, I'm here," I turned back to him. His eyes opened and Chad helped him sit up against the wall.

"What happened?" he asked.

"What do you remember?" I asked him not wanting to leave Ross's embrace.

"I got to your room, met... him," he indicated Ross. "Then it's all a little fuzzy after I finished the drink. Dear god, what do you guys put in that stuff over here?"

"You're okay," I assured.

"Yeah, but I have the biggest hangover of my life," he

replied. "And that's saying something."

"You aren't drunk," I said.

"I'm not?" he questioned. "Sure I am. I know what drunk is, baby. I remember bits and pieces but it's all so hazy." Then as if realization or memory came back to him, my Daren, the man I had loved for five years, appeared in his eyes. Reaching toward me, I recoiled but his hands were gentle this time and he passed a thumb over my cheek, throbbing with pain. "Oh my god, Nikki, did I hurt you? I'm so sorry! What did I do? Are you all right?"

"I'm fine," I stated. "Really."

His hands passed over me, cradling my face but I pulled away from him and rested my cheek against Ross's shoulder. His arms tightening around my shoulders. Daren looked at him then me, then Chad.

"What the hell happened?"

"First, I need to know one thing," Chad began.

"Who are you?"

"I'm her bestie," he replied. "Do you remember hurting my man Ross and then attacking Nikki?"

"Attacking?" his eyes flew to mine.

"You nearly raped her, you son-of-a-bitch," Chad began.

"Chad, please," I cut him off.

"What?" Daren's eyes flashed with shock. "Is this true?"

"Look at her face, you bastard," Ross growled. "And even though it's embarrassing, my temple doesn't thank you for that elbow. Look at me."

"What the hell?" he asked.

"Guys," I started. "We've been through hell and I don't know about you but I need a drink. There's a lot of stuff going on and none of this is anyone's fault but Elizabeth's."

"Who's Elizabeth?" Daren asked.

"Something you don't have to worry about," I said, then turning to Ross. "Can we go on that date now?"

Ross sighed. "Let's postpone? Tuesday night?"

"Promise?"

"Swear it," he answered.

"Then, come on, Daren, we have a lot to tell you," I said.

*Ross*

I had never been more scared than when I woke in the hallway, Chad bending over me and Nikki screaming in her room. With his help, Chad and I burst through the door but something innately primal snapped inside me when I saw Daren braced over Nikki. Now we sat at one of the high tables in the smallest bar on site, my head pounding but Nikki alive and well beside me and her ex sitting across from us rubbing his forehead after she had finished explaining what happened. In his defense, and I say this lightly, it was a lot to take in, especially for an American who never grew up with ghosts.

"I don't believe it," he said.

"Well believe it, honey because you were just possessed by the spirit of the crazy lady of the keep," Chad replied.

"Why have you stayed?" Daren demanded. "Why haven't you shut this place down? And you've allowed her to do this?" His heated gaze traveled to me.

My fist clenched. "I did nae *allow* Nikki to do a damn thing. She's an adult and can make her own decisions, damn you."

"Dare," she stopped us from fighting again. "Ross wanted me to leave but I refused. You know how I can be when I set my mind to something."

"Baby, I get that, but this isn't safe. If your father was here..." he started but let the thought trail off.

"If my father was here he would say the same thing. And Daren, I already have a father, I don't need another one. I know it's your instinct to be a father being fifteen years older, but I never looked at you like that and until now I didn't realize you looked at me that way. We are over, Daren, you wanted it, so you got it. I am not yours. I am no man's but Ross treats me like a partner, not a child."

Damn she was sexy. In a complete caveman moment, I pulled her close to me and kissed her, claiming her as mine before the one man I worried could take her from me. But the look in her eye when I pulled back told me I had nothing to worry about.

She looked over at Daren, his face downcast, eyes studying the wood of the table.

"I'm sorry," he said.

"I need one question answered," she said. He looked up at her. "Why?"

He leaned back against his chair letting out a deflating breath. "I don't know," he confessed. "I..." he huffed a sigh and thrust his hands through his hair. "I was scared. I'm sorry Nikki but I felt trapped. I knew when Ben asked Dad and me for our blessing on asking Jess to marry him I knew you would want to get married and our whole life flashed before my eyes. A house in the suburbs, kids, a dog, and I... didn't want it." That was all right by me, because I sure as hell wanted it. "So when you mentioned it, I saw my way out and I took it. I'm sorry I hurt you."

"That's all I ever wanted, Daren," she replied confidently and yet tears pooled in her eyes. Chad reached forward and took her hand. "I was hurt. Deeply hurt but it helped me find what I needed to find... myself. Without you, I wouldn't have come here."

"It was a foolish thing. But I had to come here."

"That reminds me," I spoke up. "How did you know where she was?"

"My friend from college is her agent and he found out from her publisher. Then, when I called to ask, a woman told me she was here."

"Lorna?" I questioned.

"Yes," he replied.

My hand clenched around the tumbler of whisky I had on the table. She had stepped over the line again after our talk. It was time. We would have another one soon, where I relieved her of her duties.

"Well," he tossed the whisky back and set the glass down. "I think I've made enough of a fool of myself and I have said all I can. And I see I'm not needed here," he looked down at her hand on my arm. "I'll leave as soon as I finish my drink."

Her grip on my forearm increased. Looking down at her, she pleaded with me with those damn blue eyes I never had a chance of resisting. I covered her hand with mine and looked back at Daren.

"No," I said and instantly winced at the words. I wanted him out of my castle and away from my woman, but she didn't want me to turn him out especially in the rain... though... the thought was pleasing to me. "No, you will stay the night, recover from your ordeal. We have plenty of room. Don't worry about, Nikki. She'll be staying with me."

*Nikki*

There was no place in the world I would rather be than in my lover's arms. Ross held me tightly to his side in the pitch blackness of his room. Running my fingers through his chest hair as he stroked my back, I was content and the words stumbled from my lips.

"I love you, Ross," I said.

I felt his whole body slacken, which was the complete opposite reaction from the one I had received from Daren when I told him. I don't know why but Ross's reaction felt right.

"I love you too, Nikki," he replied kissing my head. "Now sleep. You need your rest. The medicine to help your headache will start working. I love you, baby. I love you."

"Say it again," I said softly.

"I love you."

And for the first time, I truly believed it.

# Chapter Two

Ross's chest rose and fell as he breathed and my head rode the lulling motion, he was still asleep. I moved slightly away from him and was greeted by a small moan; his arm tightened around me. My fingers trailed up and down his chest until, "Still asleep?" A male voice called from the main door.

"Come on, man! What's gotten into you?" Another male voice called as the door closed.

*Oh god!* I wanted to scream. *Not them!* I didn't think I could live through the mortification as Gerard and Graeme waltzed into Ross's room. Gerard stopped dead in his tracks causing Graeme to bump into him.

"What the hell, man?" Graeme asked of his brother. Gerard just stood there with a stupid grin on his face as he looked at me cowering beneath the sheets.

"Hiya, Nikki," Gerard said brightly.

"Nikki?" Graeme questioned. He peered around his brother and pushed him out of the way when he saw me. "Nikki! Well, looks like you're settling in here pretty well!"

Ross groaned as his eyes fluttered open and he gazed at his two best friends.

"Graeme, Gerry," he grinned sleepily. "Good to see ya." Then turning to me, cowering into his side, he mirrored their stupid grin. "Morning, baby," he said before kissing me, making the twins hoot and holler. "All right, lads, ye've had yer fun, let the lady and I get up and dress."

"Hmm..." Graeme started. "Do you want to leave, Gerry?"

"Nope," Gerard answered. I looked over at him as if he had just betrayed me, it only made him grin even more. But then his face changed and immediately I felt the throb of my cheek where Daren had slapped me last night. "What did you do to her, mate? She looks beaten up. You never said you into that..."

"Shut up," Ross countered. "You know I'm no'. There's been some strange occurrences here."

"Och aye, is that what they're calling it these days?" Graeme asked. "We want details."

"Go find yer mum, she'll give ye all ye need," Ross replied.

"Where'd she be?"

Ross glanced at the clock. "At this time? Probably sharing a cuppa with mum."

"Jackie's here?" Gerard asked.

"Aye, she arrived last week," Ross explained.

"Cannae go far without mummy?" Graeme teased.

"Shut up," Ross replied throwing a decorative pillow at him. Graeme caught it, laughing but the twins left the room and Ross lifted the sheet I had tossed over my head. "All clear now, love, you can come out. They've gone."

"Thank god," I answered pulling the sheet and comforter down and under my arms.

I sent him a steely look when he chuckled as I wrapped the sheet around me and stole it from the bed as I stood. Ross still lounged completely uncovered and interlocked his fingers behind his head. I had to change the subject to prevent my eyes from wandering.

"Thanks for getting rid of them," I said.

"No worries, they like to play," he answered.

"Oh, who's their mom?" I asked.

"Marilyn," he answered.

"That makes sense," I snickered. Ross stretched and

yawned, promptly wincing when his busted lip and temple throbbed. I sat down on the side of the bed and gently passed my hand over his temple. "Thank you for saving me."

"You saved yourself, love," he turned and kissed my palm.

"Still," I shrugged. "Does it hurt?"

"A little, but it's not terrible," he replied.

I nodded, but lay down and curled up against his side again. "Thank you for not turning him out even though he deserved it."

"I know you would be worried about anything outside last night, that storm was supposed to be pretty bad," he replied stroking my arm.

"I would," I agreed.

"Did you get the answers you needed?" he asked.

"Not the answer I was hoping for but yes I did," I admitted. "I love you."

I felt his smile as he leaned down and kissed my forehead. "I love you too, Nikki."

"Where do you think the Pride is?" I finally asked. "And why does Elizabeth want it?"

"I think she wants it because that was her mission in life, it's what she died for," Ross said. "And I think the Pride could be anywhere. But I doubt it has left Scotland. I believe it may be buried."

"I want to go to Culloden," I said. "Is it far?"

"No' really," he answered. "It's about an hour and half depending on traffic and my speed."

"Do you think we could go today?"

"How about tomorrow? I think we both need a rest after the hell we went through. I also have something pressing to do today and I can't postpone it."

"Lorna?" I asked.

"I gave her another chance but she broke the league's confidentiality agreement," he replied. "She should never have said anything to Daren about you being here. That is an offence in itself, let alone I told her if she does anything like that again she was out."

"I understand," I said.

"You're not going to stop me?" he questioned.

"No," I answered. "I don't like her and I can't trust her."

"Good, me neither," he said. "Now let's shower and get down to breakfast."

When Ross and I eventually made it downstairs and into the breakfast room, Graeme, Gerard, Marilyn and Jacqueline looked up at us with the same silly grins and I could clearly see the familial resemblance between the three.

"Is it so strange for them to see you with a woman?" I asked Ross as we went to the coffee and tea section.

"No," he replied. "It's just strange for them to see me in love." I stopped. "What is it?" Ross looked over at me.

"I love you."

Ross stared in my eyes and before I could even breathe, he grabbed me to him and kissed me, twirling me around. The room broke out into applause and I wrapped my arms around his neck not letting go until we were both breathless.

Finally, Ross set me down and held me close. I laid my head on his shoulder, breathing him in. When I opened my eyes and looked over his shoulder, Daren was standing in the doorway. He looked down when he caught my eye, took a deep breath, pinched the bridge of his nose, turned and walked out. Pulling away from Ross, I gazed up at him.

"Go," he whispered.

"I'll be right back," I promised.

Following Daren out of the castle, I found him under the overhang with a single bag by his side.

"Dare," I called softly. His back straightened and his shoulders rose and fell. Slowly he turned to me, his eyes were red. Five years and I had never seen him cry. I took a step toward him but he raised his hand to stop me.

"Nikki, don't," he said. "Please," his voice was thick with emotion.

"I'm sorry, Daren," I whispered.

"Don't apologize, for god's sake," he answered softly. "You have nothing to apologize for. But... I do. I took so much from you and I can't give any of it back."

"Would you want to?" I asked feeling a sting in my heart.

"No," he breathed, looking down.

I stared at him for a long time. Taking a tentative step toward him, I spoke the words I had wanted to say for weeks.

"There were a lot of firsts with you, Daren," I started. "My first kiss, my first lover and my first heartbreak. But the one thing I need to tell you before goodbye is, you were my first love and no one can ever take that from you. You will always be the man who pulled the turtle from her shell. The inspiration and support for *Secret Revenge,* and I will never regret loving you because without you I would never have made it here. So, there were a lot of firsts with you, Daren, including my first goodbye." He didn't prevent the single tear that slid down his cheek.

"Goodbye, Nikki," he whispered "I did love you. I just wasn't ready."

"There is someone for you, Daren," I encouraged. "It just wasn't me."

He nodded slowly. "And the man for you, is waiting inside," he said.

"I believe he is," I answered.

"Be careful, Nikki," he pleaded. "I don't know or understand what's going on here, but one thing I do know is, it's dangerous."

"I will be fine," I answered.

"I know you will," he sighed. "Be well, Nikki and be happy."

"And you, Daren, be happy," I squeaked out as my throat closed with emotion.

"Mr. Boyle?" a taxi driver pulled up and got out.

"Yeah?" Daren answered discreetly wiping the tear streak on his face as he turned.

"Hopkins, sir, can I take your bags?" he offered.

"Thanks," Daren said. Once everything was situated and the cabbie opened the door for him. Daren turned back to me. We were silent for a moment but soon he took a deep breath and whispered, "bye, Nikki."

"Goodbye, Daren," I replied.

Watching as he got into the backseat of the taxi, a huge

weight lifted from my shoulders. The cab drove away and Daren didn't look back. He was officially out of my life, out of my heart and I had the closure I so longed for. Ross walked outside and rested his hands on my upper arms.

"You okay?" Ross asked.

"Surprisingly," I started. "Yeah."

"Come on, you must be hungry," he whispered kissing the shell of my ear.

"Starving," I answered.

"Well, we cannae have that," he said taking my hand and leading me inside.

# Chapter Three

## *Ross*

After breakfast, I called Lorna into my office and informed her her services were no longer required. She cried but she had made her bed, it was time for her to lie in it. She cleared out her things and I posted a job description on a job board stating the first thing I was looking for was discretion and loyalty.

Mum knocked on my office door just as I was about to call a friend from Uni who ran a staffing agency.

"Mum," I smiled and stood. "Please, sit. Are you all right?"

"Oh, yes, darling," she answered and took a seat in front of me. "Is everything all right with you?"

"Yes, why?"

"Well, I couldn't help but notice the bruise on your temple and the one on Nikki's cheek. What happened?"

"Long story," I huffed and leaned back.

"I have time," she stated.

Knowing she wouldn't stop until I told her, I leaned forward and steepled my fingers under my chin, prepared to tell her everything that happened, still keeping Nikki's confidences about her ex.

Once I had finished the story, Mum looked at me with that all-too-knowing-gaze mothers seem to have when they know something is wrong with their children.

"You have let that woman go?" she asked.

"She's gone," I confirmed.

"And Nikki's ex?" she asked.

"Also gone," I replied.

"Good," she nodded. "And you and Nikki?"

"Are prepared to give it a go," I revealed.

"Oh, love I'm so happy," she said softly. "I do like her."

"Me too," I teased. "But I sense there's something else you need to talk to me about?"

"There was something," she looked down at her interwoven fingers in her lap.

"Is everything all right?" I asked, suddenly nervous. I kicked myself for not being more available to her in the last year.

"Oh, yes, sweetheart, I'm perfectly fine," she replied and I breathed easier.

"Then what is it?" I asked.

"I was wondering..." she started. "Now that Lorna is gone, you'll need someone to help with this place." My brows furrowed but I listened. "I love Sutherland Estate, but I'm lonely up there. It's a quiet place and without you, I don't want you to feel guilty, but without you visiting or living there, there's so much that reminds me of your father, I sometimes feel I'm suffocating." She took a deep breath and continued. "I would like to move here permanently."

"Close up the old house?" I clarified.

"Yes, open it up during hunting and game times but I can't live up there by myself. Now you don't have to pay me but I would like to help run this place. You forget I ran Sutherland Estate for nearly forty years."

"No no, of course I remember, it was run perfectly," I said. "But why?"

"I miss your father," she replied as tears gathered in her eyes and in true English fashion, she cleared her throat and stopped the tears. "I need to stay busy. Or date again. And since I don't see anyone I like and cannot imagine dating again so soon, I need to stay busy."

"All right," I waved her off. I didn't want to hear about my mother dating again. "But you know I would support you if you did find someone you liked, so long as he was worthy of you."

"I know, darling, and I love you for saying that," she said. "But what do you say? Do you think I could stay on here? Help run the hotel after the retreat?"

"I don't see why not," I replied. "And of course I'll pay you."

"Oh, no darling, honestly your father took good care of us both and I don't need it. Distribute it out as raises for everyone else," she said.

"All right," I agreed.

"Now what about this assistant position you have open? Perhaps someone of the male variety? Someone who won't want to sleep with you and that way you can keep business and pleasure separate."

"I don't see myself sleeping with anyone else but Nikki," I didn't mean for that to slip out and of course my mother jumped on it.

"I knew it!" she cried. "Oh when is the wedding?"

"Whoa, mum slow down, we've only been together not even a month," I said.

"And what does that mean?" She questioned. "The first moment I saw your father in his kilt I knew and I tell you we had some fun even that first night."

"Mum, I love you but I really don't want to know about this," I replied.

"All I'm saying is, when you know you know and Connor asked me to marry him within three months of meeting me," she said.

"Don't tell me that, your father and his knew each other, I swear you donnae think I remember you both played together as children?"

"And we didn't see each other for nearly fifteen years after that," she reminded me. "All I am saying, love is if you love her and she loves you don't over think things."

"We both have too much on our minds at the moment,

maybe after both our novels are out then *possibly*."

"Once this novel is out another will come and another and another, it's time for you to settle down and start giving me grandbabies," she said.

"So that's it, huh?" I teased leaning back in my chair. "You just want some grandkids."

"Of course," she cried. "Mari and I were talking about it earlier before the twins came over. Oh and Graeme said he has to talk to you about a flat in Edinburgh? Said he needs to run something by you he heard from the agent."

"When were you going to tell me this?" I asked gently.

"I just did," she answered.

"I need to talk to him," I said.

"Where's Nikki?"

"I'm giving her the day to rest, she needs it," I answered standing. "But she's in her room, I think."

"You are an admirable man, Ross," she patted my cheek as she walked out the door. "Your father would be so proud of you. Be sure to talk to him, it keeps his memory alive and he's always with us."

Her words gave me pause. I had been angry at my dad when I found out about the cancer. I begged him to stop smoking so many times as a kid until I started doing it. But he was the most amazing man I ever met and I missed him dearly. He was my best friend. I wished Nikki had been able to meet him.

Mum left the room and I was alone. Memories of my father flashed before me and I felt the sting of tears the recently loss always brought. Sighing, I wiped my eyes and was about to leave to find Graeme but felt a hand on my shoulder. Turning, Angus stood behind me.

"Are you all right, lad?" he asked.

"Aye," I answered.

"I'm sorry, I did nae mean to listen but I heard what your mother said," he replied. "Your da' died?"

"Aye," I said. "A year ago."

"I'm sorry," he said. "I ken what it is like to lose a father. 'Tis a heavy burden for all but especially those of us who have to lead others."

"I just wish he could be here now," I confessed.

"Did you get a chance to say goodbye?"

"I did," I admitted.

"That always helps the pain," Angus nodded slowly. "I am here if you need to talk. I am nae your father of course, but I can listen."

"Thank you," I said.

"I do see how strange this is, lad," he replied. "I am a ghost and it must be odd for you."

"A bit," I confessed.

"Not to worry," Angus smiled. "I heard you were going to take Nikki to Culloden tomorrow?"

"Aye, she wanted to go."

"Good. But make sure she's careful," he said. "I will try to journey with you but I have nae been able to travel much without someone helping me."

"What do you mean, helping you?" I asked.

"Letting me in to journey with them," he explained.

"Like possession?"

"Elizabeth possess," he went on. "I would merely be there, in the back of the mind."

"Body sharing," I said.

"Aye," he answered.

"A specific person or anyone?"

"Anyone willing," he explained.

Slowly I nodded then went on, "you have my permission for tomorrow."

"I thank you," he said. "I promise it will nae hurt you."

"I trust ye," I replied. "But now I need to find Graeme."

"Which of the twins is that one?"

"The boisterous one," I answered.

"He's in the library bar," Angus said. "The other is in the main library."

"As I expected, that fits them well."

"So I gathered," Angus laughed. "Graeme is pursuing one of your staff members, a young woman."

"Annie?" I asked, she was the only young one I employed now that Lorna was gone.

"Aye."

"I'd better stop that," I said. "I promised Annie's

grandfather I would take care of her."

Angus's laugh followed me as I left the office and searched for Graeme.

# Chapter Four

*Nikki*

I skyped with dad for a little while as Ross took care of his business with Lorna. I hated he had to fire her but a part of me was glad he did. I knew I could never trust her. Marilyn and Jacqueline caught me just as I came inside and asked me to tea. I hung up the skype call with dad and joined them.

Wondering where Ross was, I looked around the room to the door where he and the twins sauntered in. Seeing them side by side struck me... there was something almost familial between them. Though Ross was dark haired and blue eyed like his mother, the bone structure was nearly the same and when they turned to look at each other, smiling and teasing, their profiles were identical. Unsure why I never noticed it before, I greeted them as they walked to our table.

"Look at you, Graeme," his mother tsked. "Whose lipstick is that on your collar this time?"

"Afraid I didn't quite get a name," he answered with a wide grin as he sat down and placed the cloth napkin across his lap.

His twin just shook his head but turned to me.

"I wanted to tell you, Nikki, I finished your book. I

couldn't put it down," Gerard said.

"I'm glad you liked it, Gerard," I replied.

"Gerry, please," he told me. "Any plans for a sequel?" Taking the tea pot from his mother, he poured his cup and passed it to Graeme beside him.

"Not as yet," I confessed. "But I do have a story I'm working on."

"Grand," he smiled.

"It features this place and of course all of you," I teased.

"Did you get my princely good looks down, darlin'?" Graeme asked.

"I don't think you'll be disappointed at how I portrayed you," I answered.

"Nikki wants to go to Culloden Moor tomorrow," Ross said. "Anyone want to join?"

"Yeah, I'd like to," Gerard answered.

"Me too," Graeme said.

"Mum? Marilyn?" Ross asked.

"I've already seen it, sweetheart," Jackie stated. "I'll pass it, makes me cry every time."

"I wish I could, loves," Marilyn replied. "But my mind is working overtime with these ghostly ideas for a romance."

"Between a ghost and a human? Seriously mum?" Graeme asked.

"And why not?" she questioned. "If I met Fearsome MacPherson... well, I love you boys but hello ghosty!"

We all chuckled knowing Marilyn was only just slightly teasing.

"It's nearly five," Gerard started. "What plans do you guys have?"

"Unfortunately, my evening will be filled with looking for an assistant," Ross said.

"What happened to Lorna?" Graeme asked.

"I had to let her go," Ross explained. "There were... issues."

"Told you, you owe me ten pounds, Ger," Graeme slapped his hand on his twin's back.

"What?" Ross asked.

"We were betting if you slept with her. I said you

wouldn't mix business with pleasure," Gerard grumbled pulling out his wallet and handing his twin the ten pound note. "You let me down, Ross."

"Oh, gee, I'm sorry," Ross rolled his eyes. "I'm not the one who took bets on their friend."

"Well we were going to bet how long it would take Nikki to get into your bed but then we both figured it would be within the week so we didn't accept," Graeme said then flinched when his mother kicked him under the table.

"Actually, I think it was within forty-eight hours, wasn't it, Ross?" I asked playing along.

"Something like that," he grinned.

"You couldn't resist me," I sighed dramatically.

The rest of tea time passed in jokes and stories of when the boys were young, but one thing I noticed was how none of them spoke of Graeme's and Gerard's father. I held the thought for later.

Ross got a phone call at the table and excused himself. Graeme and Gerard were eager to hit the golf course for a quick round while the sun was still up and I needed to work. Leaving the table with the promise to do it again soon and with Chad, I went up to my room. Wanting to check in on him, I went to his door and reached up to knock but stopped when I heard the keyboard typing and him muttering something to himself. He was busy and I knew how it could be to be in the middle of an idea and be interrupted.

Walking down to my room, I locked the door behind and went to my laptop to continue writing.

When my phone alarm buzzed seven o'clock, time for dinner, I saved my work and stood, stretching my back. A knock on my door, caught my attention and walking over to it, I grinned when I saw Ross holding a bottle of champagne, two glasses, and a to-go bag with some absolutely delicious smells.

"Room service," he said.

"How did you know?" I asked. Shrugging, he stepped inside.

"I was hungry too," he kissed me. "I wanted to curl up with you, eat, have this champagne and talk. About anything. I don't care, but I want to get to know the woman I'm in love with."

"That sounds amazing," I said. "I want to get to know the man I love too."

Curled up together on the bed, Ross and I laughed and teased each other, made out and tickled one another. I told him about my carefree mom and he told me that Marilyn and his mother would get along famously with her.

"Tell me about your dad," I said. Marilyn and Jacqueline had only mentioned him in passing. Ross breathed out quickly and I could see the pain of his father's death was still heavy in his eyes.

"Da' was..." he cleared his throat. "Da' was amazing. He taught me everything I know. Ever since I was little, he taught me my place, my position in society but most importantly, he taught me humility. We serve at the people's pleasure, not our own. He taught me in order to lead, I must first do. I should be willing to work the field right alongside my men not leading from atop a horse. I need to be willing to put me own blood, sweat and tears into the earth just like my ancestors, because that will make me a real man more than all the money, fame or women could. Since he died, I've tried to be the type of man he would be proud of."

"I'm sure he is," I said. "You are such a good and honorable man, I know he would be very proud of you; of the man you are, as I am."

"We had our disagreements of course what father/son doesn't, but I've always love him. And I miss him horribly."

"How did he die?"

"Cancer," he said. "He smoked two packs a day and had a cigar every night before bed. Graeme, Gerard and I quit smoking when he got the diagnosis and made us swear to stop."

"I'm so sorry," I replied hugging him close. "Can I ask you something?"

"Anything," he stated.

"When I saw you, Graeme and Gerard come into the tea room today, I was struck by how similar you three look. Are you related? Who is Marilyn's husband?" I asked.

Ross stiffened beside me, his jaw ticking as he clenched it. Surprised by his reaction, I turned to face him. He had nearly turned to stone, that's how motionless he was. Gently rubbing his leg, I waited for him to speak.

"Marilyn is not married," he finally said.

"Oh," I replied. "I was just curious who is Graeme's and Gerard's dad." He swallowed hard but did not answer. My stomach pitched as a thought occurred to me. "Oh god, Ross... it wasn't... I mean it couldn't have been... your dad?" I asked.

"No," Ross said quickly then sighed. "I don't know," he admitted. "No one does."

"What do you mean?" I asked.

"I mean dad and Marilyn disappeared around the same time thirty-three years ago and when he returned he told no one what had happened. Nine months later Marilyn returned with twin sons and everyone thought... especially when dad wouldn't divulge why he disappeared."

I snuggled into him. "You don't honestly think that. I mean your mom would never be so close to her if they... shared a man. I don't think as a woman, they could be so close."

"I don't want to believe it and I honestly don't. I just don't know why he wouldn't tell anyone. They could be my half-brothers and we wouldn't know," he said.

"Do they know it's a possibility?" I asked.

"Oh yeah," he answered. "In a village the size of Brora, where we all grew up, it's not hard for gossip to spread and stay with the name even years later. Graeme and Gerard were labeled 'the bastard sons of that romance writer'."

I gasped. "Oh my god, that's terrible."

"Aye," he breathed. "'Tis, but it is what it is."

"But I thought that Gerard had inherited the family distillery and Graeme had the farm..." I said.

"Reverse it," he replied. "Gerard has the farm and Graeme has the distillery. And Marilyn's grandfather and father were Scots and that is the Fergus name they took. She also goes by a pseudonym."

"And the distillery isn't in Brora," my mind trailed off trying to remember the city Graeme had said on the plane.

"No, it's in Ullapool," he said.

"I'd like to see it," I replied. He smiled and kissed me softly.

"I'd like you to see it too," he said.

After a moment, I asked, "could there be any other reason for their mutual disappearance?"

"Like what?" Ross asked drinking from the champagne flute. "And why wouldn't he tell anyone the truth?"

"I don't know why he wouldn't tell anyone, but," I paused. "Maybe... he was helping her out? Maybe he was playing the Darcy to her Lydia? Maybe he was trying to find the guy who got her pregnant."

"If he had done that why would he not say anything? Why wouldn't he talk about it? Why let everyone affected by it go through it? And my mum? She went through a lot too. I was too young to understand it, but when I was older I heard all about it," he answered.

"Maybe he didn't say anything because the truth was worse?" I offered.

"Worse than being labeled an adulterer and the children bastards?" He questioned.

"I know it's painful and I know you don't believe it, but maybe there's a side of it we don't know."

"I miss him. More than anything I wish I could sit down with him one more time."

I snuggled deeper into him and kissed his jaw.

"I know, I wish that for you too and I wish I could have one more day with my grandpa Brodie," I said.

"I would have liked your grandpa, I think," he replied.

"And he would have liked you, too."

I was crying. I didn't know why but I was sobbing harder than I have ever wept before and holding tightly to someone. Clutching them close, I finally looked up and saw Malcolm Brodie gazing down at me. He tried to smile as he soothed my hair back.

"It'll be all right, love," he whispered. "Come away."

I looked beside me and saw the pump; the old rusted pump was shiny and new.

"He should have been buried with pride back home," I cried, not knowing what I was saying.

"I ken, love, but for now he is buried with your love," he replied.

"He should be with my mother and my uncle. Not here... alone in unconsecrated ground," my eyes shot up to his. "He did nae kill Elizabeth! And I ken he did nae kill himself! He would ne'er do tha'! He should be buried with honor, no' as some pauper! Damn the English! Damn them all for what they hae done to my da'!"

"I agree, love, but ye must nae let anyone hear ye," he stopped me. "Ye ken what they would do. I swore to him I would keep ye safe and I will do what I must. I love ye, Riona, ye must ken tha'."

"Aye, I do, Malcolm and I thank God every day my da' loved me enough to give me to ye and no' someone I could ne'er love," I said. Malcolm leaned down and placed a gentle kiss on my lips.

"Darlin', trust me, I loved him too. He was like a da to me when me own fell at Culloden. No' only tha', but he was my laird. I want justice done just as badly as ye do," Malcolm said.

"We have to find the Pride, Malcolm," I replied. "'Tis the only way my father will be at peace. It has belonged to my family since William Wallace gave it to Dàibhidh Macpherson at the Battle of Falkirk. Will ye help me?"

"Aye, my darling," he answered. "I will. But ye must nae let this worry ye so. 'Tis nae good for our baby."

I buried my head in his chest, so comforted by the peaty scent that clung to his tunic.

"I love ye, Ree," I felt the rumble in his chest.

"I love ye, Malcolm," I said. "I donnae think I could survive this without ye."

He held me tighter to him. "I'm here for ye, love, always," he promised.

I opened my eyes to the pre-dawn sunlight streaming through Ross's drapes. I was cocooned by Ross's strong arms, spooned against him. I could feel his bare chest rising and falling softly behind me. Taking a moment to enjoy the feeling, I reached to the nightstand and grabbed my phone.

Ross moaned and huffed in his sleep. Not wanting to wake him, I froze. Once I was certain I did not wake him, I turned my phone on and checked my email. One from my agent saying my publisher was asking for the next book. I had a one book deal with them but they were willing to review my second to see if it was something they were interested in. Thinking of working with my agent again after breaking up with Daren and his role in finding me here turned my stomach.

Setting my phone back down on the nightstand, I spooned deeper into Ross's warmth and sighed. In his sleep, Ross's arms came tighter around me and he buried his face into my hair. I smiled. Closing my eyes, I tried to fall asleep, but I couldn't shake the dream. Could the pump be Angus's headstone? Could he have been buried in unconsecrated ground and that's the reason he haunts? I shut my eyes even tighter and took a deep steadying breath, my chest aching for him.

Unable to sleep, I looked toward the window. The sun beckoned me. I hadn't gone for a run since I arrived in Scotland. Slowly peeling away from Ross, I went next door to my room to find my tennis shoes at the bottom of my suitcase, my running spandex shorts and my tank top with built in bra I splurged my tax return on. I headed to the bathroom and pulled my crazy hair back into a high ponytail. Tying my tennis shoes, I eased back into Ross's room and hurried to the bed. My laird was still asleep. Leaning down I kissed his cheek softly.

He moaned, turned over and opened his eyes slightly.

"I'm going for a run," I whispered.

He exhaled and closed his eyes again with a soft smile. "Mm, careful," he breathed.

"I will be," I replied. He was asleep clutching my pillow to his chest in the cutest way possible before I was out the door.

"There she is!" Graeme's voice boomed behind me making me jump as I walked down the stairs. Turning, I greeted him. "Hey, Graeme."

With Ross's explanations the night before, I looked at him a little differently.

"Bleedin' hell, woman," he chuckled taking in my attire with a raised eyebrow. "Ross is a lucky sod, isn't he?"

"I think he is," I teased. "I was just going for a run."

"Mmhmm," he answered, his eyes lingering a little too long on my chest.

"Graeme," I laughed motioning to him to look up. His eyes trailed up to mine with a devilish grin on his lips.

"You know," he started. "If you ever get tired of the old boring Sutherland, you let me know. I'd light up your world."

"Thanks," I laughed. "But I do not foresee that happening... ever."

"Well, just want you to know you have options," he winked.

"I'm glad for it," I answered.

"Where is the illustrious Elliot Ross this morning? Wear him out did ya?" his eyebrows wiggled playfully suggestive.

"Well... I have run marathons in the past," I teased. "He didn't know what hit him. He's still in bed."

"Ha! I bet he is," Graeme hooted. "I knew I liked you. Now, go on your run before I throw you over my shoulder and carry you upstairs." I nodded and headed for the main doors. "Be careful?" he called to me.

"I will," I answered.

The breeze was cold and a shock to my system, but it helped clear my head. Stretching against a column outside, I inhaled the cool air and smiled. This was paradise.

Sweat was pouring off my face and down my back and chest when I finally pulled up to a stop. The castle loomed in the distance. I didn't know how far I had gone, but my little distance meter strapped on my arm said about three miles. I didn't know the grounds were so vast but I loved every view I saw.

Looking over, the pump Angus always stood beside; the pump from my dream, stood beneath an old tree. Taking a few steps toward it, I knew instantly it was his grave. He was shielded by an ash tree and white heather grew around it. Both signs of the MacPherson clan, as I found out in my research.

Kneeling before the pump, I took in the detail. There was a crest etched into the old metal; the wildcat surrounded by a belt buckled and looped around itself, the MacPherson crest. Angus wore the badge holding his plaid in place at his shoulder.

Reaching out, my fingers touched the etching and all of the sudden, Angus was behind me. His hand on my shoulder. I leaned my head against it.

"I like having ye here, lass," his soft voice said. "I feel warm and no' alone."

"Oh, Angus," I broke. "How terrible. The centuries you've

been alone. I can't imagine."

He knelt beside me and turned me toward him. Reaching up, he wiped my cheek.

"The first time I woke, my family was still here. My Riona was nearing thirty and she had three beautiful children. Malcolm had taken care of her as I kenned he would. I saw it in the loving looks between them. I was shocked to see her; so like her mother, she was. I did nae ken what had happened. Last thing I remember, I was shot by Crispin. I tried to talk to Riona but she did nae hear me and I could nae touch her. It scared me," he shook his head. "Finally, I realized what I was… a ghost… and I stopped communicating with her. I cannae tell ye how difficult it was to see her age and no' be able to do anything. I watched her become an old woman. My baby, my wee little lass," his voice broke. "When she died, I was there with her. I helped her move on."

"But you could nae…" I sobbed.

"I was buried in unconsecrated ground, lass," he shrugged. "My soul will ne'er be at peace." I choked a sob as my tears flowed down my cheeks. "Och, come 'ere, lassie," he soothed pulling me to him. Wrapping his arms around me, he laid my head on his shoulder. I held on and wept. "Donnae cry for me, lass, it breaks me heart."

"I want to help," I said. "I want to find the Pride. I want you to rest easy."

"The only way would be for me to be laid in consecrated ground beside my family," he explained.

"Okay," I pulled back and looked him in the eyes. "What do I need to do?"

"I'm a murderer and committed suicide, love, I cannae be laid to rest. That is the unpardonable sin for Catholics," he explained.

"But you didn't do it, Angus!" I cried.

"It does nae matter, lass," he replied pushing back my hair from my eyes. "According to the magistrate, my last words meant I killed her and the scene was interpreted that I had killed myself."

"You were shot in the chest," I sobbed. "How could they believe you killed yourself?"

"I donnae think they thought much about it. Crispin Blackbourne was a titled friend of the king. They needed someone to blame... who better than the lowly barbaric highlander?"

"So if I can prove you were killed and you did not kill Elizabeth, then your name would be cleared and you can be laid to rest with your family?"

"I do miss my family, my wife, my brother, my parents," he whispered.

"I swear to you, Angus," I started. "If it is within my power to help you, I will."

"I ken ye will, lass," he smiled slightly.

"So let me start with asking some questions?" I asked. He nodded and I went on. "When was the last time you saw the Pride?"

"The box it rests in was always shut and locked. But the last time I opened it was at Eachthighearn the year of Culloden," he explained.

"Who had access to it?" I asked.

"Anyone," he answered. "I did nae keep it hidden. Although only me brother and Malcolm's father, my two seconds-in-command, had a key to the door. It was kept on display behind a barred door."

"So you haven't seen it since Culloden?" I asked. Angus nodded. "Is it possible... Niall took it with him?" I asked. Angus looked at me and I could see his mind going through the different scenarios. He had never thought of that. "Is Niall still at Culloden?" I asked gently.

"Nay," he answered distractedly. "I brought him home. I rode a day after they left, arriving the day of the slaughter, two hours after the advance... I found my countrymen decimated. The carnage was sickening and the Bonnie Prince was nowhere to be found," he spat out. "I found Niall. God only knows how I did with so much death."

"I want to go. Ross is taking me today," I said.

"It's a bloody austere place," he replied.

"Angus," I started after a moment. "Why is this happening to me?"

"All in time, love," he answered leaning forward and

kissing my forehead. I closed my eyes at his touch.

"Nikki!" I heard Ross call. Opening my eyes, Ross smiled as he walked up. Angus had disappeared. "You've got to be freezing," Ross continued, pulling out of his coat and draping it around my shoulders. "Not that I donnae enjoy seeing you in tight spandex, but you should cover up in this weather," he winked. I melted into Ross's coat and leaned into his chest when he wrapped his arms around me. "Did you have a good run?" He asked rubbing his hands up and down my arms.

I nodded, resting my head on his chest, my muscles cramped from sitting. I didn't realize how cold I was until Ross's body heat began warming me and pinpricks raced through my extremities.

"Ready to go to Culloden?" I mumbled into his chest.

"I am, do you need a shower? I mean you smell fine, love I just thought..."

"Shower does sound good," I admitted.

"They don't open until nine but we can wait in line," he explained.

"What time is it?" I asked pulling away and looking at him confused.

"It's not even seven, love," he answered. "You were up at five."

"I was?" I asked.

"Aye, you were," he grinned rubbing his nose against mine and following the gesture with his lips.

"Oh, I had a dream. Riona was crying to Malcolm about Angus. They were here and she said it was his grave. I couldn't sleep after that."

"No worries, baby," he said softly. "But now, go on up and get dressed, I'll meet you out front in thirty minutes?"

"Okay," I agreed and leaned up to kiss him. "I love you."

"I love you too," he answered. "Now go."

Running up to the house to stretch my sore muscles, I hurried up to my room and to the warm shower I needed so badly.

*Ross*

I turned to Angus standing just inside the tree line.

"When do you need to…" I trailed off.

"Whenever," he replied.

"And Nikki won't know what is happening?" I asked. "Because I can only imagine how she would take it."

"That we don't trust her I believe, but that is nae true. We care about her and donnae want her hurt."

"Aye, but still," I said. "What will it feel like?"

"To you? I am no' sure," he admitted. "But it could feel a little odd."

"Will I see things?"

"Nay, but if you feel an urge to go somewhere, go. That will be me urging you. I will only want to protect Nikki and if I sense something you cannae see or feel, listen to me."

"Aye, let's get this done with then," I replied. "When will you leave me?"

"When we get back here," he assured. "You'll feel it."

Nodding, I waited, opened my arms and mind to the prospect of having him possess me. I felt the moment I let him in, I couldn't breathe for a solid twenty seconds and a tear slipped down my cheek. Finally, my body and mind became accustomed to his invasion and I gulped in much needed air. Bending over, resting my hands on my knees I took deep breath after deep breath.

"Ross?" Gerard's voice called from behind me. Turning, I saw him run up to me. "You all right? What's wrong?"

"Nothing," I waved him off. "Just couldn't get a good breath in. I'm good." My mind swirled with thoughts not my own. I needed to sit down. I had to get accustomed to it before I drove or we could have an accident. Finally, my breathing eased and my head stopped swimming. I was ready.

*Nikki*

Ross was quiet during the hour and a half drive up to

Culloden. Graeme and Gerard drove behind us. I worried about not inviting Chad but we hadn't talked all evening and I could still hear him typing as I went up to shower and change clothes.

Looking over at Ross as he drove, he wore sinful jeans, a black turtle neck, a CPO jacket with a green, blue, black, red and white plaid scarf tied in a knot around his neck.

The sun broke through some clouds and shone down on his hair turning it reddish golden brown. I couldn't resist. Pulling out my phone, I snapped a picture before he looked over. Seeing my movements, he grinned shyly.

"What?" he laughed.

"Just want to capture the moment," I shrugged.

"What are you going to do with that?" he asked.

For a moment, I hesitated, remembering his contract with his publisher and the NDA I had to sign.

"Nothing," I confirmed. "I just wanted a picture of you."

"You're not going to post it on Facebook and make us official?" he teased.

"I thought Elliot Ross didn't want his picture taken," I said.

"He doesn't," he answered. "But *Ross Sutherland* has no problems with it."

I grinned. Then, – not so sneakily – I posted the picture on Facebook with the caption; "my boyfriend is not only Scottish, but he's pretty damn hot!"

Almost immediately, I got a comment from Jess, Daren's sister and my best friend.

*CALL ME!!!!!!!!!!*

*Oh shit...* I glanced over at Ross.

"What's wrong?" how he knew, I have no idea but he glanced at me, brow furrowed.

"My best friend wants me to call her," I explained.

"Well, I'm an only child so you can tell her there are no brothers," he teased.

I laughed outright. "Sure," I rolled my eyes. "One of you is plenty. And there's always a couple hot twins behind us," I winked.

"Very true, they could use a good couple girls," he said.

"Agreed. This is Daren's sister, Jess."

"Your best friend, did you ever call her?" He asked.

"Nope," I said.

"Then you should call her now. We'll be at the battlefield in thirty minutes but we can wait in the car until you're finished," he offered.

"God, I love you," I leaned over and kissed him. Dialing her number, she answered on the second ring.

"Oh my god! Are you okay? Where the hell are you? I've been trying to call you!" Jess cried.

"Whoa, Jess, I'm fine. I'm in Scotland. I was accepted to that writer's retreat I told you about. And I'm sorry, I don't have any missed calls from you, are you okay?" I asked.

"No!" she wailed. "Ben's a jerk and I will *never* marry him! We broke up, Nikki!"

"What? Oh my god, I'm so sorry, Jess. What happened?" I asked.

"Well… he was always a bit of a chauvinist but recently he's become worse and when you and Daren broke up, which I'm still not talking to my brother because of, Ben basically took Daren's side and said some pretty terrible things."

"About me?" I asked.

"About women," she clarified. "He basically said they should stay in the kitchen, barefoot and pregnant. I mean who the hell does he think he is? Is he living under a rock? I told him I needed to rethink our relationship if that's his stance. I mean, you know my idea of marriage, I love cooking and will raise the kids. But I also have my career."

"I'm sorry, sweetie," I said.

"Enough about me," she replied. "What happened? Who is that guy? He's gorgeous. What part of Scotland are you in?"

"That guy is my new boyfriend? And yes he is gorgeous," I looked over at Ross, one side of his lip ticked up. "I'm in the Highlands right now, we're heading to Culloden Moor. But I'm staying just north of Edinburgh."

"Hook me up! Does he have a panty dropping accent?" she asked.

I grinned and turned to Ross.

"Will you say hello to my best friend?" I asked. His smirk turned into a blinding grin as he read my mind. Taking my phone, he shouldered it.

"Hello, Jess, how are ya?" he asked thickening his accent. "Oh, I'm grand, cheers, so how long hae you and Nikki been friends? Oh wow... eh no I have nae read *Outlander,* is it good? Aye? Well, I'll have tah read it... Aye I've heard Jamie is pretty hot... Och well thank ye. Aye, I'm taking her to Culloden... Oh does it? Tha's great. Yeah, some of my clan's ancestors were killed there. Great well, I'm driving so..." he looked over at me and winked. "Good talkin' to ya, Jess," I pulled the phone from him.

"See?" I teased.

"Oh. My. God! It's ungodly what that man's voice does! Does he have any brothers?"

I laughed. "Nope, he's an only child," I said as she groaned.

"I might have to come see you and find my own hot Scot," she said.

"I would love to see you and I'm sure my hot boyfriend, who is a laird and owns like two castles-" Ross held up three fingers. "Three?" I asked him. He nodded. "Oh sorry, *three* castles, can put you up." She groaned again, louder that time. Seeing the signs showing we were only a few minutes out, I sighed. "All right, love," I said. "I gotta go. I will call you later tonight, okay? Love ya!"

"Bye, babe and I'll email you if I can get a flight," she replied. "I'm serious about it."

"I'd love to see you. Let me know if you can find a flight in," I said.

"Tell her to fly in to Heathrow, I'll have MacDonald pick her up in the jet," Ross offered.

I grinned at her moan when she heard him through the phone speaker. I told her what to do and hung up after swearing to call her again soon.

"She's halfway in love with you already," I teased Ross as I pocketed my phone.

"Is she?" He replied turning into a long drive. "Well, too bad my heart is already taken."

My belly did a flip and I had a feeling I would always experience that when he told me he loved me.

"Are we here?" I asked.

"In a couple minutes, it's a long drive," he indicated the path before us. We fell back into a comfortable silence as he navigated the winding road. Finally a parking lot and visitor center came into view. Ross pulled in next to another car, a line already forming at the door.

"They open in fifteen minutes," he explained. "Do you want to get in line or wait here?"

"Let's get in line," I said already anxious to see the Moor.

"Okay," he leaned over and kissed me gently then opened his door and came around to open mine.

# Chapter Six

Ross and I took our place in line with other tourists, his hand in mine, his thumb drawing light circles on the pad of flesh between my thumb and forefinger. Graeme and Gerard pulled up and, instead of line jumping anyone, they waited patiently three couples behind us. I could hear them flirting with a couple of sisters.

I gazed around the area taking in the outside of the visitor's center. A small courtyard beyond the wall to my left, a walkway leading out to the moor partitioned by a wall to my right and an actor, dressed in traditional highland dress with wool cap, stood with his back to the wall. He had mud smeared on his face, tunic and kilt, blood poured down his forehead. I was surprised at how realistically gory he was but people were ignoring him.

Glancing his way, our eyes locked and I smiled slightly at him. His brows drew together as his eyes widened fractionally. Swallowing, I looked to Ross who stood to my left waiting patiently, his eyes focused front. The silence of the place was eerie and my gaze pulled back to my right. I jumped. The actor had moved and was now right beside me. His light brown eyes stared into mine. We were the same height but he could be no more than seventeen.

"Can you see me?" His voice was hollow.

"Umm... yeah," I answered. "Nice costume. Sorry, I don't have any coins, but-"

"Can you help me?" He interrupted me pleading.

"Um," I started looking over at Ross.

"You say something, Nik?" He turned to me.

"Hmm?" I questioned. "Oh, no I was just talking to the impersonator." I gestured beside me but the guy was gone. "Did you see him?"

"Who?"

"The Highlander?" I asked.

Ross shook his head. It wasn't like I didn't know there could be ghosts but I didn't realize it would be as soon as I arrived. I wished Angus was there to help me.

"I don't think anyone saw him but me," I confessed.

"Are you okay?" he asked.

Nodding, I squeezed his hand just as the doors opened and the line began to move.

Once inside the museum, I was surprised how austere and cold it was. However, given the somberness of the place, I was hardly shocked. I had been to Gettysburg in America but never to the main visitor center there, I didn't know what to expect. Ross squeezed my hand and went to get our tickets giving me a chance to look around the gift shop. Graeme and Gerard met me there. They were showing me a ridiculously cute t-shirt of a Highland Coo when Ross found us.

"Okay so they have tours of the moor at nine forty-five which is sold out, eleven, and one," Ross explained. "Did you want a tour or did you just wanna walk around?"

"We could just walk around. I don't think it's all that necessary," I said.

"Lads?" Ross asked.

"I've seen it," Graeme said. "I'll pass, too much to see inside," he said as his eyes glanced past me to a woman walking away from us.

"Classy, Fergus," I replied. He shrugged innocently. "Are we good? I want to go inside the main area."

"Yeah, we're good, I have your tickets here," Ross handed me one and two to the twins.

"Cheers, Ross, didn't expect this," Gerard said accepting his ticket.

"No worries," Ross replied. "Ready to look around?" I nodded and we walked through the ticket area and into the main part of the museum.

Listening to the lads tell me the significance of one thing or another, was fascinating. So many historical trinkets, jewels, letters, and paintings were on display. They even had a hilt of a gorgeous sword in a room by itself where you could sit and listen to a dramatized conversation between Bonnie Prince Charlie and his men as they planned the attack.

Branching off away from the men, I walked down another hallway reading the testimonials on the wall when the same Highlander from outside walked in front of me.

"Excuse me!" I called to him. Taking a deep breath, I prepared for what I thought could be happening. He didn't have his wool cap on then and he didn't stop when I called. I followed quickly. "Hey!" I called again. Reaching him, I tugged on his arm shocked when I felt fire pass up my arm. He turned to me and I screamed. Half of his face was gone. I could see his brain, skull and blood.

"Help me," he begged then disappeared.

"Nikki!" Ross called jogging up beside me. "Are you all right?"

"I saw him again," I confessed. "I don't know how to help him. What do I do? I wish Angus was here."

Ross pressed a hand to his forehead as if in pain. "Nikki, I need to tell you something."

Ross explained his deal with Angus in low tones. Other tourists walked by us but Ross obviously didn't want others to hear. As worried as I was for Ross, I hugged him tightly and thanked him. How could I be upset when they did it to protect me?

"Angus," I said looking into Ross's eyes. "What do I do?"

"You can only listen," Ross said but I knew it wasn't him. "And donnae blame Sutherland, it was my idea."

"I don't care who's idea it was, thank you," I said.

"Right now, just walk around the museum. It will be worse when you leave and go outside."

I nodded and as soon as Ross's headache subsided, we walked on. Ross showed me artifacts, stories, and military battle plans. There was a room with a three hundred sixty degree projection of the dramatized battle but it was a little too gruesome for me. Walking out, Ross and I found Graeme and Gerard in a section of the museum that had actual weapons and clothes from the time period to try on and use. Ross joined them and I couldn't help my grin when I saw them try to shoot a rifle, carry a dirk and targe and play with a basket hilted sword.

I walked around the outskirts of the room where all sorts of knickknacks unearthed on the battlefield lay in cases. Old bullet fragments, broken swords or dirk points, even an old rusted rosary, were encased with great respect.

I heard Ross's laugh and looked up. Graeme, as dramatic as ever, clutched his chest and pretended to fall to his knees. He received some laughs and applause from the others around him. Looking up, he winked at the same girl he had watched walk away from us earlier. She winked back and bit her lip after saying something that made Graeme laugh.

Suddenly, the same guy I had seen earlier, stood behind Graeme, looking down at him studying him. I didn't hear what Graeme said back to the girl, but whatever it was, the guy behind him grew angry, reached down and wrapped his hands around Graeme's neck.

It all happened so fast. I screamed as Graeme clutched at his throat. Ross whipped around to look at me and Gerard went down to help his brother already going blue from lack of oxygen. The ghost looked up at me, his eyes wide, empty and wild.

"He is English," he ground out, his voice rough and angry. "*Ye* would defend him?"

"He's a Fergus," I shouted, but the echo that came back

to my ears did not sound English.

Almost immediately, the ghost released Graeme and he pitched forward coughing and holding his throat. Gerard caught him and was holding him steady.

"Help me," the guy pleaded then disappeared. Everything was silent.

"Nikki?" I heard Ross say. Turning, Ross approached me like one would a wounded animal.

"I have to get out of here," I rushed out of the room through a glass sliding door before me. Ross's, or rather, Angus's voice called after me. The fresh air felt bracing as I took a deep breath. Opening my eyes, the massive expanse of the moor was before me. I couldn't imagine the carnage of battle; I never wanted to. My mind drifted to the men who had died. How many was this view the last thing they saw on earth?

The cool air cleared my head. Walking on a little, amazed to find a wide open expanse with no buildings, except those with historical meaning. Angus's words came back to me. *"If the Young Pretender spent more time with his kin, he would ken Highlanders fight best on slopes no' a wasteland."*

Looking toward an old thatched cottage off to the right of the field, I saw a young boy standing in the doorway of the house a look of terror on his face. I followed his gaze and saw two men, one in highland dress, the other a Redcoat engaged in battle. The Highlander was struck down and the little boy, no older than seven screamed something in Gaelic. Disappearing back into the cottage, he emerged with a sword nearly the same size he was. His mother appeared behind him screaming for him to come back but the boy charged the Redcoat only to be speared and fall beside his father. The mother and I screamed at the same time.

Wiping his mouth with the back of his hand, the Redcoat stepped over the bodies and headed for the woman in the doorway of the cottage. I ran after him intent on protecting the woman. The man's eyes conveyed only one thing and as a woman, I would never stand by and allow a rape. The Redcoat shut the door behind him before I had a chance to get inside.

Desperate to help her, I tried the door, it was locked. I raced around the cottage frantic to find a window that wasn't shuttered. I could hear the woman fighting the Redcoat inside but I also knew she was no match for him. Pounding at the windows, I yelled for the man to stop or to let me in. Neither happened and I could hear her screaming. I was too late to help her. A few moments later, the Redcoat walked out of the door adjusting his collar and wiping a little trickle of blood that oozed from a scratch on his cheek, he grabbed the lantern hanging beside the doorway. Throwing it into the house, the mud walls and thatched roofing caught on fire quickly.

Sauntering back to his horse, the Redcoat rode away. I tried to get inside to save the woman but the fire was too fierce and there were no screams. She was dead already.

"Help us," I heard behind me. Turning, a group of men and boys came up to me, backing me against the cottage wall.

"Please, help us," they were all in various states of dress. Blood and mud streamed down their faces, chests, legs, arms and heads. Each one had a grievous wound, some with limbs missing, portions of their head gone, or holes in their chests where their vital organs were supposed to be. They kept coming toward me, kept begging me to help them, their hands reaching for me.

"You can see us. Please, help us. Help me!" All variations of that saying were cried out. I screamed when the first hand touched me. Unlike Angus's cold flesh, this touch was burning hot. They kept coming toward me, but I had nowhere to go. I was trapped between the burning cottage and dozens of ghosts.

Turning my head away from them, I screamed again. This time, however, I didn't know what I said but a well-known hand grabbed my upper arm. I was pulled through the house to the other side then plastered to a strong, hard chest.

"I hae ye, lass," Angus said. I clutched him to me as tears streamed down my cheeks. Holding on tightly to Angus's tunic, his soothing voice calmed my racing heart. Finally, I looked up seeing Ross holding me.

"Nikki?" his voice was tight with worry.

"Ross," I sobbed. "It was terrible."

"Oh god, not again," he wiped my nose. When he pulled his fingers back, they were covered in blood.

Looking up at him, I saw desperation in his eyes. But

more importantly, the same Redcoat from before stood directly behind him.

"Ross!" I screamed but the Redcoat grinned, aimed his gun and fired. I pushed Ross out of the way and followed him down, the bullets hitting another Highlander who had raced up behind me. When the Redcoat's bullets struck and killed the man, he ran. I raced after him hearing Ross yell my name.

I didn't know how far I ran but the Redcoat had too much of a head start. Losing him, I fell to my knees and tried to catch my breath. Looking out in front of me, the same ghosts who had cornered me, encircled me, not moving. Angus's advice came back to me. I could listen. They needed to tell their stories.

"Okay," I said. "Okay," I said again a little more firmly. "I'm here. Show me what you need to show me."

There was a deafening silence, then, almost like silent whispers from beyond, each one told me their tales. After a while, I curled up in a ball on the battlefield hearing the men's blood screaming from beneath my head. Eventually the sounds stopped and I opened my eyes to see the ghosts had disappeared, save one. One man looked at me from ten paces away. I couldn't focus on him but he started walking and eventually came into view. His black hair hung to his shoulders, braided at the temples. His black, white and purple kilt pleated around his waist and his soft leather boots reached his knees. Light blue eyes bored into mine. Kneeling before me, his young face, no more than nineteen, was mere inches from mine.

"Niall," I breathed.

"Hello, lass," he whispered.

"You're here?" I asked.

He nodded once. Trying to get up, my body ached as if I had been in a battle. Niall helped me and unlike the others' touch of fire, Niall's was ice like Angus's.

"I cannae get a message to me brother, lass," he started, holding on to my forearms steadying me. "I've been trying since the day I fell on this field. I need ye to help me. Can ye do tha' for me?" I nodded. "I need ye to see this," he said.

Breathing deeply, I closed my eyes and opened my mind again to what Niall was going to show me.

*Niall*

Alistair needed me. He was wounded already. Running as fast as I could, I saw another damned English Redcoat race to my friend. Blood, from the pistol shot he had nae ducked away from fast enough, dripped off his fingertips. A front kick straight to Alistair's gut had him falling onto his back but I was there before the Red could do anything more than sneer.

Thrusting my sword home through the English before him, the bloody bastard fell with a womanly scream.

"I had it handled, MacPherson," Alistair stated from his place on the ground.

"Aye, thought I'd take a wee bit of yer glory, Sutherland. Too much'll go to yer head," I said offering my hand and helping him up. "How bad?" I asked, seeing the blood continue to drip from his right arm.

"I'll live," he grunted squeezing his hand around the hilt of his basket sword as if getting the feel of it in a hand he did not usually favor. "How does the battle fare?"

"Charlie's a fool. Angus was right," I said. "A fool and a coward. He fled."

"Nay!" Alistair shouted.

"Murray's and Drummond's divisions have been decimated," I went on. "The Farquharson's have lost heavily."

"What?" He demanded. "Nay! Me wife's brother is one of them!"

"Alistair, there's more," I said. "Several of the Sutherlands who we thought loyal, joined Cumberland."

"You lie!" Alistair cried raising his sword to me. "My clan would ne'er betray Scotland!"

"I saw it with me own eyes. Your Uncle Keith turned on..." I could nae go on.

"Who?"

"Yer father," I finally said. "They fought each other."

Alistair's eyes widened. "Did ye see him? Did ye see me da'?" Alistair demanded.

I had indeed. A greater warrior there had ne'er been. But

how could I tell this man, my best friend, and someone no older than me, his father had died so horribly? When I did nae respond, he closed his eyes for a moment, crossing himself. When he opened his eyes, they were filled with fire.

"I will kill every last one of these damned whoresons!"

"The battle's lost, Alistair," I said.

"Not until I draw my last breath!" He yelled. Crying his clan's battle cry he raced back toward the fray.

"*Eejit*," I muttered but followed him. Cutting through some English who were no older than me, I made my way toward Alistair but I could no longer see him. We were too far separated.

Five minutes passed but to me it felt like hours. I did nae even feel human while I was fighting. I was a warrior. I felt nothing as I killed a boy nae older than fourteen who attacked me. I felt nothing when I killed an old man, old enough to be my father. I put all thoughts aside. I was fighting for the future. The future of Scotland. The future of my clan.

Just as that thought entered my mind, I felt it… I was a dead man. Two pistol shots blew through my back. At first, the pain did nae register then I felt my life's blood begin pooling under my tunic. Turning around to see the coward who had shot me in the back, I came face to face with the English who had not only killed my friend Greer McKenzie, heir to the lairdship, but his young son as well and who had raped and killed his wife. The Redcoat had a sick grin of satisfaction on his face as I raised my sword toward him.

"You Scots all die the same way," his nauseating English accented voice grated on my ears. "Not realizing you are already defeated; I do believe you enjoy being overrun. It gives you purpose," he looked at me cocking his head to the side. "Look at you. You are dying but you still fight. Do you not know when you have been beaten?"

Gathering as much strength as I could, I looked him in the eyes and kept my sword steady in my hand.

"Better a warrior," I gasped out. "Than a coward who kills children then rapes the mother."

The bastard had the gall to laugh and touch his cheek where a scratch marred his otherwise untouched skin.

"Where's the Pride, Highlander?" he sobered.

I would ne'er tell and it must hae been obvious because the Redcoat kicked me in the chest, knocking me down. I landed with a painful thud. The whoreson stood over me and stomped his foot down on my chest.

"Where. Is. The. Pride?" he demanded.

"Ye'll ne'er hae it," I gasped.

"Oh, you underestimate me, Scot," he replied.

"*Ye* underestimate *me*," I reached down, grabbed my pistol from where it fell out of my belt and shot him between the eyes. If I lived, I kenned his stunned look would haunt me.

As he fell forward, I did nae want his blood on me so I rolled as much as I could. He landed beside me, dead. Hours passed, or maybe it was only a few minutes, but I felt a hand slip into mine and clutch it. Looking over, Alistair crawled up beside me. We were both dying and we kenned it. I clutched his hand as tightly as I could.

"Niall," he gasped. I could nae see what wound had finally claimed him, but one thing I kenned was we would nae survive. "Are ye there?"

"Aye, Alistair, I'm here," I answered.

"Is it safe?" he asked.

"Aye, 'tis," I replied.

"Good," he answered. I could hear gurgling as he tried to breathe. "I fear for Sarah," he said about his young bride. "She'll be alone."

"Donnae think on it," I countered.

"Our line will die with us," he said.

"Perhaps Sarah has conceived," I tried to put his mind at rest. "God kens ye've tried hard enough. Ye may even now be a father."

He held to that thought and smiled. I kenned when he passed and I am happy to say it was peaceful but it made my heart hurt. My best friend was dead. I was alone. So alone. I wanted Angus with me. I wanted our banter, our brotherly confidences. I just wanted my elder brother to tell me all would be well. Tears filled my eyes and ran down my cheeks as I thought of him and heard the groans of those dying around me. We failed Scotland. We failed our children's children. I did nae want to die. Closing my eyes, I waited for death. Then I heard him; my name being screamed from somewhere far away and hooves pounding the ground.

"Niall!" Angus screamed rushing toward me. He fell to his knees and cradled me. I finally felt safe and at peace. I could hear him speaking but all I cared about was he was there. He held me tightly. "Niall, please," his voice choked. "Stay." We locked eyes but he needed to know. Our family had a tradition. If a warrior died in battle he would be buried in the clothes he wore with only the skin revealed being cleaned. He needed to ken what I wore. He needed to ken what was around my neck. Slowly raising my hand to my chest, I splayed my fingers across my heart where I wore it under my tunic.

"Angus," I moaned.

"I'm here, Niall," he sobbed. "I'm here, brother." I could feel his tears on my face.

"Angus," I tried again. I tried to tell him but I could nae speak. "I... I..." Death was here. These would be my last words. But with them, I kenned he would ne'er find it. "I love ye."

"I love ye, too," Angus choked out.

Then the pain was gone and I was floating. Looking down, I saw Angus, still cradling my body, rear his head back and cried out.

So this was death... No' what I expected. But I kenned one thing... I could nae leave this world without telling Angus, *I* stole the Pride.

*Nikki*

"Nikki!" Ross shouted. Opening my eyes, I was on my back in the middle of the field. Graeme and Gerard were standing over me and paramedics were running toward us, Ross cradled me in his shaking arms. "Nikki!"

"Aye, I'm here, Ross," I barely recognized my own voice.

"Nik?" he breathed.

"Aye, Ross... I ken where the Pride is," I replied.

# Chapter Seven

*Ross*

I felt the moment Angus left me. He raced after Nikki but without me he was pulled back to MacCulloch castle. I held Nikki to me waiting on the paramedics Graeme and Gerard called. When she spoke, her voice different than I had ever heard, I wished Angus was still here.

"What?" I breathed.

"I ken where the Pride is," she repeated. "I mean..." she forced herself to say. "I know where it is."

"What happened?" one of the paramedics asked as he reached us and knelt beside her.

"She blacked out," I explained.

"Does this happen often?" he began examining her.

"I'm fine," she said softly. "I just need to stand." Looking up at me, her gaze questioning. "Where's Angus?"

"I'm not sure," I replied. After she was checked out by the paramedics and refused to go to the hospital, we left the moor and headed back to the car. Driving in silence, I asked her a question burning in my mind.

"Did you really mean it?" I asked. "You know where the Pride is?"

"Aye, I ken," she said then shook her head. "Yes, I know. I saw what happened. Niall took the Pride to give to the new king; Prince Charlie when they won. But they didn't so he never gave it to him. It's buried with him."

"But back then, they would prepare the dead for burial. It would have been found," I said.

"The MacPherson's had a tradition, any warrior felled in battle would be buried wearing the clothes they wore when they died. The Pride would never have been found. Enough time had passed after Niall took it to when it was found missing no one thought it could have been him."

"I can't believe you saw all of that," I mumbled.

"I don't even believe it myself," she said. "And Alastair Sutherland was your direct ancestor?"

"Aye," I answered. "His wife was pregnant when he left and gave birth to a son several months later. That boy became Laird after a long struggle for the title with his great uncle the man you met in the Laird's Solar."

"Keith," she offered. "He turncoated to the British."

"Yeah," I replied. "And is a black mark on our name and history. Soon though, Alastair's younger brothers helped his son reclaim his land and he married, had a son and so on and so forth until you get to me da' and then me."

"He was an honorable man, Ross," she answered. "And died a warrior's death. His one concern was his wife and line."

"Then I am proud to call him my grandfather however many times removed," I said.

We fell silent for a little while and after several minutes, she asked me another question, "I would like to go to MacPherson Keep. How long would it take to get there?"

"It's long been ruins," I told her. "Probably looted long ago. The Pride may not be there."

"Angus told me the crypt is hard to find. No one knows where it is unless you *know* where it is," she explained.

"And you know where it is?" I asked.

"Aye, yes," she answered. Still shaking off the effects of living so many lives in such a short time.

"We're actually going to go right passed Macpherson's lands on our way back."

"Really?" she asked then sighed. "I'm worried about Angus."

"And not to dictate but you have lived a thousand lives today, you need to rest," I said. "We can go in the morning."

"I want to go now though," she replied. "Let's get back to MacCulloch Castle first, check in there and see if Chad wants to go."

"Nikki," I shook my head. "I don't think that's wise."

"I know," she answered. "But I need to do this."

"Okay," I conceded. "Just promise me that you won't ever let that happen to you again."

"I can't promise that, Ross," she said. "It's not like I chose for this to happen but Angus and I have a connection. I don't know who I am but I know his first wife and I look identical. There must be some unfinished business and I was drawn into it. I have never in my life believed in ghosts but here I am confronted with the fact they exist. I don't choose to nearly die every time I run into one, and I won't apologize for trying to help them. I love Angus and I want him to be at peace. If it were your family wouldn't you want the mystery solved?"

"It is my family," I answered. "I am as much involved in this story as you but I'm no' dying."

"Neither am I," she placed a hand on my leg. "I love you for your protection but baby, I have to do this."

"I know, and I back you, but… I can't lose you," I said. "Okay? I can't."

"Ross, you know I have never felt for anyone what I feel for you," she began. "You will not lose me."

"Swear it," I demanded.

"I swear," she replied. "You can't get rid of me that easily."

*Nikki*

"You went without me?" Chad demanded when I found him in his room.

"You were busy with your novel," I protested. "I didn't

want to bother you."

"You went to the second most important landmark to this place and story without me!" he cried.

"I'm sorry, honey," I replied. "I didn't realize you wanted to go." He huffed and put his hands on his hips. "We're going up to MacPherson Keep to try and find the pride."

"I'm coming now," Chad stated.

"Fair enough," I replied. "Ross is in the car. I need to get some things from my room. Pack a quick bag just in case we need to stay overnight. I'll meet you out at the car in ten minutes."

Chad nodded and went about packing. Slipping out of his room, I went to mine. I lived a lifetime, several lifetimes, in just a couple hours at Culloden. The memories of all those poor souls and their stories hurt my heart. I wanted to help each of them. Hopeful now they told their stories they could be at peace, I went to work.

Rushing around my bedroom, I pulled out an oversized carryon and stuffed some clothes, shoes and toiletries. Grabbing my iPad, I zipped it up thinking I could write a little more of the story I had started a couple days ago while we travelled I had more lives and characters in my head than I could ever write. Catching the time, I needed to book it downstairs or Ross would come after me.

"Nikki!" I heard Angus call and I stopped dead in my tracks. He hadn't called me Nikki since I had arrived. "Nikki, lass."

"Angus?" I asked confused. Looking around the room, I saw him in the mirror of the secret passageway. "Angus, is that you? Are you all right?"

"Aye, lass, I need ye to trust me. I need ye to come with me," he said.

"But..." I started, looking back to the main door.

"I'll tell Ross you're all right. Please, Nikki, I need ye," he said.

"What's wrong? Is everything all right?" I asked reaching up and touching the thistle decoration. It sunk it and the mirror opened. Angus was not there. "Where are you?"

"I'm here, lass, at the bottom of the stairs," he called.

I peered through the darkness and saw his figure at the bottom. Taking two steps inside, I jumped when the door behind me closed, washing me in darkness.

"Angus?" I called. He didn't answer. Tentatively, I took a step forward coming to the edge of the stairs and braced myself against the wall. Calling his name once more, I started down the steps.

# Chapter Eight

*Ross*

Drumming my fingers on the side of my car window sill, I waited for Nikki to come back down. She insisted I stay in the car, good thing too because the way I was feeling after seeing her passed out on the moor, I would have forced her to sleep.

A tap at my window pulled me from my thoughts. Rolling it down, I saw my best friends with stupid grins on their faces. I knew this was coming. They hadn't had a chance to bust my balls for what they saw two days ago. And now we knew Nikki was all right, they weren't going to back off.

"Thanks for the show," Graeme spoke first. "Did nae know we were walkin' in on a porno set."

"Really?" I replied. "Sorry, did nae realize I needed to put a sock on the doorknob since University."

"You know, when we told you to show her the sights, we did nae mean *that* sight," Gerard said.

"Yeah, did nae know your bedroom was on the tour itinerary," Graeme replied.

Rolling my eyes, I started rolling up the window. Graeme's hand shot through, stopping me.

"Wait!" he called, a twinkle in his eye. "So how would you

rate your performance? Hot? Kinda hot?"

Again, rolling up the window, I heard Gerard laugh.

"Awe, come on, Ross," Gerard started. "Out of ten?"

Even I chuckled when I heard our code from University. Our rating of women after a night together was always *out of ten.* But somehow our old teasing and rating felt wrong. For the first time, I didn't want to share any details about Nikki and my time together. I didn't want to cheapen it.

*Where the hell is she?* I wondered. It had been ten minutes already and she was supposed to be back. I could hear the lads still laughing and teasing but when I looked at the front door, Chad bustled out. Rolling down the passenger side window, I leaned over.

"Sorry," he panted. "I tried to hurry but I couldn't find my tennis shoes," he looked around. "Where's Nikki?"

"Isn't she with you?" I asked, a sudden and sickening feeling entered my stomach. *Why the hell did I have to agree to let her go alone?*

"Uh... no, she said she needed to go to her room to get a few things," Chad explained. "And I was to meet you out here."

"What's up?" Gerard asked walking around the car. I got out and followed Graeme.

"Nikki's not here," I said.

"She's probably in her room, you know how women are," Graeme said.

Something didn't feel right. Taking the steps two at a time, I ignored the hellos and welcome backs from my staff and other authors I passed.

Finding Nikki's room, I knocked then tried the door. It was unlocked but she was gone; her mobile lay on her bed.

"Where the hell is she?" I shouted.

*Nikki*

"Where are we going?" I asked the silence. Angus guided me for a little while but we had passed the solar and now there were three doors before me.

"Take the center door, lass," he said.

"Angus," I questioned.

"Trust me, lass," he replied.

"But I can't see," I protested.

"Reach yer hand out and find the handle," he instructed.

Something did not feel right. My Angus would not ask me to do something without a reason and so far, there was no reason. Retracting my hand, I shook my head. "No, not until you show yourself and tell me what's going on."

"No!" he shouted.

"Angus!" I cried as a forceful wind knocked me back. "What the hell?"

"I'm sorry, lass," he said gently. "But I cannae have ye going now. We're almost there."

"Where Angus? Where are you taking me?" I demanded, standing.

"Hae I e'er given ye cause to doubt me?" he asked.

"No," I answered.

"Then trust me, aye?" he asked.

Dusting off my backside, I agreed. "Aye, Angus, I trust ye."

Reaching out, I took hold of the middle door's handle and opened it. Stairs leading up caught my eye through the miniscule light coming from god knows where. Tentatively, as I could smell a lot of smoke still clinging to the walls, I headed up.

Once I had reached the top of the stairs, there was another door. From the look of it, it had been boarded up and the boards removed with a crow bar, resealed and cut in half with a saw.

"In there?" I asked.

"Aye, I'm waiting for ye, lass," he said.

Opening the door, I took a step inside. Sunlight streamed through the window. Blinking, I readjusted my eyes to the light. Just as I passed the door, I heard it shut and lock behind me. Turning to look back, I tried the knob, it was locked but there was no lock on the door.

"Well," I heard a woman's crisp English accented voice say from the window. "That was tedious. Welcome, my dear. It is good to finally meet you face to face."

I swallowed the bile that collected at the back of my throat and turned.

"Elizabeth," I said seeing her raven hair cascading down her back. She laughed that same evil laugh I heard when Angus caught her in bed with Crispin.

"Oh dear me," she said turning around. "Am I that predictable?"

I could hardly believe my eyes. Jilliana, our German paranormal companion that Chad had dubbed the *mistress of the dark,* stared back at me.

"Jilliana?" I breathed.

"A good body, do you not agree?" she asked.

"Is she still alive?" I demanded.

"Why? Are you worried about her?" she asked. "How sweet. I surmise if it had been Lorna, you would not have been so keen. She is a sweet little dear, isn't she? I enjoyed stirring her jealousy. She hates you, a feeling I understand wholeheartedly. But she did not let me in. People should watch what they open themselves up to. Heaven only knows what they might get... or hell, however you want to look at it."

"And Jilliana opened herself up to you?" I asked.

"Of course," she answered. "She so wanted a *real* experience."

"What is it you want?" I demanded.

"The Pride," she answered. When I didn't answer, she continued. "Oh, do not be so foolish. I know you found it. I want it."

"*You* are dead," I said. "What's it to you?"

"I died for that damn thing," she replied.

"You whored yourself out for it," I corrected. "And you will never get it now."

"You don't know what it is, do you?" Elizabeth went on.

"I know it's rightfully Scotland's. I know it is rightfully Angus's and his decedents. You have no claim on it," I said.

"England owns Scotland. It is England's property. You have no right to it at all," she replied.

"That's where you're wrong," I stated. "Scotland is its own country, its own identity. Scotland, God's land, belongs to no one. It was free of English Tyranny for four hundred years. It will be free again. St. Andrew's Cross will fly free once more and all free born Scots will breathe a sigh of relief knowing their country is whole and free and at peace once more. *Saor Alba!*" I raised my hand in a fist high over my head. Elizabeth gave a screech and charged me, but I let my instincts take over. Aiming my fist at her, I shouted at the top of my lungs. "*Creag Dhubh*!"

All of the sudden, every one of the MacPhersons dead and gone gathered around me, surrounded me. I had rallied the souls of the Highland Warriors and they stood tall. Elizabeth screamed and fell back, but the souls were on her immediately.

Angus rushing toward me was the last thing I saw before darkness overtook me.

# Chapter Nine

*Ross*

"Angus!" I shouted. Everyone probably thought I was crazy. Pacing up and down the halls, I shouted for a ghost. Of course, only a few people knew he was a ghost but enough people knew I didn't have anyone named Angus on my payroll. "Angus!" I yelled again. "Wherever the hell you are, get here *now*!"

I reached the library bar and poured myself a shot of scotch. The alcohol burned as it slid down my throat and into my stomach.

"Is that a private bottle?" Chad asked. Opening my eyes, he, Graeme and Gerard stood before me.

Gritting my teeth against the worry, I passed the bottle and they each took a swig.

"Where the hell could she be?" I demanded.

"What did she say before she left?" Graeme asked.

"Just for me to wait in the car. She wouldn't be any more than ten minutes," I said.

"She said the same to me," Chad revealed taking another wee dram. "Told me to pack a small bag just in case we had to stay over somewhere."

"Dammit, where the hell is Angus?" I demanded.

"I'm here, Sutherland," I heard.

Whirling around, Angus stood before us. The lads gave an audible *holy shit* when they saw him. I hadn't remembered they had never seen him before but right then, I was more concerned about finding Nikki.

"Where is she?" I demanded.

"Nikki?" Angus asked.

"No, the bloody Queen of England, for god's sake! Of course Nikki!" I shouted. "She's gone!"

"Elizabeth," was all the exasperating man said before he disappeared.

*Nikki*

When I woke I was in Angus's arms, my head and body ached as if I had fought in a battle.

"Angus?" I groaned.

"Aye, lass, I'm here," he said.

"Where were you?" I asked.

"I'm sorry lass, I donnae ken what ye mean," he stated.

"She used your voice and image," I explained. "Luring me here. Where is here?"

"It's the room I died in, lass," he replied. "The room I bound Elizabeth's soul in."

I looked around remembering the room he showed me in the vision. Jillian lay on the floor near the window.

"Is she…?" My voice trailed off.

"She's alive," he said. "But Elizabeth is gone. You defeated her, lass."

"It wasn't just me," I replied. "I felt… others. What's going on, Angus? How did I do that?"

"Och, lass, hae ye no' figured it out?" he asked.

"Am I the reincarnation of your wife?" I asked hesitantly.

"Nay, love," he answered. "Ye ken the truth. 'Tis why I could contact ye after years of being alone. 'Tis why ye have the love of Scotland. Scotland runs through yer veins. Yer me kin.

Me daughter's line. Yer a MacPherson and a Brodie and those two are a deadly combination to anyone who tries to take our rights away." His eyes drifted to Jilliana. "Elizabeth used her as a vessel. Unlike me, her body was burned not buried. She had no form. Her soul was black. That woman opened her mind and body to Elizabeth allowing her passage. But you defeated her with the rallying war cry of the MacPherson Clan." Reaching up, I touched Angus's face, seeing him differently for the first time. "We're connected ya see, lass."

"I thought I was falling in love with you," I replied.

"It would have been my honor, lass," he said. "But nay, ye felt the cosmic connection of a kinship, nothing more."

"Pity," I sighed snuggling into him. "Are you all right? Ross told me you left him when I ran across the field at Culloden."

"Aye, I tried to follow you but at the last moment I knew I would hurt Ross if I didn't leave him. I am tethered here and my soul raced back as soon as my connection with him was lost."

Closing my eyes as exhaustion settled in my bones, I remembered I needed to tell him something. "Angus," I started.

"Aye, lass?" He asked.

"There was something I need to tell you," I breathed.

"What is it?"

"Something about the Pride..." I heard pounding but I didn't know where it was coming from and suddenly I was floating, then darkness overtook me and I rested in oblivion.

"Nikki," I heard softly in my ear. "Are you awake?"

"Hmm," I moaned and snuggled deeper into the chest I knew well.

"Nikki?"

*Dad?* I thought. Opening my eyes, I looked up to see Dad standing beside the bed.

"Nik, sweetheart?" Dad said. "Can you talk, darling?"

I smiled tiredly at him as he stroked my hair.

"Dad," I said softly. He smiled and I looked over at Ross beside me. "Ross."

"Aye," he gripped me tighter to him.

"What happened?" I asked. Trying to sit up, my body ached so badly tears sprung to my eyes. Ross supported me and Dad fluffed my pillow, situating it behind my back. "How did you get here?" I asked my dad when he wrapped his arms around me and gave me a hug.

"I called him," Ross replied.

"Why?" I questioned.

"Because you scared the shite out of me when I found you unconscious and bleeding from the nose so much I thought for sure you would need a transfusion. When you hadn't woken for a day, I knew it was time to call him. You've been unconscious for a week," Ross explained.

"I'm sorry," I said, reaching up and stroking his face. He leaned into my touch and closed his eyes. He looked so tired.

"Sweetie, don't be sorry," Dad replied. "We're just so glad you're okay."

"I wanted to take you to the hospital but they said you would be fine and you were just fighting exhaustion. They've had you on an IV but I bet you're hungry," Ross said.

"Starving," I finally decided.

"Good!" Jacqueline's voice came from the doorway. Dad turned and went over to her.

"Let me help you," he said taking the tray. Jacqueline smiled at him and touched his arm.

"Thank you," she said softly.

"This is much too heavy for you," he replied, setting it down on the bed.

"It's all right," Jacqueline said. "When one is a parent, one doesn't always gauge heaviness when taking care of their child."

"Very true," Dad replied. "You have raised a good man, Jacqueline."

"How many times, Travis?" she sighed. "It's Jackie."

"Jackie," he grinned. "Like Onassis? She's got nothing on you, beautiful."

Jacqueline blushed and looked away, mumbling a thank you. I looked over at Ross seeing him watching them together.

"I brought you some tea things, dear," Jacqueline came over to me. "I didn't think you should have anything heavy. The doctor just called, he'll be back over at three," she explained.

"René?" I asked Ross.

"No, our doctor on call," Ross replied.

"He said if you wake to give you some soup," Jacqueline said.

"Soup sounds amazing," I answered.

"It's your aunt's Matzo ball soup, sweetheart," Dad said.

"Even better," I thanked him. "Do you think I could shower first? Maybe go downstairs? I need to get up."

"Only if someone helps you, sweetheart," Dad replied. "I don't want you falling if you get dizzy with those nose bleeds."

"Did Ross tell you what's happening?" I asked.

"We've talked," Ross told me.

"Not sure I believe the whole ghost thing but he said you do and that's enough for me," Dad answered.

"He's real, Dad," I said. "I promise."

"I believe you, sweetheart. But let's get you up. I wonder, Jackie, would you be willing to help Nikki to the shower?"

"Of course!" she replied. "If Nikki is all right with it?"

I nodded and let the men help me up. As soon as I was on my feet, I looked around the room.

"Where's Chad?" I asked.

"Downstairs," Ross replied. "He stood watch with me and your da' every night. He was worn out. We sent him to get something to eat not half an hour ago."

I smiled grateful for his friendship and Dad's and Ross's love. But my thoughts drifted to Angus. I had to tell him what Niall told me. I knew where the Pride was.

After Jacqueline helped me into the shower, I dried off and dressed feeling refreshed and clean. I walked down the stairs leaning on Ross's arm. Entering the dining room, I was immediately greeted by applause, squeals, and hugs. Chad rushed to me and embraced me so tightly I thought I might break.

"I can't believe you woke the one time I wasn't there!" he cried as tears filled his eyes. I wiped them away.

"You were there, that's all that matters," I replied. He nodded but was soon pushed aside by two women I hadn't seen in weeks. Jess and Brittney, Daren's sisters and my best friends, wrapped their arms around me.

"We flew in with your dad," Jess replied. "I've never been so scared as when I heard you were unconscious!"

"I'm so glad you're okay," Brittney said rubbing my arm.

"I'm so glad to see you guys," I replied. "But how?" I looked over at Ross who stroked my back.

"Your hunk," Jess answered. "He took care of everything."

"I love you," I said to Ross.

Draping his arm around my shoulders, he spoke softly, "come on, let's get you seated and get some food in your belly," he said. MacDonald walked up to me and bowed.

"Please allow me to serve you, Ms. Thompson," the man could speak!

"Thank you," I replied. Ross led me to a large round table where Graeme and Gerard stood and greeted me. We all sat together and I knew all was right and good in the world.

But where was Angus?

# Chapter Ten

*One week later...*

Staring at the ruins of MacPherson keep, Highland Mountains loomed in the background. This was my family home. My heritage. My ancestors walked those ruins. Angus lived there. My direct ancestor was born there. Filled with curiosity and awe, Ross's hand slipped into mine.

"It's just so beautiful," I said looking up at him and smiling through my tears.

"Aye," he replied. "But just wait until ye see Sutherland lands there's none like it this side of heaven." I laughed. "Come on, love," he went on. "Let's find the Pride."

Almost as if I had been there before, I followed my instincts to a small mound of earth. Bending to remove the dirt and vines, we found a trapdoor in the ground. The MacPherson crest was engraved on the metal and stone.

"Here," I called. The five men, Ross, Graeme, Gerard, Chad and Dad all stepped forward. I walked back to the ladies and watched as the men tried to open the door.

"Psst," Jess hissed, her eyes on Graeme. "Is he single?"

"He didn't tell you?" I asked thinking it was odd since they had spent nearly a week together while I was unconscious and another week while I was recovering. If Graeme *didn't* say anything, that was unlike him.

"Of course, he did," she replied. "But... you would know if it was true or not."

"Yes, he's single," I confirmed. "They both are. And quite the catch. But deserve better than to be a rebound."

"Ooh, ouch," Jess winced. "Thanks, babe."

"You know I love you, Jess. I'm not telling you anything you don't already know. I've been there," I replied. "Ross came out of left field, but it had already been a little while for me. Graeme is a great guy and I would love to see you two together but honestly. Take some time for yourself. You need it."

"Graeme reminds me so much of his father," Marilyn came up beside us and I froze.

"Who is his dad?" I asked. Marilyn smiled fondly but did not reply. Instead of pressing, I turned back to watch the men work.

It was about twenty minutes later and the lads still hadn't figured out how to open the crypt. The younger ones had stripped out of their Aran sweaters to their white or black undershirts. Muscles bulged, sweat poured from their brows, curses were flying, followed by an apology to us women which made us all smile.

After another few minutes, I went to our cooler and retrieved a water bottle from the pack and went to my man. Ross stopped for a moment to accept my gift. He nearly groaned when the cold water hit his throat.

"Awe, no fair!" Graeme called as Ross drained half the bottle in one go.

"Get your own amazing woman, this one's mine," Ross yelled back while wrapping his arm around my waist and pulling me into him.

Dad laughed and yelled over to him, "so kiss her, boy and get back here to help!"

Ross grinned and pulled me even closer.

"Daddy's orders," he lowered his mouth to mine amidst whoops and hollers. "I'm calling lunch, lads," Ross called looking up seeing the sun well passed noon. The others agreed and soon we all lounged in the shade of a hundred year old oak, Ross stretched out beside me, his sweaty t-shirt outlining his torso. Looking up at me through messed up hair and sparkling eyes, Ross took my breath away.

"How is my favorite author?" he asked nearly an hour later as he pushed a strawberry into his mouth and bit down. I flushed at my thoughts as I watched him and focused on my iPad.

"I'd be better if I were alone at the moment," I whispered.

"Oh?" he asked taking another piece of fruit. "And why is that?"

"No reason," I shrugged, turning my iPad so he could read the latest part I was writing.

"Oh dear me," he hissed. "Is that a sex scene I see you writing?"

"I thought it was time," I answered. "But right now, I see my father talking to your mom and all I can think of is... oh shit, he's going to know what you did to me the other night."

Ross threw his head back and barked a laugh. Everyone looked over at us but Ross waved them off.

"I'm sure it's nothing he hasn't done before," Ross teased. "And besides I'm pretty sure he's thinking about doing that to my mom so maybe it'll give him some pointers." He winked at me and grabbed an apple from the fruit platter.

Playfully smacking his arm, "I don't even want to think about that."

"Neither do I," Ross agreed. "But if it makes her happy then I'll be happy."

We didn't say anything for a moment, but Ross cleared his throat and changed the subject. "So how is the manuscript coming along?" he asked.

"Nearly at seventy thousand words," I replied. "I think it'll be about seventy-five, maybe eighty."

His eyebrows shot up in surprise. "Is it something you can show my agent in a couple weeks?" he asked.

"Yeah, I guess," I said. "I got an email from my agent the day we went to Culloden. He says my publisher is interested in another book from me, but I don't think I can work with him again."

"No, I understand," Ross replied. "Hey, it's a great story. They would be fools not to want it."

"I would like to meet your agent," I said. "Can I meet him before I commit?"

"Of course," he agreed. "You'll like him though. He's an American transplant. Married a Scottish lass and they have three kids. He lives in Edinburgh and London."

"He sounds interesting," I stated.

"He is," Ross replied. Chewing a bite of his apple slowly, he looked up at me, stood and reached a hand down. "Walk with me?"

I looked up at him, saved my work and took his hand. The grounds were quiet as we walked, peaceful. Taking a deep breath, filling my lungs with the Highland air, I wondered how anyone could ever leave such a beautiful place. Ross and I were silent as we walked, his presence comforting. The harsh hills and mountains before us were blooming with late autumn flowers.

"What's on your mind?" Ross asked.

"I'm worried we haven't seen Angus," I started. "I haven't told him what Niall told me and I have so many questions."

"I could have sworn I felt him," Ross said. "But when I searched my mind, I didn't sense him. I'm sure he'll turn up. When we find the Pride, he'll come back."

"You truly believe we will find it?" I asked.

"Of course," he answered.

"Why?" I asked.

"Because you are a strong, intelligent woman and I know you would never leave something unsolved," he replied.

"What if this is all a wild goose chase, Ross?" I asked. "What if I'm really crazy and this is just my imaginings?"

"Jilliana explained what happened when she woke," Ross went on. "She told us how Lorna told her about the west wing and was drawn to explore. She found the room and somehow opened it. I guess she wanted an authentic experience. We found her Ouija board under the floor boards. After she conjured Elizabeth and she nearly killed Chad that evening, Jilliana wanted to know more. That's when Elizabeth tricked her into possessing her."

"I'm glad she's gone," I said.

"She's staying at the hospital for a while but she'll be back," he replied.

"I mean Lorna," I stated.

"Oh, yeah," he said. "I do blame myself a little. If I wasn't so weak it would never have happened."

"It would have happened. She loved you even before you slept with her," I replied. "You don't think she'll come back and hurt you, do you?"

"No, no she may be crazy but she's not psychotic," he replied.

"That's a relief," I said.

"Hindsight is twenty-twenty," he said. "I never loved her. I never even wanted her. She was easy and as bad as that sounds, that's who I used to be. I have changed because of you. I'm crazy in love with you, Nikki," he said. "I know your life is in America and I respect that, but my life is tied here. A lot of people depend on me and as much as I donnae like it, it's my duty. If I could work it out, do ya think ye can agree to a sort of arrangement?"

"What sort of arrangement?" I asked.

"Stay in Scotland for six months, I'm needed here mostly for the planning of the harvest and the Highland Games, late summer to fall, and then I'll come with you to America for six months. It would be a lot of traveling but I think we could do it. Mum has already started shutting up the estate up north. She's moving full time to MacCulloch to help run the place while I'm not there. I have a few candidates for assistant lined up for interviews. I want to be with you."

"I want to be with you too," I said. "But six months here and six months there? I don't think I could." Ross's shoulders fell and he looked away.

"I understand," he was saying. "Your life is in America. It was stupid of me to ask you to give it up. I'm sorry."

"Ross," I stopped him. "*You* are my life. I want to be with *you.* I don't want to split my time. I want to stay with you, here in this amazing place, with its amazing history and people. The great thing about my job is that I can do it from anywhere."

His eyes were hopeful. "And... your da'?" he asked.

"I think Scotland is looking rather tempting to Dad right now," I teased.

"I caught them kissing like a randy couple the other day," Ross laughed.

"What? No!" I grinned.

"I haven't seen Mum this happy since Da' died," he said.

"Are you okay with it?" I asked.

"Yeah," he answered. "Mum is amazing and she deserves to be happy."

"Me too, I'm happy for Dad," I said. "He deserves to be happier than anyone. All the sacrifices he made raising me, I'm happy to see he's found someone he likes."

Taking my hand in his, we started strolling back to the rest of the group. As soon as we rounded a bend of the ruins, I stopped dead in my tracks. A vision of Niall and Angus stepping down into the family crypt, appeared before me. Angus took off a very strange looking necklace, placed it into a lock, pressed down, twisted the thistle a quarter of a turn and the door opened.

"Nik?" Ross asked concerned. The vision disappeared before me as I felt Ross turn me to him.

"A thistle, Ross. It's a key in the shape of a thistle," I said. The memory of the dream, the first week I was staying at the castle, came back to me. I was running through the woods carrying something important and Angus brought me to the stables. I was carrying the thistle key but still didn't know where it was.

As Ross and I returned to the group, we heard Graeme yelling. Ross raced forward, then slowed when we saw the anger was directed at Marilyn.

"I donnae care anymore, mum!" he shouted. "I'm missing half of myself. I know you think you're protecting Gerard and me but enough is enough. I know you have your little secret, but I *need* to know! Who is my father?"

Ross and I froze as Marilyn looked down. Gerard was looking away, Dad, Chad and my best friends had vanished.

"Oh great," Graeme's eyes found Ross's. "Ross, you know I love ya, man but come on. Aren't you the least bit curious if you're my brother?"

Ross's jaw ticked. "This is not something we should be discussing right now, Graeme," Ross said tightly.

"To hell with it!" He bellowed. "To hell with the lot of you! Who is my damn father?"

Graeme looked ragged and drained as he fell back and sat down. Marilyn looked over at Jacqueline, who nodded slightly then Jacqueline's eyes caught Ross's.

"This affects you too, Ross," she said. "Come and sit down."

"I'll go find Dad," I replied.

"I wish you wouldn't," Jacqueline stopped me. "You and Ross are together now and I think this is something you should hear too."

# Chapter Eleven

Marilyn wrung her hands but didn't look up. Jacqueline sat beside her, silently comforting. Graeme's anger had subsided slightly but Gerard sat with one knee raised, his arm resting on it, his fist clenched, his gaze was riveted by the heather on a yonder hill.

"I…" Marilyn started. "I guess it's time for all of you to know the truth." Jacqueline reached out and took her hand. "Boys, please don't think badly of me. I lied to you…" she looked at Jacqueline, who nodded. "*We* lied to you but it was in order to keep you safe. When you have children of your own, I hope you will understand." Marilyn's gaze fell on me. "How much do you know, dear?" she asked.

"I told her everything," Ross said. Marilyn nodded.

"Good, then I can continue," her gaze drifted to her two sons. "Graeme, Gerard, you must understand there are some things in my past I am not proud of. Sins I hope you will not hold against me."

I looked toward Jacqueline, suddenly very uncomfortable with the direction the conversation was going. Ross's hand tightened around mine as if begging me not to leave.

Taking a deep breath, Marilyn began.

"I met your father at a party while I was staying with Jackie's family. He was dynamic, passionate, handsome. In personality, Graeme you remind me so much of him and you both are so very handsome," she looked from one to the other. My gaze followed hers to Gerard's dark blonde short hair and Graeme's longer, curly and shaggy blonde hair hanging past his ears.

"When I was younger, I was a free spirit – still am – but I have learned my lesson. You must understand, loves, no party was too small and I would always drink too much or try the latest fad." She looked down ashamed. My mouth went dry and my chest ached. Marilyn looked up at her sons again.

"I accepted... drugs from others. I am not proud to admit it to you and I know what you must think of me. Your father was the same. That's why we connected. One day, we both drank far too much and he slipped something a little something extra in my drink..." a tear slipped out of her eyes. Gerard's gaze flew to his mothers, eyes wide with fear and anger. Graeme looked stricken. "When I woke, I realized immediately what had happened. Connor found me," at the mention of his father, Ross stiffened. "He carried me to his car and drove me to the hospital. He was so angry when I told him I had been... well... what had happened. A couple weeks later, I wasn't feeling well and I hadn't seen the man again but had heard he had an argument with Connor and disappeared. I found out I was pregnant with you two and I didn't know what to do, I was so happy and yet worried that you would grow up without a father. When I told Connor and Jacqueline, Connor swore he would find him and... kill him. I begged him not to saying my boys would need a father. When there was news of him in Glasgow, Connor took me and we searched for him without success. On the way home, I cried and Connor told me he would be a father to my children. He said he felt responsible for Owen's actions."

Ross stiffened even more beside me. "Owen?" he asked, looking over at his mother.

"That's right, darling," Jacqueline said. "Your father would never be unfaithful to me and it pained him to know the town thought he had been. He was grateful you never believed the rumors."

"But..." Ross started, looking desperate. "He never said what happened. I begged him to tell me and all he said was he wanted me to stop asking and never treat them any differently than I had."

"He did that for me, Ross," Marilyn said. "I asked no one know my sin. I didn't exactly tell Owen no. We had gotten high together before and we had... been together."

"He raped you," Graeme interjected.

"He... took advantage of me," Marilyn replied. "But Connor didn't ever want you boys to think you were anything but wanted and loved. So he never told anyone and we all stayed close."

"But I don't understand," Ross started looking back and forth between the two women. "Who is Owen? Why would Da' feel responsible?"

Jacqueline squeezed Marilyn's hand. "Because Owen was Connor's younger brother," Jacqueline explained. "Your uncle, Ross. You, Graeme and Gerard are not half-brothers... you're cousins."

Silence descended on us. They were family but not the close relations we thought. My thumb drew soft circles on Ross's hand as I held it.

"All these years," Ross started, his voice cut off as he cleared his throat. "Why didn't he ever tell us?"

"Where is Owen now?" Graeme asked.

"No one knows," Marilyn replied. "He's disappeared. Dead or not, he's gone. I couldn't tell him about you. My parents had turned their backs on me when I went off to school and did all sorts of things they didn't agree with. But when they learned what had happened, they helped me. Helped us."

"Grandda' and Grandma knew?" Graeme asked.

"Yes," Marilyn answered. "I know you both probably hate me right now but I hope you will understand one day."

"We don't hate you, mum," Graeme replied. "We wish you hadn't kept it from us for so long."

"Oh, my boys," Marilyn gushed. "I love you with everything inside me. I want you to know, though the circumstances of your beginning may not have been ideal, you are so loved and I wanted you both so very much. I am certain, if your father knew about you, he would have loved you too. Connor loved you both he, I believe, almost wanted you to be his."

"Connor told me, when he was dying," Jacqueline started. "He may have failed raising Owen right but he was, in his words, 'damn proud of the men my sons have become.' He loved you both and wanted to tell you the truth and give you his brother's name but for Marilyn's sake he refrained, hoping one day you would learn the truth and not judge us all too harshly. There are things a parent does to protect their child that may not seem logical to the child, but we hope our child will one day understand and won't think of us differently. Sometimes it may seem like we are hurting you or keeping something from you but honestly it is because the truth could destroy you and we know it. God put parents on this earth to protect our children and whether you are one or one hundred we will always want to protect you. It is our instinct, it is our destiny, it is our connection to you. Don't take that from us."

Graeme took a deep breath but his eyes filled with tears. "I love you, Mum," he said. "And of course I do not think less of you. My god, have you ever thought less of me when you found out things I have done? You are and will always be the most beautiful, understanding, patient and loving woman I have ever known. Come 'ere, ya wee daft woman," he reached his arms out to his mother, got on his knees and met her halfway. Marilyn cried into his shoulder.

"I love you, Graeme," she wailed.

"Ya have ta understand," he mumbled into her hair. "A part of me was missing for thirty-two years. I needed to know. Even this."

She nodded and clutched him close. I wiped at my own tears and felt Ross's hand squeeze pulse in mine then drop.

Ross got to his knees and hugged his mother. "He was quite the man, wasn't he?" he muttered.

"He was," she answered. "The love of my life. You remind me so *very* much of him. He would be so proud of you."

They held each other for a long moment. My eyes drifted to Gerard. He still stared out at the mountains; tears were nowhere to be found. His jaw was clenched almost as tightly as his white knuckles.

"Gerard?" Marilyn called to him pulling slightly away from Graeme. "Love, can you forgive me?"

Gerard did not look at his mother when he stood and walked away from the group disappearing down the hill.

"He just needs time," Graeme said. I wasn't so sure. The look on Gerard's face held one thought... murder.

Once everyone finally returned and things had calmed down, I revealed the vision I had earlier and explained the thistle key.

"A thistle key?" Chad asked. "Great... so does anyone have one?"

"That is a verra unique key," Ross said, then turning to me, continued. "Did Angus show you where something like that could be?"

I shook my head. All I knew was it was somewhere safe. That was the message in my dream. But I had an idea on how to find it. Standing, I looked at each of them.

"I need to do something," I said. Ross made a move to stand, but I held up my hand to him. "Alone."

"Absolutely not," Dad said replacing the wine bottle in the cooler after filling Jacqueline's glass.

"Dad, please," I said sternly.

"Nik, I'm not letting you go by yourself," Dad replied.

"Dad," I stated. "I will be fine. These people... they won't hurt me. They are my people. This is my clan's land. I belong here. I need to do this."

"If you need me," Ross began.

"I know," I replied. "I have my phone and my lungs. And you know I can scream."

Ross's eyes widened as the deepest blush spread across his cheeks. As I walked away, I could hear everyone laughing and Graeme teasing him mercilessly. Walking to the ruins, I stood in the courtyard where Angus showed me the memory of Niall training with him. I took a deep breath trying to calm my nerves. A weird tingling began in the pit of my stomach.

"Angus," I said out loud once I was close enough to the keep. "I don't know if you can hear me, but I think I've found the Pride and I need your help."

I waited but nothing happened. It was strange not having him come when I called again. Still nothing. Walking on, I went in the main entrance of the ruins and called. But then I wasn't at MacCulloch castle. Could he not be here?

"Niall? Angus isn't answering me."

"Ye met me brother, lass?" I heard Angus say behind me. Turning, I smiled. I didn't realize how much I had missed him until that moment. "Where? When?"

"At Culloden," I said.

Angus looked pained. "He was there?"

"Yes," I replied. Angus looked away and closed his eyes.

"I ne'er thought he would be..."

"A ghost?" Another voice came from behind Angus. Whipping around, Angus turned toward the voice. Niall stood before us. "I've been trying to find you, brother."

"Niall?" Angus breathed. It was only then I realized, Angus had not seen his brother since Culloden and that thought hurt my heart.

"Aye, Angus," Niall took a tentative step toward him. Angus shook himself out of his stupor and rushed to his brother. They embraced tightly, burying their heads into each other's shoulder. It was a long time before either spoke. "I found my way back home, but you weren't here. I did nae ken what had happened. The MacPherson's were driven out of our land and our home was destroyed. I could nae find you. I went back to Culloden hoping someday you would come. Finally, I felt you were there because of this lass. I asked her to get a message to you." Angus finally pulled back and stared into his brother's eyes, cupping his face.

"I tried, Niall," I said. "But I couldn't find him."

"I could nae come to you, lass," Angus replied. "You were under constant supervision by more than just Ross. And though the Scottish lads believed in me, your father was no' open."

"I think he is now," I defended gently.

"What was the message?" Angus turned back to his

brother.

"I stole the Pride," Niall confessed.

"What?" Angus breathed.

"Please allow me to explain," Niall begged and proceeded to tell the story he had shared with me at Culloden. Angus listened intently. After a while, Niall spoke again. "I tried to tell you but Death claimed me before I could speak. Forgive me, brother," he looked down. "I should ne'er have stolen it. The Pride belongs to ye."

"The Pride belongs to no one man," Angus stressed. "It is the Highland Pride. It belongs to Scotland."

"We lost Scotland twice now," Niall said. "You heard they voted to stay with England?"

"What?" I couldn't believe it.

"Nay," Angus breathed.

"Aye, our Scotland is lost," Niall said.

"We will fight for it," I stepped forward. "I will not let my land be overrun!"

"She's just like your Riona," Niall chuckled.

"She's Riona's descendant," Angus explained. "Our blood kin."

"Aye," Niall replied. "And a fine credit to ye. I thank God I was able to meet her. To know our line did nae die with us."

"And she is with Alastair's kin," Angus revealed.

"That I like even more," Niall beamed.

"How did you both get here? Angus, Ross told me you needed to be tethered to someone to leave MacCulloch."

"Aye, Sutherland is right," he said. "Ross let me in again without him knowing," he held up a hand when he saw my face. "I left immediately when we reached my land. I can be either here or MacCulloch but nowhere in between."

"I died at Culloden and am buried here, I also can be in both places. But enough of that, do ye have the Thistle Key? The Pride is on my person. Nikki needs to retrieve it."

"I'm no grave robber," I said.

"Nay, you are retrieving something that is part of our clans' history," Niall replied. "You are nae desecrating my resting place."

"You are completing my promise, lass," Angus went on.

"I'll be with you every step."

"Okay, then, I need the key," I stated.

Angus looked toward what would have been the kitchen and spoke. "I left it in the one place I kenned the bloody English would ne'er look. Follow me."

We both followed him down some remaining stone steps and through an old corridor, then Niall laughed.

"Ye let it *there*? Ingenious, brother," he smiled.

"Where is it?" I asked.

"Forgive me, lass," Angus replied. "'Tis in the privy."

"The..." *oh god, the bathroom!* "That's gross."

"It's been years. Everything is dry by now," Angus said passing passed through an archway.

"Still," I whined searching my body for something I could use as a guard. I didn't know I would need to bring latex gloves.

"Here, lass," he pointed. What was left was not a typical looking toilet, fortunately. Taking a deep breath, I swallowed the sour bile on my tongue.

"Okay, here goes," I said. Kneeling down, I gulped and dived my hand into the dirt. Even after years, the smell was still there and I gagged. But soon I felt cool metal. "I found something," I said.

Pulling it out, still covered in dirt and other things I refused to think of, was a dingy thistle shaped object. Rubbing the dirt off of it, I was amazed even after all those years it still held such detail; notches where the thorns would have been on the plant, engraved grooves for the flowering part of the plant. It would have taken hours if not days to duplicate the intricacy my time, I could only image what it would have taken in Angus's.

"It's beautiful," I muttered.

"Aye," Angus replied. "Made for our family at the same time as the crypt. The door to the crypt is impregnable without this key. The MacPherson clan holds death as a sacred rite. That is why the tradition of not cleansing the body when a warrior is felled. It is an honor to fall in battle." The thought of breaching the tomb of my ancestors scared me.

"What am I going to encounter down there?" I asked.

"Your past," Angus replied. "But I will be with you."

"Everyone else will want to go too," I said. "Will that be

all right?"

"Aye, I would expect them to," he answered. "Niall is on the right of my mother and to the left of our grandfather."

Niall looked at his brother, shock registering on his face. "Ye gave me tha' honor?" he asked.

"'Twas your rightful place," Angus replied lovingly. Finally turning to me, he smiled slightly. "Ye cannae ken what it is you gave me back, lass. Seeing Niall again… makes me gladder than I have been in an age. Go now. Find the Pride. 'Tis your fate."

# Chapter Twelve

I rounded the bend and saw the group still resting under the tree. Ross and Dad stood when they saw me. I held the thistle key out to them.

"Ross, could I have a water bottle and some hand sanitizer?" I asked. He reached for the water and opened it for me. Pouring the water over the metal to wash the dirt away I was amazed at how dark the metal was. It needed a good polish. Dad handed me one of the napkins we had brought with us and I rubbed the silver. Still dark and dingy it at least had some of its former beauty returned. "The keyhole is hidden in clay near the bottom of the slab," I explained. "Angus showed me how to break the clay. Did we bring a hammer or a mallet?"

Ross laughed and looked over at my father.

"Sir, if I ever doubt you again, be so kind as to say hammer and mallet in my ear, would you?" Ross asked.

"Oh, trust me, son, I will," he winked at me. "I insisted we bring it. Saying we never know when it might come in handy." Leaning into Ross, I loved watching the two men in my life get along. Dad had never called Daren *son* in all the five years we dated. Maybe that was because they were only ten years apart.

Ross grabbed the hammer and held it out to Dad.

"You do the honors, sir," he said. Dad grinned, pulled off his flannel shirt and tossed it to me, his eyes twinkling.

"Sure, I'll play Thor," he teased winking at Jacqueline.

"Do, Travis," Jacqueline grinned. "Show us your muscles." Dad flexed!

Taking the hammer from Ross, Dad and the lads went over to the door. Removing some dirt, they revealed a clay crest near the bottom of the door. Dad lined up and took a swing over his shoulder, grunting with exertion. Jacqueline and I cheered as the clay shattered with one strike.

Stepping back, Dad took a dramatic bow as we clapped. Shouldering the hammer, he sauntered over to Jacqueline whose eyebrow was raised and a smirk rested on her lips.

Ross leaned down and kissed my hair whispering, "Time for the key, love. Are you ready for this?"

I nodded and said a silent prayer that the Pride was there. As I walked forward, silence fell across the group. Kneeling down, an impression of a thistle was visible beneath the remnants of clay. Brushing the debris away, I slid the key into the lock, pressed down, and turned it a quart of the way to the right. A mechanism groaned and clanged as the lock gave way and the door slid open to reveal stairs.

Angus and Niall appeared behind me and from the gasps of everyone, they saw them too.

"Take a torch," Angus said. Ross approached and handed me a flashlight. "It's ten steps down then curves to the right and then another five. Niall is the sixth vault."

I nodded, stood and flicked on the light. With Ross to my right and Chad to my left, we started down the stairs.

"I'm gonna wait up here," Marilyn called. "I'm not big on creepy places."

Dad hesitated as well. He was slightly claustrophobic but I could see he wanted to go with me.

"Dad could you stay with Marilyn and anyone else who doesn't want to go?" I called. "I'll be fine."

"I'll look after her, sir," Ross assured.

"I'll stay with Ms. Tucker and Lady Sutherland, sir," MacDonald stepped forward.

"I'm counting on it, MacDonald, thank you," Ross said but I couldn't help seeing how Marilyn held her breath whenever MacDonald was around. That was a match I would have to thoroughly vet later.

Turning back to the steps before us, Chad, Ross and I started down.

Ten.

Turn to the right.

Five.

We reached the dirt floor of a massive underground crypt. Plaques etched into the wall in Gaelic told dates, names and quotes of each of my ancestors. I was glad Ross was counting vaults as I was too mesmerized by what I saw to focus. It fascinated me to be able to say these people, these mighty Scots, were my ancestors. It made me proud.

"Six," Ross called out. We turned to the plaque behind the coffin as he read and translated into English. "'Niall Duncan William MacPherson, born, the nineteenth of March, seventeen twenty-seven. Died, in his nineteenth year, in the battle for Scotland's freedom, the sixteenth of April, in the year of our Lord, seventeen forty-six. Second son of Robert Gilchrist Micheil MacPherson, Laird of Castle Eachthighearn, MacPherson keep and surrounding areas. *Ar dheis Dé go raibh a anam.*' May his soul be at the right hand of God. Chad, will ye help me?"

Chad nodded, mute by the gravity of what we were doing and where we were standing. The men went to the vault and pushed on the covering. Stone on stone resounded through the large space and once it was open enough, the men stood back and looked at me. Tentatively, I stepped forward.

"This just feels wrong," Chad said.

"I know, but we have to do this," I replied. Finally reaching the edge of the crypt, I peered down. Covering my mouth as a small screech escaped me, Niall's skeleton looked up at me still dressed in his battle wear. Remnants of his tunic lay tattered on his bones and his kilt had faded to nothing. His empty eye sockets gazed up at me and the cloth they tied around his mouth to keep his jaw closed was frayed but had kept the hinge well shut. Forever in the sickening grin of death, his body was well past decay. Closing my eyes, trying to block out the image I had just seen, I felt sick. I had never seen a skeleton before, let alone one of my own kin.

Backing away, I ran into Angus behind me. His hands came around my arms and he held me gently, comfortingly.

"'Tis all right, lass," he soothed. "It'll no' hurt yet. It is an honorable thing to join our ancestors. 'Tis nothing to fear. The flesh is nothing but a vessel. Go on, we're right here."

"Niall's not here, right?" I asked. "I don't think I could handle seeing him as I looked at his skeleton."

"Nay, I asked him to wait above with the others. He'll watch out for them. I did nae think he should see his own bones," Angus explained.

I thanked him silently and with his strength, I stepped forward again. Reaching in, I ignored Chad's groaned "ugh, gross" and slipped my hand under the leather armor still on Niall's body. Feeling around the ribcage, my fingers caught a chain. I froze and my breath caught in my throat.

Slowly pulling on the chain, the crypt faded away around me. I was riveted by the trinket swinging back and forth between my fingers. An item, encased in clay, dangled from the bottom of the chain. The design was so intricate, but I had seen it before; once at the pump at MacCulloch Castle and the other on Angus's pin.

The Crest of the MacPherson's.

Looking over at Angus dressed in his day kilt, wearing his soft boots and linen shirt, he stood transfixed, staring at the little pendulum swinging from my fingers. I held the Pride – The Highland Pride – in my hand.

"Angus?" I choked seeing a tear roll down his cheek. Raising his fingers toward the charm, he hovered right in front of it.

"I ne'er thought I'd see it again," he said, his voice full of emotion. He locked eyes with me and for a moment we held each other's gaze. Sire and offspring. Kin. "Thank ye, lass. Thank ye. Ye found it."

Tears rolled down my cheeks. "You can be at peace now, Angus," I said. "Tha' is all I ever wanted."

"Aye, thanks to ye, I will get to see my wife, my daughter and my family again. Ye gave me my brother. I thank ye," he replied.

"What is it, Angus?" I asked. "What is the Pride?"

"It was encased in clay by Dàibhidh MacPherson when William Wallace gave it to him before the battle of Falkirk in 1298. Wallace was captured and murdered seven years later. When one of his limbs was sent to Perth, the Sutherlands, MacPhersons and their allies joined forces with Bruce loyalists and the Bruce himself. Dàibhidh MacPherson, the current laird, having inherited the title from his father and elder brother, commissioned the Pride to be encased in clay," Angus explained.

"You've never actually seen the real Pride? Just this?" Ross asked.

"No' in the flesh, only in paintings and tapestries," Angus replied.

"Then what is it?" I asked again, my eyes focusing on the clay still in my hand.

"'Tis the original crest of Scotland as designed by the Bruce himself and given to Wallace as the Guardian of Scotland after the Battle of Stirling Bridge. It is said to be a ring with precious stones in a design only seen when Wallace wore it. My... our ancestor was given the commission by Wallace who said; 'when Scotland is threatened, the Pride will be its hope and it will be used again when we are a nation once more.'"

"I took it to give to Prince Charlie," we heard Niall at the main entrance on the stairs. "I thought... ah, I donnae ken. I kenned it was a lost cause but I thought the magic of it, but we did nae triumph. Forgive me, Angus."

"Aye, Niall, ye are forgiven. And nay, it did nae work, but what the English failed to understand was, it is no' a ring that is the Pride, but the spirit of Scotland, its people. As long as there is pride in our country, the magic of Scotland will ne'er diminish. We need no ring, no Highland Pride. We are the pride. We are Scotland. Call me rattled in the head but I do believe Scotland will be free once again and together, brother, we fought to make that happen. Our blood soaks the soil of this land. No bloody English will e'er take that from us. Look at our legacy," he turned to me. "After Culloden, I turned me back on my king, ye remember the parchment ye found in that book?" I nodded. "'Tis my confession," he explained. "My shame. I turned my back on

Scotland and joined England for a time, but only for the good of Scotland. I ne'er gave my allegiance in my heart. But I used my position for Scotland's advantage. I was received at court, a personal friend of the king. They ne'er understood why their goods ne'er arrived or why a caravan carting new weapons were set upon by rebels... they ne'er kenned. I wrote that letter so my heirs would ken if I was hailed an English hero, my heart was always Scotland's. They lied, stole, and killed for their cause, I just gave them a little of it back."

"No' much has changed," Ross scoffed.

"And now..." Niall started. "Where is the Pride in our land? They still rule with fear and lies. When they had freedom in their grasp, they let it go by voting to stay."

"There is no pride," Ross replied. "The English stole that too."

"Then it is time the Highland Pride is back in the hands of its people," Angus said stepping toward me. "Smash the clay, lass, take the Pride to one you think deserves it and we'll pray Scotland will be a nation free of England once and for all."

"Well, Miss Thompson, it is quite the tale you tell," Ross and I sat in Edinburgh's Scottish Parliament offices with the First Minister.

"It is true, sir," Ross replied.

"I have no doubt," the First Minister said. "I may not know Miss Thompson just yet, but I know you, Ross Sutherland, your father and I were at Primary together. I have always had cause to believe in your loyalty to Scotland. You have proven it many times over, even if you do write some of those lurid and fanciful romances, eh?" He winked. Ross chuckled. "But this story intrigues me. I have heard of the lost ring of William Wallace but I did not know it was so important to our history. May I see it?"

I took a deep breath and pulled out a baggie from my purse. After we had smashed through the clay, we found the most exquisite ring I had ever seen. Slowly handing it over, I prayed I was doing the right thing but as soon as the First

Minister saw it, he sobered and a tear filled his eye. I knew then I had chosen the right man. He truly loved Scotland. Handing it over, he took it like it was made of the most precious glass and could easily be broken. After a moment, he finally spoke, his voice strained.

"I've only seen paintings of Wallace wearing this. The tales I've heard... fall so terribly short," the tear fell from his eye and he looked up at me, smiling. "And it is your ancestors who had this for so long?"

"Yes, the MacPherson's," I stated. "They were in the highlands near Newtonmore. Angus Macpherson, or Fearsome MacPherson as he was known, was laird at the time of Culloden. He lost his brother, Niall and many good and loyal men."

"As did we all," the first minister said. "Even my ancestors fought there. Tell me, were there any instructions given regarding this wonderful piece of history?"

"All I know, sir," I began. "Is that the Mac – that *we,*" I corrected. "Want it to be Scotland's."

"It is Scotland's alone," he vowed. "There is room in the Edinburgh Castle vaults beside the Stone of Scone. I believe that would be a good and secure place for this on display for all to see."

"Sir, that is exactly what Angus would have wanted," I said.

"You're a writer, are you not?" he asked.

"I am," I replied.

"This is a tale worth telling, not just for Angus MacPherson but for Scotland as well," he said.

"I have actually begun writing it, sir," I revealed.

"Excellent, let me read it and I will personally write a recommendation to any of our Scottish Publishers," he offered.

"Thank you, sir," I replied.

"And I want you to be at the ceremony," he said. "As Scotland's guest of honor."

"I would love to, sir, but the retreat is up in a couple weeks and–"

"Nonsense," he cut me off. "I will deal with Customs myself. You are a Scottish hero! We would be honored to have you and since you found us a national treasure, as well as having a Scottish citizen as a grandfather – Brodie, correct? – then we can start the paperwork for granting you citizenship, if that is something you would like."

"I would love that," I gushed.

"Good," he clapped.

"Oh and one other thing, sir," I said. He nodded. "Angus MacPherson gave his life protecting Scotland. He has been labeled a murderer and a suicide. Sir, that is not true and I can prove it. I have his written confession that he is no friend of the English."

"I know the tale. Killed his second wife and her brother then himself, aye?" the first minister asked.

"No!" I said a little too adamantly. "I'm sorry. But that's not true. Crispin Blackbourne killed Elizabeth and shot Angus. Angus was defending himself. His last words of 'I killed her' were meant as a euphemism meaning because of his accusations and because of what happened with the Pride, Crispin killed her."

"I see, well, we shall have to remedy that," he replied. "I will officially pardon him and make the announcement at the reveal. Do you know where he is buried?"

"In unconsecrated ground at MacCulloch Castle," I said.

"We'll exhume him and give him a proper burial. He was Catholic, aye?" he asked. I nodded. "Good," he smiled and handed the Pride back to me. "Hold on to the Pride for now. It belongs with your family. I will be in touch. We may have lost the vote, but Scotland's fight for freedom is far from over. So long as there are men and women willing to do whatever is right, Scotland's legacy will never die."

# Epilogue

*Six months later...*

I finished the reading of my newest novel to a crowd of over one hundred in the banquet hall of Edinburgh Castle. The Highland Pride was safely in the vaults beside the Stone of Scone with a memorial plaque dedicating it to two MacPherson brothers, who gave their lives to protect it and Scotland's freedom; Niall and a fully pardoned, reburied beside his wife and father, Angus MacPherson

The crowd applauded and Ross helped me down from the gallery to the main area. Cocktail tables were set up around the room and waiters passed hors d'oeuvres and drinks. Another small table, with my novels stacked on top, stood at the far end of the room and people had already begun forming a line to purchase the novel. Ross's and my agent took credit cards and cash as Ross stood beside me handing me books.

After a while, my hand ached from signing but the line never seemed to end. Glancing over at Dad, I saw him sipping a glass of champagne beside Jacqueline and the former First Minister. He caught my eye and winked then turned back and laughed at something the Minister said. Jacqueline touched Dad's arm affectionately. Ross and I had had the shock of our lives when we walked in on them in bed together. Since then, they hadn't made their relationship a secret.

We had not seen Gerard since the day of his mother's confession and even after Ross and Graeme went out to look for him, there was no sign. Ross told me it wasn't the first time Gerard had disappeared. My besties flew in for the book launch and ceremony. I caught Chad's laugh from the other side of the room. Looking over, he stood with his arm resting on Frank's shoulder sipping his third glass of champagne. Catching my eye, he winked and turned back to the conversation.

"Baby?" Ross nudged a book at me.

"Sorry," I said, taking it and opening the cover. "What's the name?"

"Angus MacPherson," his voice said. I looked up sharply. Angus stood before me smiling.

"You're here," I breathed.

"Aye, lass," he stated. "I had to come see ye."

"Where have you been?" I wanted to hug him. I missed him so much.

"Ye fulfilled my vow, lass. Ye found the Pride, ye cleared me name. Ye gave me peace," he said. "I can rest now."

Tears ran down my cheeks as I suddenly realized, I may never see him again.

"Will I *ever* see you again?" I begged.

He smiled slightly. "Nay," he answered. "I'm going home," he looked up and Ross and I followed his gaze. Riona, his first wife and my absolute likeness, stood by a window.

"Come home, Angus, *mo chridle*," she said.

"Ree, this is our daughter's descendant," he explained.

"Aye and she's beautiful," Riona said smiling at me.

"She takes after ye, woman," Angus grinned. Riona laughed, a sweet melodious tinkle.

"With yer temperament," Riona replied.

"Thank ye," he winked. Lifting a hand toward him, she beckoned him to her.

I looked back at Angus and could feel the love he had for her flowing from his eyes then, he looked down at me.

"Thank ye, Nikki," he said.

"I love you, Angus," I whimpered.

"I love ye too, lass," he smiled. "Ye may no' see me again, but I will always be wit ye. When ye need me, call for me, aye? Ye'll feel me, I promise." I nodded letting my tears fall. "Take care of her, Sutherland," he said to Ross.

"I swear to you, Angus, I will," Ross said putting a hand on my shoulder.

"Then my task is done," he said. "I am at peace. Remember me, lass."

"I will never forget you," I swore. "Don't go. Not yet. I..." as if reading my thoughts, he smiled and opened his arms to me. Racing to him, I threw my arms around him. Instead of the cold shock I normally had when I touched him, Angus felt more real and human than ever before. I held on tightly letting my tears wet his tunic.

"Donnae cry, me wee lassie," he whispered. "I'll always be in yer heart and I'll always be yer kin. I promise you will ne'er be alone."

"I will miss you so much," I cried into his shoulder.

"I ken, but 'tis time for you to let me go," he said.

"I can't," I replied holding him tighter.

"Ye must," he gently pushed a little on my hips to separate us. "We both need to move on."

"You were the one constant in this crazy time of my life," I said.

"Aye, I ken you believe that," he replied. "But he is the one who will always be with you."

Finally, I pulled back and nodded. We locked eyes and I memorized his face; the straight jaw, the dark brown stubble, the cleft in his chin, his soft crystal blue eyes, straight nose and high forehead. I wanted to remember every detail about him. When he kissed my forehead, I took a deep breath of him, even though I knew he had no smell I thought of peat, musk and early morning dew on windswept grass, that was my Angus. When he pulled back, he smiled, nodded to Ross, locked eyes with me again and stroked my face. Then he was gone.

Closing my eyes against the pain, I sat back down at my table and Ross clutched my shoulder.

"He's at peace," he said.

"I know," I smiled. "And that makes me glad. But I will mourn him."

"That is all any of us could ever want. To be loved enough to be mourned," Ross said. Squeezing his hand on my shoulder, I turned to the man who was next in line.

"Are you all right?" The man asked. I smiled and wiped my tears.

"Yes, sorry," I apologized. "What's your name?"

"Angus Farquharson," he replied.

"Angus," I repeated. "That's a good name."

A sigh of relief escaped me as I fell onto the bed back at MacCulloch Castle. Ross turned on the fireplace, went to the mini fridge and brought back a bottle of Krug Champagne. But looking around the room, he sighed.

"Well, I had some glasses," he said.

For some reason, I found that very funny and burst in hysterical laughter. Maybe it was the stress of the day, maybe it was the excitement of the book launch and dedication of the Pride, but whatever it was, I was exhausted and everything was extremely funny. Ross looked over at me, a lopsided grin on his face.

"Yeah?" he teased.

"I'm sorry," I said.

"I'll give you something to laugh about," he pounced and tickled me before I could stop him. Shrieking, I wrestled with him attempting to stop the tickle torture. Finally, he had me successfully pinned and leaned down to kiss me. "Now do you want me to open this bottle or are you going to laugh at me again?"

"Bottle," I gasped. "I promise I won't laugh." But as soon as I said it, I started laughing again. Kissing me hard, he stopped me but then left me breathless as he rolled off the bed and continued his search for the missing glasses.

Disappearing into the sitting room he emerged with two crystal flutes. "Better than whisky tumblers," he said.

"I don't know," I sat up on my elbows and watched him pop the cork. "It would have been very rugged, my laird."

"I do try," he winked as he poured. Handing me the fizzing glass, he raised his in a toast. "To great success to you and your novel, my love. To many more and to the completion of a task set before you centuries ago."

"*Sláinte mhath*," I toasted.

I let the crisp bubbly liquid ease down my throat and reveled in the flavor. When I opened my eyes, Ross had bent to his knees and was raising my leg. Pulling off my high heel, he began to massage my calf. Groaning, I leaned back on my elbows trying not to spill the champagne. Oh, it was heaven.

"I love you," he said, placing a gentle kiss on my knee.

"I would love you to never stop doing that," I moaned as he switched legs. It was about five minutes later and me feeling completely boneless, when he finally spoke again.

"I'll always love you and I will always massage your aching legs for you," he said.

"For what in return, Sutherland?" I raised a droopy eyebrow.

"The rest of your life?" he asked.

My eyes popped open. I sat up in time to see him rise to one knee and hold out a box in his hand; it was open to the most exquisite diamond ring I had ever seen.

"Ross," my words caught in my throat.

"I love ye," he started. "I fell in love with ye when I first read your book and even more when I first saw ye in Heathrow, drinking that glass of white wine berating yourself for being... you. Did you know, I was supposed to take off an hour before but Graeme's bag spilled open on the steps of his London flat and it took us that long to clean it all up? Fate had other plans for us that day. I cannae promise life with me, Nikki will be anything more than this. But I swear to love ye always. I will treat ye like a queen. I will honor and respect you for the rest of my life. I want to make all of your dreams come true. Could you see yourself with me? As your husband? God willing, having a family with me and being mine for the rest of time? Be my wife, Nikki. Will you marry me?"

I was staring at him and then the ring. I could see it on my finger. I could see Dad walking me down the aisle to Ross dressed in his full kilt, Graeme and Gerard beside him and Jess and Britt waiting for me on the other side. I could see us raising a family in this castle and in his estate north in the Highlands. I could see us growing old together and lying side by side every night. Yes, I could see it. Yes, I wanted it.

"I could think of nothing else I would rather want than a lifetime of your shenanigans, Ross Sutherland. Yes, I will be your wife. Yes, I will be by your side and dear god, yes I will marry you!"

He let out a quick breath and beamed. Raising himself up to kiss me, we were breathless by the time he pulled back to slide the ring onto my finger. Leaning forward again, I stopped his lips.

"One condition," I said.

"Anything," he prompted.

"You *have* to wear your kilt at the wedding," I stated.

Ross reared his head back and it was his turn to laugh that night.

The End

Thank you for reading! When I first started writing this novel it was during the Scottish vote for Independence and followed a family vacation to Scotland and Ireland in 2013. My heart will always be in Scotland, my maternal grandfather's land. His love of Scotland was instilled in my mother who instilled it in me. I am very pleased with *Silent Whispers* and hope you enjoyed it too! Please follow me on Facebook and Twitter for more information on latest releases.

www.ingramcontent.com/pod-product-compliance
Lightning Source LLC
Chambersburg PA
CBHW070309040726
47501CB00018B/1322
* 9 7 8 0 9 9 0 9 9 1 5 7 1 *